UNLEASHED

AN OMEGA THRILLER

BLAKE BANNER

RIGHTHOUSE

ISBN-13: 978-1-63696-342-6

ISBN-10: 1-63696-342-0

Cover design by: Damonza

Printed in the United States of America

www.righthouse.com

www.instagram.com/righthousebooks

www.facebook.com/righthousebooks

twitter.com/righthousebooks

THE OMEGA SERIES

ONE

There was no woman in my life.

I sat on the white sand, looking out at the vast, pale blue sweep of the Gulf of Mexico, with the warm sand on my bare feet, and realized that the thought was an empty, desolate one, but it was also a liberating one. I stood. I had been swimming, and the late afternoon sun was drying the salt in my hair and on my skin. It felt good. I turned and started pushing through the sand toward the big house on stilts that I had rented on the southwestern tip of Galveston Island. My car, an original, matte black, 1968 Mustang Fastback with a modified Zombie 222 under the hood, stood in the shade of the house, waiting for me. I smiled. I was thinking about a cold beer, maybe two, a steak and some margaritas at Pier 32, in Freeport, to while away the evening.

I pulled on my boots, put the Eagles on the sound system and rolled onto the San Luis Pass Road. The Zombie will accelerate from naught to sixty in one and a half seconds. Forty-five seconds was how long it took me to cover the mile from my house, across the bridge, to San Luis Island. There, I braked hard to take the long curve that follows the bridge, then straightened up and covered the fifteen miles to Freeport in seven minutes. The twin engines are silent, so the only sound was the battering of the wind and the Eagles, telling me to come down from my fences.

I rolled into the Pier 32 parking lot, climbed out of my car and stood a moment, watching the copper afternoon turn slowly to evening, smiling and feeling good inside for the first time in many months.

Inside, it was dark by contrast with the sunlight outside. Lee Mathis was singing something about the rain and JD was behind the bar, going a little gray in his long beard and his ponytail, but otherwise unchanged from when I'd first met him, sixteen years ago, when I was sixteen. I leaned on the counter and he ignored me while he polished a glass. Then as he put it down and picked up another, he said, "You're smiling. What the hell's wrong?"

He looked at me then and gave a laugh like a truck running out of gas. I grinned and said, "Give me a brew, and try not to get your beard in it."

He pulled a draft into an iced jug and put it in front of me. "I'm serious. You ain't showed up around here for more than ten years? Then you show up out of the blue, for the last two weeks you hardly said a damn word and I ain't seen you smile once. Now today, you come in with a big, stupid grin on your face. What happened? You got laid?"

"Long story, JD. But you're right. I'm feeling better today."

"The ocean'll do that for a man. I been meaning to ask you, how're your dad and your brother?"

"Both dead."

He didn't react, just kept polishing the glasses. "Sorry to hear that." After a bit, he smiled without looking at me. "I remember…" He shook his head and laughed, "You was a real son of a bitch. What was you? Sixteen? Seventeen? You'd come in here with the money you stole from your dad's wallet, 'Come on, JD, gimme a beer. It's my birthday. I'm twenty-one.'" He gave his slow, spasmodic laugh again and pointed at me. "'And gimme a whiskey chaser, too. What's your best whiskey, JD?' You remember that?"

"Yeah, I remember. I also remember you served it to me."

"If you'd been my son, I would have whipped your ass. I'd a been proud of you, but I'd still've whipped your ass. But you wasn't my son, so I wasn't gonna turn away good money. Also, it made me laugh when your dad came in lookin' for ya. 'Have you seen my son? Has he been in here?'"

I smiled. "You told him if his son wasn't twenty-one, he hadn't been in here, 'cause you wouldn't 'countenance no underage drinkin' in your establishment.'"

We both laughed.

"You used to come most every year, at least twice."

"May and November. We used to rent a house from the Colonel. Don't know what his real name was, we just called him the Colonel."

"Harry Burgess. Used to be in the air force. He owns a lot of property 'round here. He was a friend of your dad's. They were pretty tight."

"Yeah, I've been avoiding him. Guess I'll have to say hello at some point."

"Well, now's your chance, Lack. He's comin' in later to have dinner. He's booked a table." He gave his head a little twist. "I ain't one to gossip, but there's somethin' going on with that old goat. He's been hangin' around with some chick, 'bout half his age. Fine lookin', too."

A small crowd came in and I told him when the kitchen opened, I'd have a steak and fries out on the terrace. He went to serve his customers and I strolled onto the deck, where they had tables set for dining overlooking the water and the wooden piers, and, about a mile away, the vast, blue sweep of the Gulf.

The sun set slowly behind me. I had another beer and watched the sky turn from blue to pink to dark, and then the stars pierced the darkness. JD had set up some flaming torches along the wooden railings, and as the night closed in, they lit up, casting a warm, wavering, amber light over the tables.

By that time, the terrace had filled up and a couple of young waitresses were serving the tables. One of them brought me my steak and a fresh beer, and as I was cutting into the meat, I heard a voice I hadn't heard since I was a kid.

"Well, I'll be doggone! If it ain't Lacklan Walker, as I live and breathe! You used to be a skinny kid. What happened to you?"

It was the Colonel. He had aged in the years I hadn't seen him. He had lost a lot of hair and what he had left was gray, but at sixty-something, he still looked strong and vigorous. He was standing, staring, smiling, with a young woman in jeans and a white blouse by his side. She must have been in her late twenties, slim, but with a generous feminine figure. Her hair was dark and cut short, and though she wasn't beautiful, her full lips and large eyes made prettiness something extreme. She was very attractive. I stood and moved around the table. We shook and he embraced me.

"God darn! You've grown into a man! Let me look atcha!" He stood back and held me by the shoulder. "How long's it been?"

"Too long." I gestured at my table. "I know you've come for dinner, you're welcome to join me."

His face said he was pleased at the invitation. He turned to the woman he was with and said, "Well, we'd love to, wouldn't we, honey? This is..." He hesitated a moment. "This is Emily, my... um..."

I took her hand and we shook while he mumbled something. "I'm Lacklan. We used to rent a holiday home from the Colonel a few years back."

Her smile was as warm and pretty as the rest of her. She gave a small, nervous laugh and said, " Hi..."

We sat, and after a brief, awkward silence the Colonel said, "I was sorry to hear about your daddy."

I nodded. "Yeah." Then I shrugged. "You ride with the Devil, you get burned sooner or later."

"I don't know nothin' about that, but I *do* know he had a nose for makin' money!" He laughed. "I've missed his advice in the last few years, I can tell you that! We're doin' OK, real estate is always solid, you know that, but the closure of the factory was a blow."

My interest was more polite than real, but it was good to talk to an old, familiar face, so I asked, "What factory is that?"

Emily gave a small laugh. "It wasn't a factory, Harry."

He shrugged. "What do I know? Whatever the hell it

was. QPS. They leased a property of mine out near Chenango, eighty-two acres, gave me a nice return each year, I can tell you."

"They closed down?"

"Big market crash few months back? Hit them real hard."

Suddenly, I was interested.[1] "A software company?"

"Yup. Parent company was a solid American enterprise, but they sold out to a European firm. 'Parently, funding dried up all of a sudden and they went belly up. But tell me 'bout you." He frowned. "Your daddy said you was in the English army?"

"I was ten years with the Special Air Service. I left a couple of years ago, with the rank of captain."

It was Emily who answered. She looked curious. "The SAS? That's an elite special forces unit, isn't it?"

I nodded.

Her cheeks colored. "Wow, I'm impressed."

"Don't be. It was something I happened to be good at, but I am not proud of it."

It was the Colonel who answered. "Don't sell yourself short, boy! And don't sell your regiment short. Ain't nobody stupid enough to pretend war is a good thing. But there's plenty who are stupid enough to believe we can get by without an army. You show me a world where there ain't no Putin, no Kim Jong-un, no ayatollahs and no Islam, and I will *consider* the possibility that we could do without men like you and me. You know what hell is, Lacklan? Hell is a world where good men stop fighting for what's right an'

---

1. See *Kill: Two*

just." He turned to Emily, who was giving me a very disturbing smile. "Am I right?"

"I'm afraid you are."

I noticed she had no accent. She could as easily have been an educated New Yorker as an educated Californian, or from Iowa. She was hard to pin down.

They had obviously ordered before coming out, because a waitress brought them a couple of steaks, a bottle of wine and two glasses. As he poured and they started to eat, I smiled at her, then at the Colonel, and asked, "So, how do you two know each other, if that's not being nosy?"

He froze halfway through cutting his steak and I saw his cheeks color.

She smiled back at me and put her hand on his shoulder. "Harry is my father."

I stared at him for a moment and grinned. "I had no idea you had children, Colonel."

"Well, neither did I, to tell you the truth, Son."

Emily laughed. "Harry was stationed at McGuire Airforce Base, in New Jersey. My mother lived in Trenton..."

He scowled at his plate like it was being unreasonable in some way, by sitting there with food on it. "I told her to come back to Texas with me. She didn't want to. And never did tell me she was pregnant. I had no idea I had a child, or I would'a done the right thing."

Emily shrugged as she poked a piece of steak in her mouth. "Mom died a couple of years back and, going through all her stuff, I found photographs and letters and all kinds of stuff she had never shown me. And among it all, I found a letter to Harry that she had never posted, in which she told him he had, 'a beautiful little girl!'" She laughed prettily. "So I came out here to meet my daddy."

The Colonel had a big, stupid grin on his face. "Happiest day of my life."

I raised an eyebrow. "And that was two years ago?"

She nodded. "Two years ago last month."

I raised both eyebrows. "So you just stayed?"

She laughed again and gave his arm a hug. "We got on so well, didn't we? It was like we'd known each other all our lives. So I decided to stay and make up for lost time. I sold the house in Trenton, got myself a place here and I've been looking for a job—not as hard as I should—but sometimes Harry lets me help him, don't you, Daddy?"

She gave him a kiss on the head. He seemed to swell. "She's a great help to me, Lacklan. As long as I'm around, she don't need to worry about a thing."

I glanced at her and a shadow seemed to pass across her eyes; for a moment, her smile seemed strained. It was so brief, I wondered if I had imagined it. I said, "It's a big change, from Trenton to Freeport."

"And a very welcome one. Tell me, Lacklan, will you be staying?"

"For a time."

The Colonel grinned. "Say! You kids should get together some time! Go out and do stuff!"

It caught me off guard and I think I just sat and blinked at him for a while, but Emily beamed. "Well, that would be marvelous! We could go swimming! You have *the best* beaches where you are, or we could go to the races in Chenango! Harry never has time to do anything, do you? And I do get bored sometimes!"

There was a hot twist in my gut I could only describe as fear. I had a momentary flashback of sitting outside my house just a few hours earlier, realizing I felt good about having no woman in my life. All I could do was nod a lot, lick my lips and make vaguely positive noises. She didn't seem to notice, but plowed right on and arranged a picnic on the beach, a day at the track and a day of sightseeing in Houston.

We finished our meal and she was still talking. The waitress came and took our empty plates away. The Colonel and Emily ordered a couple of rum and Cokes and I had an Irish whiskey straight up and a black coffee. All the while, I was thinking about how I could get out of the engagements she had arranged. My instinct was to be blunt, but she was a nice kid and I didn't want to hurt her feelings, or upset the Colonel.

While they talked, I sipped my whiskey and decided to make some vague excuse about being tied up for the next few days. But as I drew breath to speak, she looked me straight in the eye and said, "Your house is the first one over the bridge, isn't it? On its own there, on the beach, with the blue roof."

"Yup."

She winked at me. "Well, don't go straying too far, Mister, I'll be dropping in on you one of these days for a day of bathing and barbecue."

With no fixed dates to avoid, all I could do was say that would be great and I was looking forward to it.

"But I'd better be getting home now. It was great seeing you again, Colonel, and really nice meeting you, Emily. You know where I am."

She winked again. "Sure do. Gotcha pinned."

I stood and the Colonel got up and gave me a big hug and a pounding on my back. She rose too and gave me a kiss on the cheek, for just a little too long. I left them on the terrace, waving to me, and made my way through the bar and into the parking lot.

I drove back slowly, listening to the surf and watching a fat moon suspended over the ocean, touching everything with yellowy light. I crossed the bridge, left the Zombie among the big stilts under the house, and climbed the wooden stairs to the veranda. There were two large, plate-glass sliding doors that gave access to the living room. I slid them open, switched on a single lamp and carried a bottle of Bushmills and a glass out to the big terrace. There I sat in the rocking chair, with the table by my side, looking at the immense ocean under the moon and thinking about the Colonel and Emily. I decided she had some kind of story. However happy she might have been to connect with her dad, she must already have been willing to let go of her past and her childhood. There could not have been much left for her in Trenton to give it up that easily.

Then I decided that whatever her story was, I didn't want to know about it. She was pretty, cute, hot as a jalapeno pepper, and had trouble written large all over her. Plus I had found my freedom at last, had just started enjoying it that afternoon. I was not going to get involved.

Period.

That was when I heard the whine of a slowing car, heard it pull in under the house and stop, saw the headlamps making long, black shadows of the stilts across the white sand, heard a single car door slam, and feet climbed the wooden steps up to my terrace, my home, my refuge.

TWO

HER WHITE BLOUSE WAS FAINTLY LUMINOUS IN THE moonlight. It made her look like a ghost, standing on the deck at the top of the stairs, watching me in silence. I sipped my whiskey and felt unreasonably irritated. The surf sighed on the beach and the breeze moved her hair slightly. It was hard to make out the expression on her face, and when she spoke, her voice was unexpectedly loud.

"Please don't think me forward."

I repressed my irritation and said, "Sure, sit down. You want a drink?"

She gave a small laugh. "I think I need one."

"Rum and Coke?" She didn't say anything, but I thought I saw her nod. I stood and said, "Grab a seat."

I went inside, found a tall glass and filled it with ice, then half filled it with rum and topped it up with coke and a slice of lemon. I carried it out to her. She was sitting on the edge of her chair with her hands clasped between her knees. I handed her the drink and sat in the rocker.

"What's on your mind, Emily?"

She glanced at me and took a long pull of her drink before answering.

"I said I'd drop in. Maybe I'm just visiting."

"But you're not."

She looked at the moonlight on the water. "I knew you were SAS."

I frowned, hard. "What's that supposed to mean?"

"JD told us you were back three weeks ago. Harry was so happy, couldn't stop talking about you. He loves you like his own family." She paused as though she expected an answer. She didn't get one, so she kept talking. "He said you'd been in a special ops unit in England. I figured it had to be the SAS."

I sighed and tried not to sound blunt. "You're not making a hell of a lot of sense, Emily. Why does it matter that I was in the SAS?"

"I'm sorry."

She went quiet and stared at the deck with her hands clasped between her knees again. I repeated my question.

"Why is it important, Emily, that I was in the SAS?"

"I'm in trouble, Lacklan."

A wave, slightly larger than the others, slapped hard on the beach, and then there was a deep sigh as it withdrew. I said, "I'd figured that out already. That's why you left New Jersey."

"Yes."

"You thought you'd got away, but the trouble followed you here."

She nodded. "Yes. I guess it always does, right?"

I smiled at her. "And you figure the SAS can solve your problem. You don't think small, I'll give you that."

She smiled, but didn't quite make it to a laugh. "I have no right to ask. I'll pay…"

"Let's not get ahead of ourselves. Tell me what the problem is first, then we'll see what the best way to tackle it is."

She straightened her back and took a deep, shaky breath through her mouth. "I am going to be murdered. If somebody doesn't help me, I am going to be killed."

"Who by?" I think she expected me to be shocked, because she looked at me sharply, like the lack of emotion in my voice was offensive to her in some way. I said, "I stopped being surprised by killing twelve years ago, Emily. It's a job, like any other. Who do you think is going to kill you?"

She shuddered. It may have been the breeze off the ocean. It was getting colder.

"His name is Gregor."

"Russian?"

"Yes."

"Mafia?"

"Yes."

She didn't say any more and I sat and watched her for a while, trying to read her face and her posture. Finally, I said, "I am struggling here, Emily. I am struggling to visualize any kind of situation in which you would be involved with the Russian mob."

She puffed out her cheeks and I caught a glint in her eyes that might have been tears. "I haven't told Harry everything about Mom. I kept it to the kind of stuff he would want to hear. But there was more. She really had to struggle after he left, to survive, and raise me on her own. Sometimes, when things got really hard, she..." She stared up at the moon for a while, then spoke in a rush, forcing the words out. "Sometimes she had visitors: men. When I was small, I didn't realize what that meant. But as I got older, it slowly dawned on me that they were clients."

She picked up her drink and turned it around in her hands for a bit, then took a long pull. After she had swallowed, she started talking again, but there was a repressed sob in her voice now.

"When she died, I kind of cracked up. I went to pieces. She was young still, and we were close, like friends. I really depended on her, we shared everything, talked about everything. I was holding her, cradling her head, when she passed."

Another shaky breath. I didn't say anything. I knew where this was leading, and I let her talk.

"So, I lost my job because I took too much time off work, nursing her and then recovering from her death. Grieving. Consequently, I was really hard up. I simply didn't have enough to pay the mortgage, the bills, insurance... let alone buy food." She paused. "This is so humiliating. In the end, in desperation, I did what I knew Mom had done. I went to a club where I knew girls went to pick up clients. Almost straight away, Gregor approached me. He owned the club. He told me if I wanted to work there, he would take a cut." She shook her head. She wouldn't look at me. "He is the most terrifying man you can imagine, Lacklan. Huge, bald, and his eyes..." She paused, frowning, searching for words. "They are dead. You look at him and you know he has seen and done the worst things the human mind can possibly conceive, and it has left him cold. He is a horrific creature. He terrifies me."

I sighed. "So you told him you'd changed your mind, and he told you it was too late."

She nodded. "That night he made me do things... and then again, afterwards." She looked away and wept silently for a while.

I handed her a handkerchief and she blew her nose. I asked her, "So how long ago did your mother really die?"

She gave a small laugh. "You don't miss much, do you?"

"No."

"Three years ago. After a year of working for Gregor, he'd got bored with me, and there were a couple of new girls he liked on the scene anyway. So I asked one of his lieutenants if I could take a few days to go and visit my dad in Seattle. I told him he was ill and dying. I guess he thought I might inherit something, and he could get his hands on that. Anyhow, he said yes, and I came out here. For a couple of years, it was idyllic." She gave a little laugh. "I guess they were looking for me in Seattle."

I smiled.

She went on. "Harry is a wonderful man. We became real friends and—more than that—family. I look after him and he looks after me."

She stopped and went silent again for a while. Then she said, "I have no idea how they tracked me down, or why they bothered. I am not valuable to them. But a couple of weeks ago, they turned up."

"Was Gregor with them?"

"Yes, and four of his men. He said I had broken our contract. He wanted a hundred thousand dollars for the memory cards with the photographs and videos, or he would show them to my father, and publish them online. It would destroy Harry. It would destroy his standing in the community, and it would break his heart."

"Do you plan to pay him?"

"I have no choice. But I know that when I do, when he has the money, he will kill me."

"What makes you say that? Right now, you're the golden goose. Digital pictures and films can be reproduced to infinity. He could have you paying over and over for the next twenty years. And he must know your father has money."

She gave her head a small shake. "I managed to convince him that Harry is not all that paternal, and we have a very tentative relationship. I told him I'm on a kind of probation, that he would drop me like a hot brick if they tried to blackmail him. I also convinced him that a hundred grand is all I have. It's not a lie. It's all I have left from the sale of my house. So once I pay him, I will no longer be any use to him. Also..." She looked at me across the table for a long moment. A chilly breeze made her shudder. "There's the location. The place he's chosen, he can kill me, drop me in the bayou and there will be no trace of me."

I nodded. "When is this exchange due to take place?"

"I told him I needed a couple of days to get the cash together, and I would contact him tomorrow to fix the date."

"Good. Fix it for tomorrow night. Tell them you want to see the cards, disks and any other material they have. They may or may not bring them, but it's worth a try. You get out of town first thing. Go to Houston. Spend the day there. I'll call you when it's over."

She gave a small laugh that sounded almost hysterical. "Just like that? What are you going to do?"

"It's best you don't know. But I'll persuade them that they should take the money and leave you alone."

She laughed again. "You make it sound so easy." I didn't answer and she asked, still smiling, "How much will this cost me?"

"I don't want payment, Emily. Your dad's an old friend. Just promise me you will never get into anything like this again. I don't want the Colonel getting hurt."

"I promise. Neither do I."

I stood and she stood too, and came close to me. She put her hands on my chest. "Is there no way I can thank you?"

I took her hands and held them between mine, looking hard into her eyes. "I'm going through a divorce right now, Emily, and I am not somebody you want to get involved with. But if we ever do make love, it will not be payment for services. It will be because we like each other. You are not a negotiable commodity."

She withdrew her hands and took a step back. "I'm sorry."

"Where is the drop due to take place?"

"On the Old Angleton Clute Road. When you pass under the FM 2004, you find you're in a forest. Follow the road straight for a mile after the bridge. You'll come to a clearing where there's a kind of parking space, just before that there's a track that leads into the woods. Follow the track for two hundred and fifty yards and you'll come to a clearing. You'll know it because there is a large tree on the right that collapsed in a storm a couple of years back, and on the left there is a large, swampy bayou." She hesitated a moment. "What time shall I tell them to be there?"

"Tell them to be there at twelve midnight." I frowned. "The way you describe it, you know this place pretty well. You've been there before."

She nodded. "Of course. I went to have a look, to see if I could set a trap for them. But I was too scared. I couldn't do it."

I grunted. "What about the money?"

"I withdrew it from the bank this morning. I've been driving around with it in my trunk."

"OK, give me the money. You go home, make the call. Tell them you'll have the cash tomorrow night. You going to be OK?"

She shrugged. "Can't I stay?"

"No, you can't be seen with me again until this is over, Emily."

I walked her down the steps to her car. She opened the trunk and handed me a small, black sports bag. I unzipped it and looked inside. There was a sealed paper parcel, about eighteen inches long, six inches deep, twelve inches across. It was heavy. She said:

"It's all there. They counted it out in front of me, twice."

I nodded. "OK. I'll take care of it."

She kissed me on the cheek. "I don't know how to thank you. I am so grateful I could cry. I can't believe that you would do this for me, Lacklan. It seems incredible..."

"Let's talk when it's over, OK?"

She gave a small nod and I watched her climb in her car and slam the door. The engine whined and she reversed toward the road with her headlamps blinding me. Then she turned and for a moment, the amber funnels picked out the twisted trees on the far side of the road before she accelerated away, back toward Freeport. As her red tail lights disappeared into the darkness, I stood for a while, thinking. I shuddered. The night was growing cold. I turned toward my car.

When I had decided to come to Galveston Island from Erick Redbeard's place in L.A.[1], I'd had Kenny bring me the Zombie from Weston with a full kit bag, but I hadn't looked at it since it had arrived. I went now and opened the trunk. The kit bag was my old green canvas bag from the Regiment. I opened it and pulled out my hickory take down bow, twelve aluminum arrows with razor-sharp broad-heads. There was a Heckler and Koch 416, two Sig Sauer p226 with the extended magazines, a Maxim 9, a Fairbairn & Sykes fighting knife, my Smith & Wesson 500 in case I needed to blow down any walls, and four cakes of C4, because you never know when plastic explosives are going to come in handy. He had also packed a variety of detonators, a box of listening bugs and a pair of night-vision goggles.

I smiled at the recollection of him when he handed over the vehicle. He'd raised an eyebrow and said, "When you mentioned you aimed to relax and recuperate, sir, I thought it best to prepare a *full* kit bag, just in case." He was a kind of extreme Jeeves on steroids. The only thing he'd left out was the rocket launcher.

I took out the knife, slipped it into the sheath in my boot, rammed a magazine into one of the Sigs and slipped

---

1. See *Kill: Two*

that into my waistband. I had a feeling that before long, I might be having some visitors. Then I closed the trunk, looked around and sniffed the air. The only sounds were the surf and an owl somewhere, calling for a mate. I told him he was a fool and that he was better off on his own, but he ignored me and kept on hooting.

As I climbed the stairs back toward my terrace, I thought about Gregor, and wondered if he would be at the drop. I hoped so. I wanted to talk to him. I dropped the bag on the table, poured myself another Bushmills and stood holding my glass, chewing my lip and staring at the moon.

After a bit, I put down my glass without drinking, opened the bag and took out the parcel of cash. I carried that inside and put it on top of my wardrobe. Then I went back out, drained my glass, locked up the house and went down to the Zombie again, whistling softly through my teeth. The first requirement for a successful operation is good preparation; and the basis of good preparation is good reconnaissance. So I climbed into the Zombie and headed silently through the night toward Freeport, the Old Angleton Road, and the woods.

THREE

The next day I spent mainly lying on the beach, swimming and doing not much of anything else. At nine A.M., she phoned me to say she was on her way to Houston. I told her not to call me again until it was all over, and she hung up without saying anything, like she was mad at me.

At one P.M., I barbecued a sirloin steak on the beach and ate it between two hunks of fresh bread with a cold beer. Then I slept for an hour in the shade of the stilts, had another swim and spent the afternoon reading a book on my sofa, about a world where it was always raining, and the elite were trying to escape to Mars. Two years ago, I would have thought it was stupid. Now I wasn't so sure.

As evening fell, I went for a two mile run along the shore to warm up, spent an hour training in the sand and then at nine, I climbed in the Zombie and went to the drop point. My advantage was surprise, and I was going to exploit that every step of the way.

I took it easy and arrived at nine forty-five. I had found a place the previous night, off the track and just before the designated exchange point, and now I backed the Zombie in among the shadows and killed the lights. After that, I spent an hour carefully inspecting the area for traps and snipers. It was an unnecessary precaution because they thought they were going to meet cute, vulnerable Emily there. But unnecessary precautions can often turn out to be life-savers.

At eleven, I got back in the Zombie, cocked my Sig and settled to wait.

They arrived at eleven forty-five. They were in just one car, a dark Ford Explorer. They rolled past me, maybe ten feet away, passed the fallen tree, came to the edge of the bayou and turned to wait. They killed the lights and got out. The closing doors were a staccato volley in the darkness. I slipped on the night-vision goggles and the world became a strange green and black place. I counted four men. One of them leaned against the radiator and lit a cigarette. He was six feet, big but athletic. He had a goatee and short hair, black jeans and a black T-shirt. He also had an air of authority. I pegged him as the leader of the operation.

Beside him with his arms crossed was a fair-haired man in his early twenties. He wasn't smoking, and he looked gym-fit. A third guy had gone to piss by a tree. He was well over six feet, with a huge back and a long, black ponytail. He was wearing what looked like an Italian suit. He had a big gut and something about him told me he ate people for breakfast. He wasn't gym-fit. He was a ruthless son of a bitch.

The fourth guy was holding an assault rifle and was staring out and up into the trees. He was also dressed in black jeans and a T-shirt and had the air of a combat-hardened soldier. None of them was Gregor, but they were all dangerous men. I had to use the element of surprise, and keep it coming.

The Zombie is totally silent. So when I fired her up, the first thing they knew about it was when the headlamps came on full beam. I pulled off the goggles and watched the four men for a moment, squinting and shading their eyes. Then I rolled out silently and moved up the path toward them until I was thirty or forty feet away. They were still shielding their eyes and had gathered around the hood of the Ford. I dimmed the lights and climbed out, holding the sports bag in my left hand.

I heard the assault rifle cock, the other three guys pulled automatics and there was a click, click, click. I raised my hands, with the sports bag dangling from my left thumb. Where I was standing, behind the door, behind the headlamps, all they could see was my silhouette, but it must have been clear I wasn't Emily.

The guy with the goatee trained his automatic in my general direction and, squinting in the light, said, "Who are you? Why you are here?"

I said, "Take it easy. I'm here for Emily. She thought the forest air would be bad for her health. Where is Gregor?"

He spat on the ground. "The arrangement was Emily comes. This is bullshit!"

I shook my head and put a smile in my voice. "No, not bullshit, tough shit. Now, do you want to do business or do you want to talk?"

There was some cussing in Russian followed by some consulting in Russian. The big guy with the ponytail and the

Armani suit jerked his chin at me and growled, "Kill little piece of shit."

But goatee snapped, "You bring it?"

I said, "It's in the bag. Now, what about your part of the deal?"

The big gorilla went to the back of the truck and pulled out two bags similar to mine, only bigger. They were full and looked heavy. He brought them to the front of the truck and raised them for me to see. I studied them a moment, thinking hard. I shrugged and spoke, half laughing.

"Are they all there? I don't want to come back again next year. How can I be sure that's all of them?"

As I had expected, they all looked at each other and frowned. Goatee said, "What the fuck? Don't play fuckin' games! What you fuckin' talkin' about?"

I shook my head. "Never mind. Have your man take six long paces and put the bags down. Then I take six long paces, collect the bags and leave this one behind. I check the contents right here, you collect your bag and check the contents there. Everybody happy, we all go home. Agreed?"

There was some more guttural muttering and the gorilla took six long paces, which placed him about twenty feet away. He put down the bags and stood leering at me.

"Now you come."

I smiled and waved him away. "Go back, pal, I am not looking for a bear hug tonight."

He grunted and walked back to his comrades. I took six long paces of my own, dropped my bag and picked up the two he'd left. I figured each one weighed a good fifty-five pounds. I hefted them back to the Zombie, then turned to watch the gorilla lumber back, pick up the bag and carry it to the goatee.

The goatee and the blond unzipped it. The guy with the assault rifle trained his weapon on me and the ape aimed at me with his automatic. I smiled and put my hands in my trouser pockets. Goatee pulled out the package and frowned at it. I pressed the detonator and a quarter of a pound of C4 vaporized his hands and pretty much tore him and the blond in half. The blast wave shattered the windshield of the Ford and hurled the gorilla and the guy with the assault rifle to the ground. They lay there deeply concussed and groaning.

As a back up plan, in case plan A didn't work out, I had placed the HK 416 under the fallen tree. I walked over now and retrieved it. I made my way toward the guy with the assault rifle. As I passed the gorilla, I shot him in the back of the head. Then I rolled the last survivor on his back and knelt with one knee on his chest. There I paused, hearing the sound of a reversing engine. The skid of tires on gravel, and then a car accelerating away, fast, toward Freeport.

The guy under my knee was still groaning, and his pupils were the size of soup plates.

"Do you speak English?"

I had to ask him twice, but finally he said, "Da..."

"Where is Gregor?"

"Fuck you..."

I leaned back and pressed the muzzle of the HK416 against his right kneecap. "If I squeeze the trigger, it will tear your leg off. Now, where can I find Gregor?"

He groaned some more and said, "He always at Caribbean Casino on Caribbean Island, Jamaica Beach. He is owner. He always there."

"Thanks."

I shot him between the eyes.

I dragged them all to the bayou and rolled them in. The big gorilla was difficult. He must have weighed four hundred pounds if he weighed an ounce, but with the help of the Ford and a length of rope, he went in too. After that, I put the two bags in the trunk and drove back to my house at a nice, leisurely pace, letting the sea breeze batter my face and blow away the stench of death. The moon was rising, in its first waning, but it was still brilliant and cast a faint, turquoise sheen over the world.

I parked the Zombie under the stilts of the house and, with some difficulty, carried the two heavy bags up the steps to the terrace. Between them, they weighed easily a hundred and ten pounds, and I was out of breath by the time I got there. I opened the sliding glass doors, dropped my luggage on the sofa and poured myself a generous glass of whiskey. I knocked it back, then locked the doors, went to my bedroom and retrieved the parcel Emily had originally intended for the drop, before I'd replaced it with half a cake of C4. I dropped it on the sofa with the two bags, poured myself another whiskey and sat in an armchair, sipping Irish and contemplating the three peculiar articles.

I had a pretty good idea what the two sports bags contained, and it wasn't memory cards for a camera. But the package in the middle was a real mystery: something the Russian Mafia apparently wanted real bad. Finally, halfway through my second whiskey, I got up and unzipped the two bags. As I'd assumed, they contained hundred dollar bills, bound into tight packages of one hundred: each package worth ten thousand dollars. I did a rough calculation and decided that there was five million dollars contained between the two bags. I made a dozen random checks and all the money seemed to be both present and authentic.

I picked up the parcel Emily had given me and sat back in the armchair, asking myself, what nature of a thing is eighteen inches long, six inches deep and twelve inches across, and worth five million dollars? Then I asked myself, how did Emily come to be in possession of such a thing, and why would she be selling it to the Russian Mafia?

I shook my head, pulled out a pack of Camels, poked one in my mouth and lit up with my old, battered brass Zippo. I shook my head because that wasn't the question either. The question was...

I blew smoke at the ceiling, framing the question carefully in my mind. A good question is worth a million good answers. The question was: why did she want me to make the exchange, believing I was paying them money, when she must have known full well I would realize immediately it was the Russians paying me, and not the other way around? Why would she arrange such an elaborate ruse, when it would so obviously become transparent right away? It didn't make any sense at all.

Unless...

I pulled the knife from my boot and cut open the paper packaging. I tore it away and found I was looking at a sleek, shiny black cube that was perfectly featureless. It was hard to tell what it was made of. It felt like either ceramic or highly polished steel. I ran my fingers over it very slowly, with my eyes half-closed, seeking for the slightest seam or crack. I found nothing on the top or sides, but on the underside, exactly half way along the front edge—or back edge depending how you looked at it—I felt two minute, parallel ridges about half an inch apart. I applied slight pressure between them and the top of the cuboid levered open.

Inside, resting on a bed of red felt, was a smaller replica of the box, perhaps twelve inches long, three inches deep and six inches across. This time, however hard I searched, I found absolutely no features of any kind. And this perfectly featureless cuboid was what Gregor was prepared to pay five million dollars for.

I spent an hour thinking, smoking and drinking whiskey. In the end, I phoned Emily and said, "It's all sorted. You can come back tomorrow."

There was a small gasp on the other end of the line, then silence, followed by, "Is there any... was there any problem?"

"None at all. We'll talk when you get here."

"My God... I can't believe it..."

"I'll see you tomorrow."

I hung up, carried everything into the bedroom, dumped it on the bed and went to sleep on the sofa in the living room, with my Sig in my hand.

At five, I got up and went for a swim in the ocean. After that, I spent an hour training in the sand, then returned to the house to have a shower and make a cooked breakfast of bacon, eggs and mushrooms, with a large pot of black coffee. I ate on the terrace, watching the sunrise and deciding what I was going to do that morning.

The first thing I did was to call Kenny and give him some very precise instructions. "Call me the moment it's done, will you?"

"Of course, sir, as soon as the café is open."

"Be waiting at the door."

"I shall, sir."

Then, I dragged the two bags of money to the Zombie and threw them in the trunk. Emily's bag I dropped on the floor in front of the passenger seat. I made the drive to Pier 32 in a leisurely ten minutes, parked in the parking lot and strolled into the bar. It was empty at that time of the morning, but JD was behind the counter polishing glasses again. I climbed on a stool and put Emily's bag in front of me.

"How come you're always polishing glasses, JD? How come you never wipe down the bar and talk about dames like the rest of your profession?"

"I'm a Master of the thirty-second degree. We don't do that kind of shit. Apart from wasting my time with stupid questions, what do you want, young Lacklan?"

"To drink coffee, Old Wise One, and reminisce about when I was a young hell raiser."

"Most people 'round here would be glad to forget those days. You were lucky not to wind up in jail."

I watched him pour my coffee and observed, "You were lucky not to wind up there with me."

"True enough."

"You remember my dad's associates used to come down to visit him to talk finance and business?"

He did his imitation of a truck out of gas. "You used to steal their wallets. Son of a bitch! I don't know how you never got caught."

"Remember I used to bring them up to the bar with my jacket over them, and you'd keep them in the fridge, under the cokes? Then we'd share the spoils."

He nodded for a while, staring at the bar and smiling. "I remember, all right. You said it was OK because your dad's associates were all crooks. You used to say, 'It is no crime to steal from a thief.'" He raised an eyebrow at me. "You still think that way?"

I shrugged. "I don't know, JD. I think most laws are there to justify theft, not prevent it. Just so long as that theft is by the state or its allies. I'm not above helping the little guy if the occasion calls for it."

He nodded and my phone rang. I answered:

"Kenny."

"Good morning, sir. It is all organized, just as you requested."

"Thanks, Kenny. Any problems?"

"None at all, sir."

"Good, see you soon, old friend."

I hung up and climbed off the stool. "Thanks for the coffee and reminiscing with me, JD." I dropped some coins on the bar and walked out. He watched me do it with a small smile on his face.

After that, I drove to Clute, East Main Street, and parked in the post office parking lot. I sat there for a while, smoking, staring at the building and thinking, then I got out and went inside, to send a small package priority mail express, to be delivered within twenty-four hours.

Finally, I went to the parking lot, got in my car and headed south, back toward the coast and the Bluewater Highway. It was almost ten o'clock, and I was beginning to feel it was high time I paid Gregor a visit. I had a few questions I needed to ask him, and I was pretty sure he had a few burning questions that I was eager to answer, too. Plus, I had five million bucks that were burning a hole in my trunk, and I wanted to get rid of them.

FOUR

I TURNED NORTH AND EAST ONTO THE BLUEWATER
Highway and put my foot down for the twenty-five miles of
perfectly straight road that took me to Jamaica Beach, on
Galveston Island. I covered the distance in somewhat less
than thirteen minutes and, just outside Jamaica Beach, I
slowed, turned into Indian Beach Drive and followed it to
the one mile bridge that crossed to Caribbean Island, where
Gregor had his casino.

Caribbean Island was slightly less than half a mile across
and devoted exclusively to a variety of bars and restaurants
situated around a central casino. They had managed to
circumvent Texas' very strict laws on gambling by
persuading the state authorities to accept a claim from one
Bob Auia, that he was descended from the Karankawa tribe,
which had inhabited that part of Texas until 1860.

Bob Auia had amassed a body of evidence that, he
claimed, proved his lineage as one of a very small number of
Native Americans descended from the Karankawa, or

Carancahua, tribe. He had also acquired the services of a leading Houston law firm which lodged a claim, on his behalf, for one billion U.S. dollars, against both the State of Texas and the Federal Government. The claim was naturally never heard in a court of law because it was settled out of court with an undisclosed sum of money and the grant of the island as an Indian reservation for those few remaining descendants from the tribe. Having secured this singular victory, he promptly went into business with a Russian associate and built a casino, exempt from the state laws relating to gambling, by its status as a reservation.

What happened to Bob after that, nobody was very sure, but it was rumored that he retired to a luxurious estate somewhere in California and left his Russian partner to run the casino. That had been over twenty years earlier. Whether Gregor was that same Russian partner, or whether he had taken over from him, I didn't know.

The island had been planted with abundant palm trees and a rich variety of tropical gardens in order to emulate its namesake. At the center of the island was a large and highly ornate building that seemed to be modeled on the Kremlin, and made gaudy seem restrained by comparison. I parked in the lot out front, beside a Rococo fountain with a statue of Poseidon vomiting an endless stream of water onto a dolphin's head, grabbed the two bags of cash from the trunk and climbed the nine marble steps to the main entrance.

The foyer was carpeted in violet and had a vast, crystal chandelier suspended from the ceiling and a total of four gleaming, white, full size statues of David (the Galleria dell'Accademia in Florence only has one), two at either end of the lobby. On the right, there was a broad, wooden staircase that rose to the second floor and was big enough to have a palm tree in a vast earthenware pot on the first landing. Sharp right, just inside the door, there was a pale oak desk with a pretty, dark-haired woman behind it.

She observed me with a fixed smile and an odd mixture of curiosity and disquiet. Her eyes shifted from my face to the two large sports bags I was carrying and up again. I dumped them on the floor in front of her desk and said, "I need to talk to Gregor."

Her expression didn't change, but she blinked and said, "Gregor?"

I leaned down, picked up one of the bags and dumped it on the counter. I unzipped it and let her look at the money for a while. Her expression became the sort of thing you see on a five year-old's face when they go for the first time to Disneyland. I zipped it shut again and said, "I need to talk to Gregor."

The disquiet had gone from her face, never to return, and she said, "Of course. Your name, sir?"

"The man returning his five million dollars."

She blinked a few times and picked up the internal phone. She pressed a button and waited a moment. "Mr. Ustinov? There is a gentleman here asking to see you... Well, he says his name is, 'the man returning your five million dollars,' sir. Yes, sir, he is alone... Yes, sir." She hung up and said, "Somebody will be right down."

Thirty seconds later, two men came down the broad staircase. They had the unmistakable look of special forces gone into private enterprise. One of them was tall and lean with very short hair, an expensive Italian evening jacket and a burgundy bow tie. His pal was shorter and stockier, with a clipped beard and a short ponytail, a cream tuxedo and a black bow tie. He was the one who spoke to me.

"What you want?"

"Again? I want to see Gregor."

"What you want with Mr. Ustinov?"

"If I had wanted to talk to you, I would have asked to see the asshole with girl's hair and the IQ of road kill. But I don't and I didn't. I didn't because what I have to discuss with Gregor is none of your damn business. Either take me to him or get out of my face."

His lip and his left nostril curled. He muttered something to his pal in Russian and his pal leaned forward to grab one of the bags.

As a general rule of thumb, if you are hitting something soft, like a belly, it is best to use a closed fist, and if you are hitting something hard, like a skull or a jaw, it is best to use an open hand. It isn't always true, but often enough, it is. On this occasion, it was. As the guy with the burgundy bow tie leaned forward, I bitch-slapped him twice, first backhanded and then with my palm. Then I made cups out of my palms and smacked them both simultaneously over his ears, bursting his eardrums.

His pupils dilated wide, he said, "Ah..." staggered back a couple of steps and fell on the violet carpet, holding his head and vomiting.

The guy with the ponytail reached for his piece, but I already had my Sig in my hand. I said, "Do I need to explain in more detail?"

He frowned at me like I was being unreasonable. "You cannot take pistol into Mr. Ustinov. Is not allowed."

I sighed and pistol-whipped him. Then I turned to the girl behind the counter. "Where is Gregor's office?"

She swallowed hard and looked at the stairs.

I said, "Up the stairs, first on the right?"

She made a slight sideways move of the head.

"Second on the right?"

An imperceptible nod.

I pointed at the internal phone. "If I see you reach for that, I'll shoot you. Understood?"

Another nod.

I grabbed the bags and climbed the stairs, keeping an eye on her. When I got to the second floor, I saw that the first door on the right was a gents' restroom. The second was a large, walnut door. I knocked on it and a deep voice like a geothermal disturbance rumbled something inside. I turned the handle and went in.

The room was large, thirty or forty feet square. It was furnished as you'd expect, with lots of mahogany, red Wilton and chesterfields. At the far end of the room, there was a huge, oak desk, and behind it, broad double windows looked west, over the gulf. Silhouetted against the nearest window was a huge, bald man in a dark suit. He had his back to me and the morning sunlight was reflecting off his head. He spoke quietly and said something in Russian. I kicked the door closed with my heel, crossed the room and threw a hundred and ten pounds worth of cash onto his desk, knocking over an ink well and sending his landline and internal telephones crashing to the floor.

He turned and scowled at me, saw I was alone and scowled at the door, then back at me.

"Where are Zoltan and Peter?"

"I'm not your damned information service, Gregor, and I am not here to waste time. There's your five million bucks. Count it. It's all there."

He took a couple of steps toward the desk. His face said he was struggling to make sense of what I was doing. I decided to help him.

"You're not dealing with Emily anymore, Gregor. You're dealing with me. The four men you sent to kill her last night are dead. Most of their bodies are in the bayou, though bits of them are still scattered across the grass and in the branches. Am I getting through to you? Do you need a translation?"

He shook his head and came a little closer.

"Good." I pointed at the two bags. "Emily is OK with being insulted. I am not. When you are ready to make me a realistic offer, you let me know."

He came to the desk and slowly unzipped the bags and looked inside. Then he raised his eyes to look at me and I saw what Emily had meant. His face was reptilian. His mouth was a thin, lipless line, turned down at the corners, and his skin was leathery. His eyes were hooded and a pale amber color. They were completely devoid of feeling. It was as though he was filled with rage, but rage for him was not so much an emotion as a state of being.

"You have it?"

"Yeah."

"We agreed with Emily, no auction."

"I told you already, Gregor, you're dealing with me now, not Emily. Emily is finished."

"Who are you?"

"That's none of your goddamn business. You want the

box, come up with a realistic offer. I'll be back tonight. If you haven't got an offer for me by then, kiss it goodbye. Are we clear?"

He gave a single nod. "Da..."

I crossed the Wilton, stepped through the door and went down the stairs to the foyer. The girl behind reception watched me all the way. The two thugs in evening dress had disappeared, but there was still a stain on the carpet.

I stepped into the morning sun and went to my car, parked by the pseudo Renaissance Chinese water torture, and drove back toward my house at a leisurely pace, letting the sea breeze slap me around a bit and ruffle my hair. I was wondering how high Gregor would go in his next offer, and who the potential buyers would have been at the auction Emily had apparently agreed not to have.

It also struck me that the fact that she had agreed not to have an auction might be a clue to the reasons for some of her behavior, and might suggest an answer to some of my questions.

What it did not help to answer—at least not in any obvious way—was the big, burning question: what the hell was that black tablet that Gregor feared she might auction on the open market, that was worth many times the five million he had offered her for it?

I was beginning to have a suspicion, but I did not want to believe it.

I pulled off the road and parked among the stilts that held my house high above the sand. Then I climbed the wooden steps to the veranda and sat looking out at the surf. The wind had picked up and what had been lazy splashes on the shore that morning were now becoming curling breakers, five and six feet high. As I watched them curl and tumble toward the shore, I wondered when Emily would call. My gut told me it would not be until that evening. She would want to see me that evening on her own ground.

A voice in my head asked suddenly, who was she?

A gust of wind rose and battered the house, lifting a host of sandy ghosts and dragging them along the beach, only to die down just as quickly and lay the specters to rest again.

Ghosts. I turned the word over in my mind. Whoever she was, Emily was scared. Was she scared of ghosts? The ghosts of her own past? Was Gregor one of those ghosts? Or was this elaborate plan nothing more than a way to make good her escape from ghosts she had left behind in New Jersey; Gregor nothing more than a ticket, a means to acquiring her financial independence, a means that had at the last minute turned unexpectedly dangerous?

There was, at that stage, no way of knowing, but one thing was clear. The story she had told about being blackmailed by Gregor and the Russian Mafia was a complex, well thought out, credibly delivered lie. She had been very believable when she told it. And yet, she must have known from the start that as soon as the exchange took place, I would know she had lied. More symptoms of fear? Or something deeper and more complex?

There was no way of knowing until I spoke to her. I sucked my teeth, stood and made my way to the door. Even then, I told myself, as I unlocked it and went inside, even then I might not get all the truth.

My phone rang. I checked the time. It was eleven thirty-five. I pressed green and sat in my armchair.

"Yeah?"

"Lacklan, it's Emily. Can you talk?"

"Sure."

"What happened last night?"

"Not over the phone. Where are you?"

"I'm still in Houston. I won't be back till this evening. Can you come over then?"

I smiled to myself. "Sure. What time? What's keeping you in Houston?"

"My car broke down. It's being fixed. Can you give me some clue as to what happened?"

"Not really. Everything was fine, why are you so anxious?"

She was quiet for a long while. Finally, I said, "Emily?"

"Yes, yes, I'm here. It's just... Did they give you what they were supposed to?"

Now I was quiet. After a moment I said, with a smile audible in my voice, "I'm pretty sure they did."

"And you gave them what you were supposed to give them?"

"Without a doubt."

Her voice was becoming tense. "And there were no problems...?"

"There were no problems, Emily."

I could hear her breathing becoming quick and heavy. "But then, Lacklan, I don't understand. You must surely have questions for me. And, are you telling me that there was no... That they went away with the parcel...?"

"Emily, I didn't say that. I may have questions for you, or not, but we are not going to discuss this over the phone. You understand? Now I want you to relax and trust that I have done the right thing. I'll see you this evening at about six. Where is your house?"

She was quiet again, like she was thinking. Finally, she said, "Lake Jackson. Where Lake Road meets Bayou Road, on the lake."

"I know it. I'll be there at six. Can you be back by then?"

"Yes, I'll be there."

"And Emily? Relax. Everything is fine."

After a moment, she said, "All right. I'll see you then," and hung up.

I went to the kitchen, pulled a beer from the fridge and cracked it. I stood swigging from the bottle, looking through the plate glass doors at the blustery sea and asking myself, "Who is Emily...?"

FIVE

EMILY'S HOUSE WAS SET AMONG A COUPLE ACRES of broad, green lawns, dotted with cedar elms and partially concealed from the road by a hedge of cypress trees and poplars. There was no gate, but an asphalt drive ran from the road to a concrete parking area outside her front door.

When I arrived, the sun was almost setting and the trees cast long shadows across the lawns and against the side of the house. It was a two-story construction with white walls and gray slate roofs. It wasn't small, and it wasn't cheap.

I rang the bell and she opened it almost immediately. She didn't say anything, but stepped back to let me in, then closed the door behind me. We were in an oddly-shaped hall with parquet flooring and a broad, wooden staircase curling up the left-hand wall in a semi-spiral. Ahead, the hall opened into a living area and a dining area that was on a mezzanine floor. A large, over-stuffed sofa and two similar chairs stood on a beige rug in front of a large, open fireplace, where a couple of logs were burning. At the back of the room, there was a vast, sliding plate glass door that showed more lawn and a swimming pool.

She led me through and gestured to the sofa. "Can I get you a drink?"

I studied her face a moment before answering. I thought she looked scared. I said: "Whiskey, straight up, thanks."

She went to an antique credenza where there was a tray of decanters. I watched her pour a generous measure into a crystal tumbler. She brought it over and handed it to me with both hands, like an offering. I took it and smiled.

"It's quite a house."

She caught the tone in my voice and I saw her eyes flick over my face. "It's not mine. It's Harry's. He lets me live here."

I went and sat in one of her overstuffed armchairs, with my back to the plate glass doors. She came and sat close to me, on the sofa. I was waiting to see what she would say, if she would offer an explanation without being prompted. She didn't. She said:

"Are you going to tell me what happened?"

I sipped the whiskey. It was good, old and smooth.

"What were they paying you five million bucks for?" She shifted her eyes from my face to the beige carpet. "You must have realized that when I saw the bags, I would know that you had lied. Or didn't you realize how bulky five million bucks would be? It's fifty thousand hundred dollar bills. Two sports bags. That's a lot of memory cards, Emily."

"I'm sorry."

"That's not good enough."

"I don't know what to say."

"There is no magic form of words that is going to make

this OK. You lied to me, you duped me, you put my life at risk. There is only one way this goes now. You come clean and tell me what is going on."

She took a deep breath and sighed, shifting her eyes to look at the orange flames wavering in the fireplace. "Would you believe me if I did?"

"There is no 'if'. You are going to tell me. Then we'll see if I believe you."

Her eyes shifted again, this time to look at me. Her brows twitched into a frown. "And if you don't?"

"Let's take it one step at a time. What were they paying you for?"

She remained silent for a while, watching me. She was trying to read my face. "You didn't look?"

"You going to answer every question with a question of your own? I looked..." She straightened, there was a small intake of breath. I pretended to ignore it and went on. "I found a black, carbon fiber box that was impossible to open."

"You didn't force it?"

I sat back and crossed one leg over the other. "I figured if it was worth five million bucks, it might be smart not to damage it."

"How did you know..."

"Enough. I ask, you answer. What is it?"

She put down her drink, clasped her hands and slipped them between her knees. "Even if I wanted to, I couldn't tell you."

"Bullshit." I said it without any particular emphasis, but she looked up, wide-eyed, as though she was shocked. "Cut the act, Emily. I know already that you are a consummate liar. You gave an Oscar-winning performance at my house the other day. You had me almost convinced. But you won't hoodwink me a second time. So let's start again, from the top. And I'm warning you, I am running out of patience. So I advise you not to answer with another question."

"All right, I'm sorry. What do you want to know? If I can, I'll answer."

"Let's start with this: what made you lie to me about the photographs, when you must have known I would spot the lie the minute they handed over the money? You may be many things, but stupid isn't one of them."

"I was scared that if I told you the truth, you wouldn't help me, but I gambled that by the time they handed over the money, it would be too late for you to back down and you'd see it through."

"That's a hell of a gamble."

She gave a small shrug. "Not really, Harry had told me quite a lot about you. You don't get to be a captain in the SAS by backing out of a fight because something unexpected happens..." She paused, still staring at her hands. "And five million dollars in cash is not something most men would give back, once it is handed over."

I nodded. It made sense. I asked: "Who did you have hiding in the bushes?"

She shook her head, then looked me in the eye. "Nobody. Perhaps Gregor had somebody watching. I already told you, my problem is that I am alone."

I let it go and asked, "So what is in the box that is so valuable to Gregor?"

She made a gesture of helplessness and stood, walking away from me toward the plate glass doors. I turned to watch her and saw the last of the copper light fading from the sky.

"I have no right to expect you to believe me. All you know of me is that I lied. But we all do things, bad things that we would not normally do, when we are desperate, when we are in fear."

I rose and went to the fireplace so I could watch her. She was a shadow, a silhouette, with the last of the evening light touching her face.

"I would have done almost anything, however wicked, however awful, to get out of that situation. Now it's over, perhaps I can start to rebuild my life." Now she turned to look at me. "Where is the money, Lacklan?"

"All in good time, Emily. First, answer my question. What is in the box?"

"Enough information to destroy Gregor, the organization he runs from the casino on the Caribbean Island, off Jamaica Beach, and several of his superiors, leading all the way up to the top of the *Shulaya* clan in New Jersey and Russia."

"Information? How?"

"Because I was his personal assistant back in Jersey." She took a couple of steps toward me. "It's a long story, Lacklan, and you probably won't believe me. I wouldn't blame you if you didn't. The *Shulaya* are a powerful clan, they're based in Jersey, but they are trying to make inroads into Texas. It's not as easy as you might think. There is a lot of resistance to them. That's why they took over the casino, as a kind of beachhead, but their sights are set first on the cross-border drugs and prostitution rackets, and ultimately on oil and political corruption. They don't think small, and they are supported by the state back home."

It didn't sound incredible. It sounded very believable, but then, I told myself, everything she said sounded believable.

"You want to tell me how you came to be Gregor Ustinov's personal assistant?"

She gave a small snort of a laugh, took a couple of steps and sat on the arm of the sofa. "I answered an ad in the local paper."

I laughed out loud.

She smiled. "It's God's own truth. The ad was for a receptionist and admin assistant at a local gym. It turned out the gym was owned by a Russian, and the Tae Kwon Do and Krav Maga classes were taught by a Russian special forces veteran. Bit by bit, as I took on more responsibility, they let slip scraps of information: it was a money laundering operation, money from various criminal enterprises was fed through the gym... And every scrap of information they let slip was followed by a promotion or an increase in my salary. At first, you turn a blind eye, but by the time you can't ignore it anymore, you have unwittingly become an accomplice."

It had grown dark. She rose from the arm of the sofa and walked to the door to flip a couple of switches. Half a dozen large, fat lamps came on and the plate glass in the doors turned black. She pulled the drapes and sat on the sofa.

"Put another log on the fire, will you?"

I hunkered down, added a couple of logs and stood again, feeling the warmth of the flames on the back of my legs.

"What made you leave?"

"I'm ashamed to admit that in the beginning, I told myself I had a job and I should be grateful for that, what the owners got up to in their private lives was none of my business. But as time went on and they drip-fed me more information, reeling me into their organization, I began to realize what the Russian Mafia was really about. You see it in the movies and on the TV, but until you see it in real life..."

She paused, as though remembering something she would rather forget.

"I was eventually promoted to be Gregor Ustinov's personal assistant. I'll admit, to begin with, I was quite excited. He seemed to have a very glamorous lifestyle. He traveled a lot and was obviously very rich.

"Apparently, he had taken a shine to me and liked the way I worked. He gave me a very generous pay increase and, after about a week, I was invited to a small gathering at the gym. When I got there, they were all drinking champagne, and in the middle of the dojo they had a man tied to a chair. He was what they called a *bratok*. Like a soldier. He had been in charge of collecting protection money from a number of brothels, but he had been skimming money off the top and keeping it for himself. They forced me to watch as they beat him to death. After that, they told me I was an accomplice, one of the clan. One of them.

"Then Gregor used to take me places with him. Sometimes, it was just a casino or a restaurant, or one of his yachts, other times it was one of his nightclubs, and I met girls who had been abducted in the Eastern Block, addicted to heroin and brought out to the States as sex slaves. In the end, it became more than I could bear. So I gathered all the information I could, stored it and escaped."

"So the whole thing about Harry being your father..."

"Is true. And about my mother's death. It's all true. It was what gave me the impetus, the courage, to escape."

"So what was your plan?"

"Initially, I thought of going to the FBI."

"That would have been the smart thing, why didn't you do it?"

"Because my lawyer told me I faced a real risk of doing time myself. I would probably also end up on the witness protection program, and never see Harry again."

"So you decided to blackmail the Russian mob instead? That has to be the stupidest idea I ever heard in my life."

She gave the floor a rueful, lopsided smile. "Thanks. You sure know how to make a girl feel good about herself." She looked at me, but I wasn't going to take it back. So she went on. "What they will discover when they examine the documents is that I have kept several key pieces of evidence back, and those have been lodged with an undisclosed attorney. If any harm comes to me or my father..."

"The oldest ploy in the game."

"I suppose so, but it's effective."

I had a number of questions that were crowding in on my mind, but I decided not to ask them yet, because I wanted to see how this new situation played out. So instead, I said, "Only, this time it isn't going to be so effective, Emily."

"What do you mean?"

"Things just got a little more complicated."

She sighed and flopped back in the sofa. "You want your

cut of the five million. How much? Half? More? All of it? I notice you haven't given it to me yet."

I smiled. "That's not complicated, Emily. That is very simple and straightforward. No, I don't want your money. The complication is that I didn't give them the box."

She sat forward. "*What?*"

"I killed them, took the money and the box."

"Are you out of your *mind?*"

I sipped my whiskey and returned to my chair. She was barely three feet away from me. Her eyes were wide and bright. Her brows were drawn forward into a scowl. Yet I couldn't find fear or alarm in her face. What I saw was curiosity disguised as fear.

"I killed them, and after I had killed the first two, I heard a car reversing away, then speeding back toward Freeport."

"That had nothing to do with me."

"Then I sat and had a good think about these five million dollars and this enigmatic box, and I decided what I was going to do."

Now her cheeks colored and the curiosity in her eyes turned to anger.

"And what have you decided to do, Lacklan?"

I smiled. "I put the box somewhere where neither you nor Gregor will ever find it, and after that I took your five million bucks back to Gregor at his casino and returned them to him."

She stood and stared down at me with wide, furious eyes. Her voice was shrill. "You did *what? You returned the money? Why, for God's sake? What is wrong with you?*"

We stayed like that for a moment, her staring at me like

she wanted to shoot me, and me carefully studying her expression. Finally, I said, "Sit down."

Instead, she marched to the credenza and mixed herself a stiff martini with plenty of gin. Then she turned to face me and rested her ass against the sideboard.

"Would you please explain to me why you decided to give *my money* back to Gregor Ustinov?"

"I told him he was negotiating with me now and that I found the offer of five million dollars insulting. I told him where he could find his four dead soldiers and that I would be back tonight to hear his improved offer."

She went very still. "My God," she said after a moment. "You are insane. You will get us all killed."

I raised an eyebrow. "All? Don't you mean both?"

She didn't answer. She just kept staring at me.

After a moment, I asked her, "Aren't you even a little curious?"

"About what? Forgive me, I am still reeling at your..." She seemed to search the air for a word and eventually came up with, "*Temerity!* To steal *my* property, *my* money, and then give it back and demand more...!"

"Are you?"

"Am I *what?*"

"Curious."

"*About what, for goodness' sake?*"

I frowned and narrowed my eyes. "About what Gregor said."

She took a pull on her drink. "Of course I am, but I imagine he told you to go to hell and is at this moment burning down your house, on his way here to murder me!"

I shook my head. "No."

She watched me carefully.

"He reminded me that you two had agreed there would be no auction."

She looked quickly away. I waited. She didn't say anything.

I smiled. "So tell me, Emily, what kind of report on criminal activity is kept in that kind of sleek, black box, and is auctioned off to the highest bidder? And, if we hold out and don't sell to the Russians, who else is going to be bidding?" I labored the irony in my voice. "The NYPD? The Galveston County Sheriff's Department? Perhaps the FBI...?"

She looked at me long and hard. "No," she said at last. "The CIA."

SIX

WE REMAINED IN SILENCE FOR A WHILE, SHE sitting, staring at the fire, I leaning with my elbow on the mantelpiece, watching her, waiting, while the fire crackled and the light from the flames bathed her face with wavering light.

Eventually, she said: "I don't blame you for being cynical, Lacklan, and I don't blame you for doubting my word. Perhaps I should have come clean from the start and told you the truth, but be honest." She looked into my face with eyes that said they had been hurt once too often. "How many men do you know who would have helped me if they'd known what I aimed to do? Would you, if I had come clean?"

"Yes."

She gave a snort, then seemed to regret it and sighed. "Even if that's true, how could I have known it?"

I shook my head, moved to the chair and sat down. "You couldn't have."

"So how can you blame me for elaborating on the truth? I am in desperate danger, through no fault of my own. Have you any idea what those men would do to me if they caught me and I had no protection?"

"I know exactly what they would do to you. Which is why I keep telling you to cut the crap. Stop playing games, Emily. First you ask me to believe that two sports bags full of money, weighing over a hundred pounds, are in fact a couple of memory cards, and now you want me to believe a feature-less black box eighteen inches long, six inches deep contains enough documentary proof to bring down one of the biggest clans in the Russian Mafia—and that the CIA are prepared to bid millions for it. How stupid do you think I am? What the hell is going on in your head, Emily?"

She fell back on the sofa, covering her face with her hands, and half-shouted, "*God!*" She dropped her hands by her side and spoke to the ceiling. "Why do you have to pick at *everything*? Question *everything?*"

"Because it's not just your life on the damned line! You asked for my help, and if I am going to risk my life for your crazy plan, I expect you to come clean with me."

She didn't react. She stayed lying back, staring at the ceiling. Finally, she spoke in a dead, monotonous, almost mechanical voice. "The information is in a digital format. It contains more information than you could possibly imagine. There are bank accounts, transactions, contracts of every imaginable type. More than half of it relates to money laundering operations through major international financial institutions, but there are also payments for deliveries of prostitutes from Chechnya, Ukraine, Brazil, Colombia, Mexico..."

She paused to sit up, resting her elbows on her knees.

"There are details of cocaine and heroine shipments, and payments going back years, we are talking about *tens of billions* of dollars. There are payments for assassinations, bribes and blackmail. Some very significant names are involved—and most important of all—there are details relating to the relationship of senior members of the Russian government, including the president, to the leading *Pakhan* in the Russian Mafia, to the godfathers. Believe me, there are several governments around the world who would give a lot to get hold of this information."

I raised an eyebrow, sighed and shook my head. "And you got hold of all this from working in a gym?"

"*Oh for goodness' sake, Lacklan!*" She stood and walked across the room, then turned suddenly to glare at me. "*Why won't you listen to me?*"

"I'm listening, Emily. I'm just not hearing anything I can believe."

"No! I did not get all of that information from working at the goddamn gym! *I told you!* I was promoted to be Gregor's personal assistant! And *that* made me privy to a great deal of highly secret information! I got all that information from working on yachts, in restaurants, at meetings in investment banks in New York and Hong Kong. *And* I had access to his computers! Is that clear enough for you?"

I was quiet for a long while, turning her story over in my mind, following it through from beginning to end. After a while, I frowned at her and asked:

"So you watched that guy get beaten to death, and you stayed in your job..."

Her voice was shrill: "*Of course I did!*" She stared at me, breathed and then repeated more quietly, "Of course I did, Lacklan. Maybe *you* can kill four men with your bare hands and walk away as though nothing had happened—but look at me, for God's sake! I am a small woman! I weigh barely a hundred pounds! I haven't got your physical strength... *or* ten years training in the SAS! If I had tried to walk away after what I had witnessed, they would have killed me! I *had* to pretend I was with them, gain their confidence, encourage them to trust me! You do what you have to do to survive. You know that!"

She paused, her shoulders sagged and she spoke more quietly. "And over time, I was able to gather the information I needed to make the break and protect myself."

It made sense, and however much I prodded her, she was sticking to that story. I moved to the armchair and sat facing her. "So you sat on the information for two years."

She nodded. "Yes. My mother had died and I had found my father. That part of what I told you was true. I got away and at first, it seemed they would not come after me. I confess I was chicken. I let the days slip by and run into weeks and then months, enjoying being with Harry and feeling safe. Having an almost normal life. But it was a fool's paradise and in the end, they caught up with me."

Suddenly, her face seemed to contract. She got up and rushed across the room, dropped on her knees in front of me and clutched my hand. There were tears in her eyes.

"Please, Lacklan, stop punishing me. I've been living in hell these last few years and I am fighting to get out, but I can't do it alone. Please help me. Please stop attacking me. Perhaps I should have told you the truth from the start, perhaps I should have come clean, but how was I to know?

You can't blame me for being careful. I have leveled with you now. I have told you the truth. I have told you everything there is to know, please help me. I am *begging* you."

I nodded. "Get off your knees, Emily. Don't ever kneel."

She ignored me and asked, "What have you done with the box, Lacklan? If they get their hands on it, I..."

She trailed off and I waited, smiling.

"I wondered how long it would take us to come to this. If they get their hands on it, you are defenseless against them... and yet. And yet it was *you* who got me to deliver it straight into their hands. You want to explain that to me, Emily?"

She got off her knees and sat, perched on the edge of the sofa. "The money..." she said, "It would have been enough to..."

I interrupted, "You're still bullshitting me, Emily. You know damn well that five million bucks would have done nothing to protect you, or your father, from an organization like that."

She didn't answer. I sighed, stood and moved toward the door. She snapped, "Where are you going?"

I turned. She had gotten to her feet and now took a step toward me. I said, "When you're prepared to come clean and tell the *truth*, then we can talk. But as long as you are trying to hoodwink me, I have no reason to talk to you. Meantime, I have an auction to organize."

"No! Lacklan, wait!"

I waited.

She closed her eyes. "I had somebody there."

"I already know that. Who? Who was it?"

She swallowed. "Jerry. The name will mean nothing to you. He..." She covered her face with her hands and dropped onto the sofa again. She looked ragged. "I am *sorry! I was desperate! I keep telling you I was desperate! Can't you understand that? Why won't you listen?*" She dropped her hands to her lap and looked up at me. There were genuine tears on her cheeks. "He was there to... If you didn't kill them, he was to start a fire fight."

"I could have been killed."

"He was also there to protect you."

My voice was bitter with irony. "Gee! Thanks."

She wiped her cheeks with her fingertips. "From what Harry had told me about you, I was pretty sure you would not hand over the money, and you would probably try to take them out. So I asked Jerry to keep an eye on you, and if things didn't go as they were supposed to..."

"Meaning if I didn't do as expected and kill them."

"He was to shoot the man with the automatic rifle."

I frowned. "How did you know there was a man with an automatic rifle?"

"There is always at least one, it's procedure. But in any case, Jerry told me."

"So he takes out the assault rifle, triggers a firefight and I take care of the rest."

"He would have given you cover."

"You could have got us both killed. Who is this Jerry?"

"A colleague. It's best you don't know him."

"You're quite something. The cute, demure girl next door. Gregor lost more than he knows when you walked out. You shouldn't be in the Mafia, you should be in the GRU, organizing operations."

"Please stop it. That's not fair. I did what I had to do. I didn't ask to be press ganged into organized crime."

"You did what you had to do? You recruited me, tried to seduce me, reeled me in, played me—the works! That was a damned sight more than you *needed* to do! What you *needed* to do was go to the Feds and come clean!"

"Lacklan, *stop!* You must realize I would not have done any of this if I had not been desperate. I *have* come clean. I have told you all the truth. Can we please *stop* this now!"

I didn't answer. I stood looking at her and thinking. Finally, I said, "I am going to go. I am going to go to the casino and see what kind of offer Gregor is prepared to make. While I'm there, I will also make sure he understands you and your father are off limits. I need to think about what you've told me. We'll talk again soon."

She took a couple of steps toward me. "Lacklan, you're scaring me. Please tell me where it is. You have to!"

"I don't have to tell you a damned thing."

"You can't do this!"

"I've done it already. And if you're smart, you'll stop trying to play me. I can help you, Emily, and I am willing to, but not if you are going to keep doing crazy stuff like this. All you'll achieve is to get yourself, and everybody else killed —or worse."

We stared at each other for a while in silence. Her chest was rising and falling like she'd been running. "You will help me then?" she said at last.

"I am helping you."

"You are going to the casino now..."

"Yes."

"All right. And you will contact me tomorrow?"

"I'll let you know what Gregor says."

She took another step toward me. "Lacklan, don't cut me out. I need to be a part of this."

"No. You don't. You need to stop acting crazy. We'll talk, but first I need to know you're done with your wild plans."

She closed her eyes. "All right... I have just..." She opened them again and they were moist and pleading. "I've had nobody to turn to till now. Can you understand that? I have had to deal with everything all on my own."

I nodded. "I get it."

She sighed, then said, "Will you take me to Harry's house? I don't think I can be alone tonight."

I raised an eyebrow. "What about Jerry?"

She looked startled, then frowned. "Forget about Jerry."

"Forget about the guy you dispatch with a rifle to assassinate Russian mobsters? That's not going to happen. I'll postpone it for tonight, but I won't forget."

Her face flushed and she spoke through clenched teeth, "*Enough!*"

I figured she was right and she had had enough for one day. In any case, I was curious to see what I was going to find at the casino. So I nodded and said, "Let's go."

We didn't talk in the car. She called her father to tell him she was coming and then sat with her arms crossed, staring out the side window so I couldn't see her face. I didn't know if she was mad, scared or crying. Most likely, it was all three. I dropped her outside the Colonel's house, she got out, slammed the door and ran through the big gate and up the drive. I saw the front door open, bathing the path in warm light around her black silhouette and the Colonel's. She hugged him and kissed him, they went in and he closed the door.

I pulled away and headed toward Galveston Island. At Surfside Beach, I turned north and accelerated along the Bluewater Highway, leaving the lights of Freeport behind me. The moon had not yet risen, but the sky was a mass of stars, distant and icy. I drove fast, with the windows open and the night sea air battering my face and cooling my head.

At San Luis, I slowed for the bends before the bridge, and then accelerated again across the mile wide expanse. There is no town on the Galveston side of the San Luis bridge, and mine is the only house. So it was pitch dark, apart from the slight luminescence of the white sand and the foam from the waves. That fact made the twin cones of light from the headlamps all the more noticeable as they pulled onto the blacktop off my track, and accelerated toward Jamaica Beach, bathing the sides of the road in amber light, with the two red taillights chasing them into the darkness.

For a moment, I thought about going after them, but then I thought better of it. I pulled over beside the house and ran up the stairs to the terrace. The lock had been picked and the sliding doors stood gaping onto the blackness inside the house. I pulled my Sig and cocked it, though I knew there was nobody there now.

I snapped on the light and looked around. It was as though a tornado had passed through the house. The sofa and the armchairs had been gutted. The rugs had been pulled up and every floorboard inspected. Every drawer had been pulled out and emptied onto the floor. Every cupboard stood gaping and empty, every cushion slashed. The kitchen was in a similar state, as was the bathroom. There was not a nook or cranny in the house that had not been searched, but equally, there was nothing of any value missing.

I left the house as it was and went back to the Zombie, rolled onto the road and continued my journey toward Jamaica Beach, and the Caribbean Island Casino.

When I got there, the parking lot was almost full. The windows of the elaborate, palatial building were all a blaze of light, and the hideousness of the Rococo fountain was enhanced by green and blue spot lamps located within the water. I parked the car and climbed the stone steps to the foyer. There was a different pretty girl behind the desk this time. I told her, "I'm here to see Gregor Ustinov. He's expecting me."

"Your name, sir?"

I smiled. "He doesn't know my name."

She wasn't fazed. "Oh, you must be Mr. Lacklan Walker. Mr. Ustinov is engaged in a meeting at the moment. Will you please have a complimentary drink in the cocktail bar, and he will join you very shortly." I hesitated a moment, wondering whether to go up anyway, but she gestured at the big mahogany doors with the brass handles, and the doorman in the violet coat with a violet top hat, and I figured I could use a complimentary drink.

It was not the kind of casino James Bond would have felt at home in. There were a lot of fat people in baseball caps, Bermuda shorts and shirts with parrots on them, standing at slot machines giving their money away, so my jeans and my linen shirt didn't look that out of place. I found the cocktail lounge, ordered a Bushmills straight up and told the barkeep in the violet waistcoat it was on the house. He didn't seem to care. He even threw in a free bowl of peanuts.

I took a sip, climbed on a bar stool and turned to survey the bar. That was when I saw Rand, all four hundred and forty pounds of him. He was about ten or twelve feet away, in a white tuxedo with a burgundy cummerbund and black pants with a satin stripe. His bow tie was black. He was watching me and his expression was one of narrow-eyed curiosity: like he was doing mental arithmetic over and over and didn't buy the result he kept getting. I smiled on the left side of my face, where it is more rueful than ironic.

He said: "Lacklan Walker, late of her Majesty's Special Air Service. I heard you'd been making a nuisance of yourself, but I did not expect to meet you here."

"Rand Peabody, allegedly of the United States Central Intelligence Agency. I can't say I would be surprised to see you anywhere, especially a dive like this. Have a drink. It's on the house."

His eyebrows shot up toward his bald scalp. "Is it, by Jove! In that case, I'll have a vodka martini, shaken, not stirred!"

SEVEN

He sipped and asked me, "Why are you here, Lacklan? In my experience, whenever you show up somewhere, things start exploding and people start dying. Are we safe?"

I shrugged. "What can I tell you? I yam what I yam. Actually, I'm on holiday. We used to come here when I was a kid."

"Is that so?"

"It really is. Ask anyone."

He nodded a few times with a bland smile on his fat face. "I never figured you for the casino type. I had you down more as the beach bar, steak house type."

I ignored the comment and asked him, "What about you? What brings you here? You still with the Company?"

He chuckled comfortably. "I am in the intelligence *gathering* industry, Lacklan. If you want news, switch on the TV."

I switched my smile to the right, where it was more

ironic. "Haven't you heard? That's all fake news. So what kind of intelligence do you hope to gather on Galveston Island? Feel like sharing?"

He took the olive from his drink with fat, pointed fingers and pressed it into his mouth. As he chewed, he eyed me and said, "That depends on what *you're* sharing."

"You here for the auction?"

He raised an eyebrow. "Auction?"

"Feel like sharing?"

He tried to read my face and found only a blank page. So he nodded. "OK, we could share a bit. What auction?"

I shrugged. "I heard there was an auction. If you're here for the auction, you must know what one."

He thought about it, looking around the bar. "I guess I could be here for the auction. What do you know about it?"

I shook my head. "Uh-uh. I committed myself by admitting I know there is an auction. Now it's your turn, buddy. Commit."

He waited a long time, then nodded. "I'm here for the auction. I thought you were here on holiday?"

"I am. Who else is here?"

"So far, just me—and you. Who are you representing?"

"No Europeans or Brits? No Chinese...?"

"Uh-uh, not yet. But I'm guessing they'll come. The ones I was expecting to see were the Saudis..."

It was a calculated statement and his small, hard eyes watched me carefully for a reaction. I nodded and said, "So I guess you're here on behalf of Israel as well as the U.S."

"Joint interests," he said.

"Right."

His eyes narrowed and he grinned. "You don't know

what the hell this is about, Lacklan. You sniffed something on the air and you're prowling around, looking for an angle."

"That may or may not be true."

"Who are you representing? You're not here for the Brits."

"What makes you so sure?"

"Because I know who they'd send, and it wouldn't be a rhinoceros like you."

I gave him a lopsided smile. "You're right, of course. In fact, Rand, I am the auctioneer."

He didn't say anything. His face went hard and his eyes were small diamonds.

I said, "Feel like sharing some more?"

He drained his glass. "I don't know," he said. "But I think your date has arrived. I'll be in touch. Let's do lunch."

"Yeah, I'd like that."

He moved away, like a galleon in full sail easing its way out of a crowded harbor. And as he left, Gregor approached. He didn't acknowledge me. He just leaned on the bar. When he'd been served, he spoke without looking at me.

"So. You are here. What you want?"

I turned my stool to face him and shook my head. "Uh-uh. That's not the way it works. You make me a new offer. I tell you if I like it."

"Five million was final offer. Where is Emily?"

"Let's understand each other and save time, Gregor. If you go near Emily, her family or her friends, if you drive down her street or send one of your gorillas near her, if you ever mention her name again or even think about her, the deal is off and you will never—*never*—get your hands on the box. Is that much clear?"

"Is clear."

"Good. Now, shall I tell you what five million bucks buys you? It buys you my attention for five minutes. The next five minutes. If, by the end of that time, you haven't said something more interesting, I'm going to go and have a chat with my friend from the Central Intelligence Agency."

"We said no auction."

"You agreed that with Emily. I already told you Emily is finished. You're running out of time, pal, and I am running out of patience. Have you got a serious offer or not?"

He still hadn't looked at me. He was leaning both arms on the bar, staring at the polished wood, with his bald head reflecting the overhead lamps. I could see the corner of his left eye twitching. "Maybe," he said at last, "I can go ten million."

"Maybe? *Maybe* you can go to ten million? When will you know? You had all goddamn day to sort this out, Gregor. What? You thought I wasn't serious when I killed your four goons and came in here to give you your damned money back? What do I need to do to convince you I am serious?"

Now he turned to look at me with eyes that had seen suffering and pain beyond endurance and grown calloused against it. "You don't talk to me like this. I will gut you..."

"What you do in your wet dreams is no concern of mine, Gregor. Make me a serious offer or stop wasting my time." I stood. "And another thing, I'm sending you the bill for refurnishing my house. I'm insulted you think I'm stupid enough to keep the box where your gorillas could find it.

Next time you damage my property, I'm going to level your damned casino. I hope I'm beginning to get through to you, Gregor."

"I don't know what you talkin' about. Give me card. I call you tomorrow."

I gave a small, humorless laugh and scrawled a number on a paper napkin. As I put the pen away, I said, "Don't leave it too long, Gregor. I think you're a pussy, and Emily was stupid to get involved with you in the first place. The auction is on, as of now."

I crossed the bar to where Rand was talking to a well dressed couple in their early fifties. I knew Gregor was watching. I placed my hand on his massive shoulder and said, "Forgive me for interrupting, Rand. Call me tomorrow if you're free and we'll do lunch."

He searched my face a moment, nodded and pulled a card from his inside pocket. He handed it to me and said, "Call if you need to talk. Till tomorrow, then."

I stepped outside and sat for a while with my ass on the hood of the Zombie, smoking and looking at the stars over the Gulf. I wondered who Jerry was for a while; then I wondered if he was anybody, or just another one of Emily's fantasies. Finally, I decided there was no way for me to know until I had extracted some more information out of the relevant people. So I dropped the butt on the gravel and trod on it. Then I drove back to my vandalized house.

There, I did what repairs I could to my mattress with bits of duct tape, left the sliding doors open and tied a length of fishing line across the opening, secured at one end to the wall and at the other to a precariously balanced carton full of empty beer bottles. That's the kind of high tech security an

EMP won't neutralize. I slept peacefully for four hours, with my Sig in my hand and my Heckler and Koch 416 under my improvised, duct-taped pillow.

I rose at six to go for a morning swim and a couple of hours' practice on the beach and, shortly before nine, I climbed the steps, planning to call my landlord about the burglary, and telling myself it had been either Gregor or Emily. My money was cautiously on Gregor, but I had decided that whoever turned up first that morning would, in all probability, be the guilty party. As it turned out, the first person to show that morning, at just before ten, while I was sitting down on the terrace to eat fried bacon and eggs, was Harry, the Colonel, Emily's father.

He parked his Ford pickup on the sand beside the house and struggled up the stairs. He looked slightly yellow, had hollow eyes and sweat beading his brow. He was breathing heavily. I stood as he reached the deck and went to him.

"Colonel? Are you OK? What happened?"

He came to me and gripped my arms, staring up into my face. "Lacklan, is Emily with you? Tell me she's with you, please!"

I shook my head. "No, I left her at your place yesterday evening. I watched her go in the door."

"Yes..." He nodded several times, almost convulsively. "Yes, but she's gone."

"What do you mean, she's gone, Colonel?" Before he could answer, I ushered him toward the table and told him to sit down. I handed him a paper napkin to wipe his brow. "Take a minute, relax, get your breath."

I went into the kitchen to get him a cup, then came back

out and sat opposite him. As I poured his coffee, I said: "Now, tell me what happened, from the beginning."

"It must have been half past seven or eight when she came in. She looked upset. I sat her down and gave her a drink, and asked her if she was all right. She assured me she was OK, it was just what she called a 'bad hair day' and she needed some company. So we chatted for an hour, watched some TV, and at half past eleven or twelve, we went upstairs. She often stays over after a meal, so she has her own room, her own bathroom, she keeps some clothes there... You understand."

I nodded and he went on.

"This morning, I rose at seven thirty and went down to make breakfast. She is usually up by half past seven or eight, but this morning, there was no sign of her. I gave her till eight thirty and went up to knock on her door. There was no reply. I finally went in and her room was completely empty. There was not a trace, like she'd never been there. Her bed had not been slept in. Her phone, her purse—everything was gone. It was as though I had dreamed the whole thing!"

"So you called her..."

"Her telephone is either switched off or has no signal."

"You went to her house?"

He frowned, like my question was somehow absurd. "No. I came straight here. Why would she go home before half past seven in the morning? And even if she had, she would have left a note. And why would her phone be switched off? The only thing I could think of that made any sense at all was that she was with you. I thought perhaps you called her last night..."

I thought for a moment, looking out at the surf rolling in off the sea. "Why? Did she receive a call last night...?"

He hesitated. "I'm not sure. I wear earplugs to get to sleep. I have very sensitive hearing. I thought I heard her talking, it may have been a phone call. That would have been midnight or very shortly after."

I looked at my watch. It was five past ten. "Colonel, don't you think you're jumping the gun a bit? She might have got up early, made the bed and gone home or into town. She didn't think to take her charger with her last night, maybe her battery is flat."

He shook his head. "Lacklan, I *know* something is wrong. For the last few weeks, I have known something was wrong. I can't put my finger on it, but she has been...*different*." He ran his fingers through his gray, wispy hair, looking around him, searching for the right words. "It's as though she were on constant alert, waiting for something bad to happen. She's been needy, clinging, always wanting to be around me, as though that made her feel safe. Take last night, for example. This is totally out of character. Something has happened to her, believe me. Somebody has taken her..."

"Have you called the police?"

He shook his head vigorously. "No!"

"Why not?"

"What if she *has* been kidnapped? They might kill her!"

I nodded, still thinking. "What do you want me to do?"

"Can't you find her? Get her back?" He shook his head, imploring me with his eyes. "Lacklan, I couldn't bear to lose her. In the last two years..."

"I know, Colonel, she told me." I hesitated. "How much do you know of her life before she came out to Texas?"

He became serious. "Only what she has told me. She doesn't talk much about her life before... before she came to look for me. I know she had to struggle financially. I know she worked as a receptionist, then got promoted to the director's PA..." He faltered. "I have often suspected there was more, things she didn't want to tell me about, especially lately. She's been so edgy..." He stared at me suddenly, frowning. "*Scared*," he said. "She's been scared..."

His eyes shifted from my face over my shoulder and his frown deepened. He sat forward, staring, noticing for the first time the state of my living room. "What in the name of...!"

"I was burgled last night."

He got up and went to stand in the doorway. The glare of the bright morning sun had cast the inside of the house into darkness, and it was only as he stepped over the threshold that he got the full extent of what had happened.

"Dear God, man! When did this happen?"

"While I was with Emily?"

He turned quickly to search my face. "Is there some connection? Has she confided something to you, Lacklan? I need to know!"

"I don't know anything, Colonel. And if something has happened to her, then we are wasting time. You need to go home. She might turn up, or there might be a ransom call. I'm going to go to her house, see if I can find something there."

He watched me say all this with a deepening scowl. "You

know something. Goddamn it, Lacklan! Don't lie to me! What has happened to her?"

I sighed noisily through my nose. "Whether I do or not, we are not helping her by standing here arguing. Go home, Colonel, and wait there. I'll see what I can find out and I'll be in touch. You got a key to her place?"

He nodded, but his scowl didn't lessen. He pulled a latchkey off his key ring and gave it to me. Then he turned and made his way down the stairs. As I watched him go down, I thought he looked like a very sick man, older, suddenly, than his sixty-odd years.

I called the landlord and told him I'd been burgled. He told me he'd be over that morning with someone from the insurance company and see about replacing my essential furniture by that evening. I thanked him, told him to let himself in, and went down to the Zombie, wondering if Emily had been kidnapped, or if this was just another fantasy episode in her unfathomable game. After my conversation last night with Gregor, it was hard to believe that he would snatch her. On the other hand, men like Gregor could be unpredictable.

And then there was Rand, and the Company. I had no idea how much he knew or, perhaps even more important, who had informed him that there was going to be an auction. It was conceivable that the CIA had snatched her, but then again, I had told Rand I was the auctioneer, so why not snatch me instead? Did they think they could use Emily as leverage over me? And then there was the big imponderable: if the CIA was there and knew about the auction, who else was there? Mossad? The Saudi GID? Al-Qaeda?

Without knowing what the damned thing was, it was impossible to know who would have an interest.

I climbed into the Zombie and sat drumming the wheel with my fingers. One thing was clear. However compelling the evidence was, that Emily claimed she had against Gregor, it was not enough to have Rand Peabody and the Company getting involved in an international auction, bidding millions against the Kremlin and the Russian Mafia. Was there anything, I asked myself, looking at the waves through the massive stilts under my house, was there anything about Emily that was true?

"Who," I asked aloud, "Who is Emily...?"

Then I reversed onto the road and headed south over the bridge, toward Lake Jackson and Emily's place on Jackson Lake.

EIGHT

I was half expecting to find her at the house, but as I moved down the drive, among the trees, there was no sign of any kind of activity, and the drapes in the windows were pulled closed. I parked outside her garage and used the key the Colonel had given me to open the front door.

Inside, it was dark. I stood motionless on the threshold for fifteen seconds, listening to the house. There was nothing. It was still and silent: no movement, no creak of boards, no breathing. I closed the door and crossed the parquet hall to the living and dining area.

The drapes were pulled closed over the large, sliding doors that gave onto the lawn and the pool at the back, casting the room into a kind of penumbra, where shadows merged with each other and played tricks on your eyes. But even so, it was easy to see that the sofa had been moved about three feet back and now sat askew in the middle of the room, the lamp table at the far end of the sofa had been overturned and the large, cream lamp lay on the beige carpet, with the shade broken, torn and twisted.

The fire which had been burning the night before was now ash and embers. Small trails of smoke rose from it, and there was a smell of soot in the air. The nearest of the two armchairs had been shoved to one side, and between the fireplace and the farthest armchair, the poker lay on the rug. It had left stains, some of them were soot. The others, I was pretty sure, were blood.

Sitting in that farthest armchair, staring at me with incurious eyes, was a man. He was about thirty, with long, stringy hair that seemed to be reddish in color, though it was hard to be sure in the gloom. He had a long beard of the same hue that reached to his solar plexus. He had on brown corduroy pants, a pale blue shirt and a beige bomber jacket. His heavy, horn-rimmed glasses were on the floor and there was a thick trickle of blood from a blow to the right side of his head. The blow hadn't killed him, though, and neither had the toothpicks under his nails. They had probably made him talk, but what had killed him was the kitchen knife that had been rammed through his sternum.

I stepped to him, taking care not to tread in any soot or blood, and checked his pockets. He still had his wallet. I pulled it out and looked at his driver's license. His name was Jerry Fines. So he did exist. Or at least, he had existed.

I wiped my prints off his wallet with my handkerchief and put it back in his jacket. The rest of his pockets didn't yield anything of interest, and neither did the rest of the house, but it wasn't hard to work out what had happened. He had been picked up by somebody who knew he was an associate of Emily's. He had been forced to call her and arrange a meeting at her house. That had been the call the Colonel thought he'd heard. After the call, they had killed him, and when she had arrived, they had taken her away.

I thought about Rand. It would be easy for the CIA to monitor her calls and find out who her close associates were, and it was well known that they were not above using torture. But I would have expected the Company to be tidier, cleaner and more efficient. Besides which, they could have picked her up directly, without going through Jerry. It also struck me that Jerry would probably have been of interest to the Company anyway.

This, I told myself, looking around at the mess, definitely had more the look and the smell of the Russian mob; and if it was the mob, it meant that my threats last night had meant nothing to them. All I had managed to do was make them mad.

I went out, closed the door and climbed into my car. Then, I drove slowly toward Pier 32, trying to think. As I went, I called the Colonel.

He answered and babbled: "Lacklan, is that you?"

"Yeah."

"Did you find her?"

"No, not yet. Listen, did you ever meet a friend of hers called Jerry?"

He was quiet for a moment. "No, why?"

"I found him at Emily's house. You need to brace yourself, Harry. He had been tortured and murdered. I figure they forced him to phone her. That was the call you heard. He asked her to meet him at her house, and when he'd hung up, they killed him. When she arrived, they abducted her."

"Oh, my God! But *why*, for heaven's sake?"

"I don't know yet, Harry. But I'm going to find out."

"Do you think she...?"

"Don't lose hope. We'll sort it out. Now, listen to me, you need to call the cops and tell them you're worried about Emily. Ask them to check on her house. Do not tell them you contacted me, you understand?"

"Yes, yes, of course."

"I'm going to try to find her. I have some ideas, but I can't do anything if I have the local PD or the sheriff watching my every move."

"I understand."

"I'll call you as soon as I know something."

I hung up and called Rand. He answered, "Keep it short and sweet."

"Have you got her?"

"I have no idea what you're talking about."

"Let's have a drink at Pier 32."

"I'll be there in fifteen minutes."

I pulled into the near-empty parking lot, left the car near the entrance and pushed in through the doors. At that time of the morning, the place was quiet. JD had his elbows on the bar and was looking at his cell phone, laughing quietly to himself.

"How come you're not polishing glasses?"

He didn't look up. "I joined the zombie revolution. I sold my soul to social media."

"You have a soul?"

"Not anymore."

"Another giant bites the dust."

"What can I tell you?" He put his phone away and smiled at me. "What's happening?"

"Not much. I got burgled last night."

He frowned. "No shit? They take anything valuable?"

"Not a thing."

He narrowed his eyes. "That's good, then. If I hear anything, I'll let you know."

"Appreciate it, JD. I'm just going to have some coffee out on the deck with an old friend. Send him through when he gets here, will you? You'll know him. He's the size of a small moon."

"You got it."

He poured me a large cup of black coffee and I carried it out to the veranda, where I sat in the shade of a blue and white parasol and waited for Rand. I didn't have to wait long. After ten minutes, he rolled up in a gleaming red Jaguar XE. He climbed out, waved to me, walked through the dark saloon, paused at the bar to talk to JD and then joined me on the terrace. He lowered his massive form into the chair opposite me and said, "Who is 'her'?"

"I've been asking myself the same question."

"Don't be cute. Are we going to fence and play games, or cooperate?"

"I don't know yet."

He raised an eyebrow. JD brought out a draft beer, placed it in front of Rand and withdrew back into the shadows.

"When will you know? Shall I go away and come back when you've been enlightened?"

"How did you find out there was going to be an auction?"

He sipped his beer, then wiped a foam moustache from

his upper lip with the back of his wrist. "That's classified information."

"Then we are going to have to fence and play games, which is a shame, because I have information you need, and you have information that I need."

"You said you were the auctioneer. You should know who sent us the invite."

"I am the auctioneer now, Rand. I wasn't the auctioneer before. I took over. Does that make sense to you?"

"Mm-hm... When did you do that?"

"Yesterday. I'll tell you what we'll do. I ask you a question, and if I'm wrong, you tell me I'm wrong. OK?"

He shrugged and took another pull.

I said, "Your invite was sent to you by Jerry Fines."

He didn't say anything. I sipped my coffee, then as I set down the cup I said, "Jerry Fines is no longer involved in the auction."

"Why not?"

"He has a bad case of death. The cops are probably discovering his body 'round about now."

He tried to hide it but I could see that he was mad. "Did you kill him?"

"No, think it through, Rand. If I had, would I then call you and ask you if you've got her?"

He frowned. "Jerry is a girl?"

"No."

We stared at each other a while, trying to read each other's faces while giving nothing away. Finally, I said, "Was he one of yours?"

He hesitated half a second, then said, "No."

"So you were trying to recruit him."

He didn't answer, but after a moment, he said, "Who is 'her'? Who did you think we had taken?"

I sighed and decided I had nothing to lose. "All I know is her name is Emily, and she was an associate of Jerry's."

He looked at the sky. His eyes were narrow and I could see them shifting, jerking this way and that. Finally, he shook his head and said, "I don't know of any Emily. But you would be wise to come clean and share what you know with us, Lacklan."

I gave him my best lopsided grin. "Sure, I know that, Rand. Because the CIA are such a caring, sharing gang of nice guys. Equally, you know you would be wise to reciprocate."

He grunted. "Who killed Jerry?"

"Till ten minutes ago, I thought maybe you did. Now I'm thinking maybe it was Gregor Ustinov. You got any ideas on that score, partner?"

He shook his head. "What about this auction, Lacklan? You know there can't be an auction, right? It's us, or nobody."

I frowned and smiled at the same time. "Yeah? How's that?"

"Come on, Lacklan. I know you can be a ruthless son of a bitch, but I also happen to know you're a patriot and you believe in those old values of freedom and democracy..."

He trailed off and I had the interesting impression that his eyes and his mouth were engaged in two completely separate tasks. I kept watching as he furrowed his brow and squinted, hesitated a moment and then started to laugh.

"Oh, man! Oh, *man!* You don't know what you've got, do you?"

I made the face of innocence. "I don't?"

"Son of a gun…! Who dares wins, right. You're what the Irish call a chancer."

I shrugged. "I'm guessing it's not a digital record of the crimes of the *Shulaya* clan, and their links to the Russian government?"

"That what they told you it was?"

I nodded.

He frowned. "Lacklan, you need to come clean with me. Who is this Emily? and where is the…?"

He hesitated. I said, "The box?"

"OK, the box. Where is it?"

"Here's the thing, Rand. I don't know who Emily is, aside from being the best liar I ever met in my life." I shrugged again, more elaborately, and sighed. "And as to the box, I am going to follow Napoleon's advice, when in doubt, do nothing."

"You know he lost, right?"

"You tell me what it is, and I will decide what to do with it. While you think about it, I am going to try to find Emily, and see who turns up for this auction."

His face was tight. "We can help you find her."

"No, thanks."

"Lacklan, if you sell that box to anybody but the U.S. government, you could be guilty of treason."

"So you say. Convince me. Tell me what it is."

"What it is is classified."

I shook my head. "Says you. Not good enough, Rand. Get authorization if you have to, but I am not handing that box over to anyone gratis until I know what it is."

He sighed, chewed his lip and drummed his fingers on the table. "Not much point threatening you, I guess."

"Let's not go to that place, Rand."

He chuckled and his expression changed to one of good-humored gossiping. "Say," he said, jerking his chin at me, "are the rumors true?"

"What rumors?"

"About Timmerman, and the European stock market crash[1]..."

I gave an imperceptible nod, then said, "Let's keep it friendly. Tell me what it is, we'll discuss what happens to it. Who else can I expect to turn up at the auction? Can you tell me that?"

"I can guess. The Brits will send someone. They'll probably be among the highest bidders. Europe, China for sure, Saudi. Maybe others." He made to stand. "I have to go and make a call." He hesitated. "Lacklan, I know your history and your background. I know you've been to some dark places and come out alive. But believe me, you have never been in this much danger before. You don't want to make an enemy of the U.S. Government. Keep us on side."

I showed him a face with no expression. "I appreciate the advice, Rand. Let me know what your boss says."

He walked out and a moment later, I watched him squeeze his huge bulk into his red car and drive away. I sat for a while after he'd gone, watching the seagulls circling overhead, occasionally crying out in what sounded like a Greek chorus of despair. I knew how they felt.

The CIA had not known about Emily. Jerry had been

---

1. See *Kill Two*

her front man, her hit man, her all-purpose gofer. Two got you twenty he had been in love with her—she was not a hard woman to fall in love with. He had served her faithfully and paid the ultimate price.

On the other hand, Gregor knew about her. That was odd: Gregor did but the CIA didn't. That was as odd as it was interesting. I wondered if it meant that other intelligence services were also in the dark about her, and I decided there was a good chance it did. Then I got to wondering how those intelligence services were intended to contact Jerry for the auction, and how he had planned to contact them. He'd had no cell phone on him when I found him. Chances were, I decided, that he and Emily had used a computer at a secure location.

As far as I could see, I had only two avenues to explore: Gregor and Jerry. Jerry meant finding out where he had lived and going through his apartment with a fine-toothed comb for some clue as to who and what I was dealing with. It wasn't promising, but it would have to be done.

On the other hand, Gregor was going to play out one of two ways, either he would contact me to negotiate the box in exchange for Emily, or I would go and blow up his casino and beat Emily's whereabouts out of him before sending him back to Putin in twenty-four small boxes.

I had just made up my mind to go and find Jerry's address when my phone rang.

"Yeah, Walker…"

"Is Gregor. I think we meet now."

"You have a better offer for me?"

"Yeah, we make better offer. You come to my office this afternoon."

"I don't want to waste my time, Gregor. What kind of offer are we talking about?"

"Four times previous offer."

"That's it? Nothing else?"

"Is good starting offer, we can negotiate."

I hesitated a moment, frowning to myself. Was he deliberately not mentioning Emily because he wanted to see if I would mention her, as an admission that I gave a damn? Or did he simply not have her?

"OK, I'll be there at two. And Gregor, you should be aware I already have another offer."

"From U.S. government. I know. I have seen."

The line went dead.

NINE

It didn't take me long to find Jerry's address. He was listed in the White Pages and had a house on Ralph Street, in Clute. When I arrived, the sheriff was already there, with a couple of deputies who were putting up yellow tape that said the house was a crime scene. He was a tall, rangy man in a denim shirt and a handsome white hat. As I parked at the end of the drive, he watched me, then strolled down to the sidewalk with his thumbs in his belt.

I climbed out of the Zombie and approached him, frowning like a man who is wondering what is going on. He waited for me to speak.

I said: "This Jerry Fines' house?"

He nodded slowly. "Yup. Who're you?"

I shook my head like I was saying I was nobody. "We have a mutual friend. Her father asked me to look in on Jerry and see if she was with him. Is he OK? What happened?"

"I'm still waiting to find out who y'are, Mister."

"Walker, Lacklan Walker. I'm here on holiday."

"Who's your mutual friend?"

"I know her as Emily. She's Colonel Harry Burgess' daughter."

He raised an eyebrow at me. "I've known the Colonel for thirty years, and he ain't got no daughter, Mr. Walker."

I smiled. "That's what he thought. She turned up a couple of years ago from New Jersey."

"I know Emily, too. My understanding was they were friends."

"They've kind of kept it quiet."

His face was eloquently expressionless. "Is that a fact?"

"I was as surprised as you are when he introduced me to her." My mind was racing, trying to fit together all the pieces I was suddenly beginning to see. I kept pushing and he kept looking at me like he was a scientist and I was some new kind of bacterium. "In fact, last night I was with her at her house and dropped her off at the Colonel's..."

"You were with her last night at her house?"

I nodded. "Sure."

"Where would that be?"

"Lake Jackson, Bayou Road..."

"At what time were you there, Mr. Walker?"

"Sometime between six and seven. Sheriff, what is this all about? Is Jerry OK? Is Emily with him?"

"Sometime between six and seven you dropped Emily off at the Colonel's house. What did you do after that, Mr. Walker?"

"I went over to the casino on Caribbean Island."

"Anyone confirm that?"

"Sure, Rand Peabody was there. We had a drink. I have his number right here..."

He sighed and looked at me with distaste. "It's OK, I have Mr. Peabody's number."

He labored the possible double meaning. I frowned. "Why are you asking me for an alibi, Sheriff? What has happened to Jerry? Is Emily with him?"

He watched my face carefully as he spoke. "Jerry was murdered last night, Mr. Walker."

"Murdered?"

"At Emily's house. Emily was not with him."

"But that's..."

"You just got through telling me you dropped her off at the Colonel's place."

"Yes, but she went out after that and he hasn't seen her since. I told him to call you. I'm surprised he hasn't..."

He nodded. "He called. He just didn't tell me she was his daughter. Why'd you think that is, Mr. Walker?"

I shook my head again. "I have no idea, Sheriff. I'm just here on holiday, the Colonel and my father were friends back in the day." I frowned, like I was thinking. "I wouldn't read too much into it, though. From what she told me, he never married her mother. He didn't even know she was pregnant. He may just be trying to protect her from any scandal."

He grunted. "Maybe so."

"So Jerry was killed in *her* house? While she was out?"

"Looks that way..."

"That's bizarre. Poor guy. And you have no news of Emily?"

He shook his head. "Went to her house looking for her, found Jerry Fines instead."

"How was he killed?"

"Stabbed through the heart, after being tortured."

He was still watching me closely, trying to read my reactions. I squinted at him and repeated, "*Tortured?* What in the world for?"

His eyes now said he was losing interest. "If I knew that, I'd probably know who done it. Have you got any information for me, Mr. Walker?"

"I wish I had. I mean, unless..." I frowned. "Where did he work?"

"He's been out of work since the factory closed."

"Factory?"

"QPS."

"Oh, yes. But he wasn't self employed, or have his own private business..."

"No. Why?"

I shook my head again and sighed. "No, nothing, Sheriff. I'm afraid I have nothing for you. Have you informed the Colonel?"

"Uh-uh, not yet."

I walked back to my car with his eyes burning holes in the back of my head. I drove slowly back to Pier 32, had a burger and a beer and then made my way to Gregor's casino. I arrived at ten minutes to two, parked by the grotesque statue and climbed the stairs. This time there was no reception committee and the girl at the desk told me to go right on up.

My knock was answered with a "Come!" and I pushed in.

He was sitting behind his desk. Zoltan or Peter, whichever the one with the ponytail was, was standing behind his right shoulder, silhouetted against the big window. Gregor had a large, white linen napkin stuffed into his collar and he was spooning something I assumed to be caviar onto crackers and stuffing it in his mouth, between his teeth. He also had a bottle of vodka on his desk, and a shot glass. I stood a moment looking at him chewing, and he looking back at me. I said, "Is that compulsory?"

He jerked his head, which I took to mean, 'what?'

"Eating caviar and drinking vodka if you're a *pakhan* in the Russian mob?"

He shrugged without looking at me and said, "I like. Sit."

I sat.

"You want?"

"I prefer my eggs fried."

"Drink?"

"Irish whiskey."

He mumbled something without looking up from his plate that sounded like "*Peter, Poluchit yemu Irlandskiy viski.*"

Peter scowled at me and went to get me a glass of 'Iraldskiy viski'. While he was doing that, I said, "The CIA tells me the little black box is worth a damned sight more than twenty million bucks."

"You don't know what is."

He stuffed caviar in his mouth, chewed, and looked at me with dead, amber eyes. Then he knocked back a shot and refilled his glass. Peter put a cut crystal tumbler half full of Bushmills in front of me. I sipped. It was superb.

"Maybe I do and maybe I don't, either way it's not relevant. What's relevant is that the American government tells me I have a legal and moral duty to give it to them."

"You are talk a lot of..." He sighed and scratched the

inside of his ear, then looked up at Peter who had returned to his position behind him. He said, "*Der'mo...?*"

"Shit."

He nodded, "*Da, spasibo*, shit. You talking a lot of shit. CIA will take box from you and pay nothing. Maybe they lie, promise much, but give you only big fuck in end. English SIS, European INTCEN, do the same. They take from you, but give nothing."

I laughed. "You telling me the only people I can trust are the Russian mafia? Boy! Then I really am screwed!"

He nodded. "Is irony, I know." He said it without smiling. "But is true. If we are in Russia, is no true. But we are here. Options are limited. We do not want many complications. Easier is give you lot of money in cash, take you in boat to Belize, you put money in bank, everybody happy." He shook his head. "CIA, MI6, INTCEN, Mossad... They offer more, but kill you, never give you money."

I took another swig and sighed. "For that matter, Gregor, what guarantee have I that *you* won't kill me?"

He shrugged and pulled down the corners of his mouth. "For what? If you knew what is this box, you would not ask stupid question. You can be easily hero in Russia for this box. We happy to give you money. Is not a lot of money, twenty millions. We happy to make you hero of Russian people too. Is easier this way."

"You want to tell me what this box is?"

He smiled for the first time and rumbled like a Harley. The smile faded and he shook his head. "No."

"You said it's not a lot of money. How about you double it?"

"No. I tell you what we will do. Thirty millions, and you can have Emily."

So there it was. He had her.

"Is she still alive?"

"Yeah. Why not?"

"Did you hurt her?"

He squinted at his wrist and made pinching motions at it with his fingers. "Little bruises, from taking her..." He looked up at Peter and they exchanged a few words and shrugs in Russian. Then he looked back at me, still squinting. "Just little bruises on wrist and arm. Nothing serious."

"Why did you kill Jerry?"

He frowned at me like I was talking word salad at him. "He has to die. He has seen Peter and boys. They have put..." He jabbed the fingers of his right hand at the fingers of his left. "...sticks, in his nails. He cannot live after this. Is liability."

I nodded. "Sure, that's very reasonable. I understand." I took a deep breath and drained my glass. "I need to meditate on this, Gregor. I am going to go home—to what is left of my home after your visit last night..."

He shook his head. "Again this. We do not visit last night, Mr. Walker." He approached a second smile, but gave up before he got there. "What for? I know box is not in your house. You have hidden, or maybe you don't have at all. If you have, only you can get box. So we have you, instead. You don't go home. You stay here. In the end, only we will have box, Mr. Walker. I explain to Emily already, there is no auction. Box is for us."

I eyed Peter. I had taken him once before and I knew I could take him again. What worried me was that they knew that too. He gave an unpleasant smile. I looked at Gregor and shook my head. "Sorry, Gregor. I'm going home. I'll call you tomorrow."

I went to stand, but as I did so, the floor moved and tilted up toward me. It slammed me hard in the face and I struggled to push myself up with my hands. The room tilted again and I felt a foot on my shoulder, shoving me over on my back. I fell and looked up at the ceiling. Everything began to spin and then I saw Peter's bearded face leering down at me, only a few inches away. The next thing I saw was his fist. I felt a powerful pain in my head and everything went black.

———

CONSCIOUSNESS BEGAN to seep back into my mind. First, I was aware of the small jostles. Then I was aware of the sound, a deep humming. Next it was the smell of mustiness and oil. I opened my eyes. It didn't help. I still couldn't see anything, and I wondered for a moment if they had blinded me. I tried to rub my eyes and realized my hands were tied behind my back, and my ankles too were bound. Then it all began to make sense. I was in the trunk of a car.

There is not a lot you can do if you are tied up in the trunk of a car. With what little mobility I had, I felt around for a tool of some sort. There wasn't one. I drew my knees up to my chest and tried to loop my arms over my ass, to feel for my knife in my boot, but the trunk was too confining, and in any case I was pretty sure they would have found and removed the knife, along with my Sig.

I had no idea how long I had been in there, but the drive seemed to go on for maybe ten or fifteen minutes. Then the sound of the engine changed and we slowed, grinding and thudding over uneven ground. I bumped around for a bit and banged my head a few times until we finally came to a halt and the engine died. Next there was a short volley as four doors were slammed closed, and a moment later the trunk opened. I was surprised to be looking up into a night sky. It meant I had been out for at least four or five hours.

Peter was leering down at me again through his straggly beard, a dark, unpleasant form against the stars. He reached down, grabbed me by the scruff of my neck and hauled me out of the trunk. Then he let me drop onto the sand. Pain stabbed through my shoulder joints and I rolled on my back. There were four of them towering over me. I recognized Gregor as well as Peter. The other two I didn't know. I wondered if they were going to give me a kicking, but instead they closed the trunk and one of them hunkered down to cut the bonds on my ankles. Gregor said:

"Stand."

I got to my feet. Now I could see we were on a long stretch of beach. There were lights in the distance, and a headland, but it was hard to make out exactly where we were. Small waves lapped at the shore and faint, silver starlight touched the surface of the water, mixing rich blue with inky black. About a mile out, I could see the glow of four or five lamps on the sea. Looking more closely, I began to make out a schooner, maybe white or cream, riding at anchor. Closer, on the wet sand, where the small waves were breaking, there was a wooden speedboat with a guy standing beside it. Peter shoved me toward the dinghy and said, "Walk."

I walked, pushing through the sand, wondering what the

hell was coming next. I said to Gregor, "You know if you kill me, you never get the box, right? You understand that."

He grunted and climbed in the front passenger seat of the boat. I was shoved in the back and Peter got in beside me. The other three grabbed the prow and heaved us backward into the water. One jumped in the front behind the wheel, and the other two clambered in the back. The engine roared, we banked right and accelerated toward the yacht. Obviously dialogue was not the big thing with the Russian mob.

We slapped over the waves for a minute or two, then rounded the stern of the schooner and slowed to pull up beside what looked like a retractable staircase. Peter held the boat steady and Gregor climbed up the steps to the deck. Over his shoulder, he said to me, "You come."

Peter showed me my knife. He said, "You are two kilometer from shore. There are sharks here, and twelve men with guns. Don't do nothing stupid."

He cut the bonds on my wrists and I followed Gregor up the stairs. The others came up behind me, with their weapons drawn.

She was about a hundred feet long, with two masts and a raised cabin amidships, with narrow walkways on either side. Warm light was spilling from the cabin and I could hear voices inside, laughter and music. Gregor was standing at the door, with the light making shiny patches on his face and his bald head. He was watching me.

"Peter will settle you in. I will come in a while to talk with you."

He went inside the cabin. There were noisy greetings and Peter shoved me toward the bow. One of the others went ahead and opened a hatch in the foredeck. I peered down and saw an iron ladder leading eight or nine feet into a dimly lit space with a rough, wooden floor. Peter said, "Go down."

There were four of them, they were armed and they were all watching me with interest. I thought about taking them, but the risk was too high, and I still believed the black box was a trump card. I moved toward the ladder.

Peter kicked me in the back of the knee, I fell forward and crashed through the hatch, clutching the rungs of the ladder as I went down. I jarred my shoulder and fell in a heap on the floor. Peter came down after me, smiling, and behind him the other three. I looked around me. It seemed to be some kind of cargo hold with a dozen crates piled against the walls. Behind me a pipe, maybe six inches across, rose through a hole in the floor and disappeared through the ceiling. Light was from a single, bare bulb.

Peter jerked his head at me. "Get up."

I got to my feet and he pulled a pair of cuffs from his back pocket. Again he jerked his head. "Stand by pipe."

I stood with my back to the pipe. He pulled my arms around behind it and cuffed my wrists. There is a myth that if you tense your thumb you can add half an inch to the diameter of your wrist, and if you do that when you're being cuffed, you can then slip the cuffs off by relaxing your hand. It is true that you can add half an inch to the diameter of your wrist. It isn't true you can then slip off the cuffs, you need more than half an inch for that. The fact was, unless I pulled the pipe out of the floor, I was not going anywhere.

After he'd cuffed me, Peter came back around and said something in Russian to the other guys and they climbed the ladder onto the deck and left. He turned to me and smiled.

It wasn't a friendly smile. I knew what was coming, and all I could do was roll with the punches, and try not to focus on the pain.

He worked on me for a good five minutes. Five minutes is a long time when you're being beaten. He was good, experienced. He hit me hard enough to hurt and to weaken me, but not so hard as to knock me unconscious. He started with a few backhanders to my head that left my ears ringing and my head spinning, and then he started pounding my belly and my floating ribs with his fists, until I felt nauseous and light-headed. Eventually, I slid down the pipe into a sitting position. Then he sneered at me and said, "You prefer to be kicked? Stay there, I will kick."

I looked up at him. "Un-cuff me, then kick me."

I pushed myself back to my feet and he went to work on my face again, with an open hand. The taste of blood in my mouth was strong, and I could feel my left eye swelling. My lip felt like I'd just had an anesthetic from the dentist. He was strong, and his open-handed blows were making me dizzy.

Finally, he stopped, out of breath, and went to sit on a crate. He took a packet of cigarettes from his pocket. They were called Apollo-Soyuz, and I wondered for a moment if I was delirious from the blows. He lit one and sat smoking and staring at me. I laid it on. Slid to the floor again and groaned, but I didn't have to lay it real thick. I was bad. My body hurt all over, I was dizzy and weak.

Then there was the rumble of a big diesel engine firing up, and the yacht began to tremble and shake. After a moment, footsteps overhead told me somebody was approaching. The hatch opened and Gregor's huge, bald form lumbered awkwardly down the steps. Once he was down, he turned to look at me. He seemed to fill the whole space. I squinted up at him. The bare bulb reflected of his shiny head.

I said: "Have you gone completely out of your mind? What the hell do you think you're doing, Gregor?"

"Now," he said, "We go sailing, and you tell me where is box."

TEN

I PUSHED MYSELF BACK TO MY FEET WITH difficulty, wincing at the pain, and stared at him.

"Exactly how stupid do you think I am? If I tell you where the box is, my life isn't worth a damn. You think I don't know that?"

He sat on one of the crates, watching me with amber, reptilian eyes. "Of course, but by time we have finish with you, death will seem like nice idea. Anyway." He shrugged and pulled his lipless mouth down at the corners. "I think maybe you have not box. I think maybe Emily has box."

I shook my head. "Uh-uh. Emily hasn't box, Gregor. And for that matter, neither have I."

"Where is box?"

"There is only one way, Gregor, that you will get that box, and that is by handing over thirty million bucks and Emily. That was the deal, that's how it works. Continue on this path, and by nine A.M. tomorrow morning, the box will be safely in the hands of the CIA."

He gave a single nod and looked at Peter. Peter walked over and drove his fist into my belly. I retched and sagged, and gasped for breath.

"I ask again. Where is box?"

When I had gotten my breath back, I raised my head to look at him. "Ask yourself, Gregor. What would you have done in my position? Let me explain something to you. Let me explain something to you, so that you fully understand this situation."

Peter moved to hit me again, but Gregor raised a hand and muttered something in Russian. I went on.

"Emily told me you were blackmailing her."

"I? Blackmail her? How?"

"She told me you used to employ her as a whore. She said you had pictures and films, and you were demanding a hundred grand for the return of the material."

"This is lie."

"Of course it is. I know it's a lie, Gregor. I saw it was a lie when she gave me a package that was clearly not money, and your boys handed over two sports bags that were obviously *full* of money. Now, let me ask you, what would you have done at that point?"

He was listening carefully, but he didn't answer.

"Let me tell you what I did, because this is something you need to know. I looked in the box and I saw something I did not understand. Here was an object—I had no idea what it was, but clearly it was worth *a lot* of money—so I sent it immediately to my attorneys in New York, with instructions to dispose of it in such a way that only I can recover it. Now, ask yourself, Gregor, is that not what you would have done? Isn't it what any intelligent person would have done?"

He nodded a few times, then turned to Peter. Peter went to work on me again, methodically pounding my belly and my chest, and then my face, while Gregor smoked and watched. This time Peter used his fists. They were big and hard, and they made a mess. Still, he was careful to make it painful, but not so damaging that I would no longer be of any use to them, or that I would become numb and stop suffering.

By the time Gregor had finished his cigarette, Peter was out of breath and his boss told him to stop.

"I think, Mr. Walker, that you are under impression that Russians are all stupid. We are not stupid. You ask me to believe that woman who has never met you before, ask you to deliver money for blackmail, and you agree to do this. Why? Is most stupid story I ever hear."

I swallowed the blood in my mouth and fantasized for a moment about killing first Peter and then Gregor. Finally, I spoke through swollen lips.

"My father and the Colonel, Harry Burgess, were friends when I was a kid. She has convinced him that she is his daughter. Maybe she is. He was stationed in New Jersey just before she was born. He introduced us, hoping we would become friends."

"And? So?"

"He told her I used to be in the SAS."

"Oh. You were in British SAS?"

"For ten years. That's why she chose me to help her."

He grunted. "So you think, if they are paying five million to stupid, naïve girl, probably it is worth ten. And you will impress me by bringing money back and tell me, is an insult."

"That is exactly what I thought."

"Who dares wins. This is your motto."

"Yes."

He grunted again. "We see. In few hours, we are in Mexico. Then I will talk with Emily, and we decide who has box, and how we are going to get the box. You are arrogant, stupid man, Mr. Walker, and Emily is stupid woman. I want kill both of you. I want do it slow and painful. It is best for you to cooperate with me."

"I have told you the truth. Think about it. It makes sense. Why would I do anything else?"

"We see. Now I am eat and have some wine, a nice woman. I have a couple on the board. I cannot decide. Maybe I have both. You have rest from beating. We are in Mexico at one or two in morning. Then we see what happen next. Good night, Mr. Walker. We will see later."

He stood and climbed the iron ladder with heavy, clanking feet. Peter followed him, onto the deck, and dropped the hatch with a loud, wooden slam. I sank to the floor and closed my eyes for half an hour while I tried to think of what to do. I had badly miscalculated my position with Gregor. I had also miscalculated his personality. Taking risks was not something he did as a last resort, like most people. Taking risks was something he did as a way of life because he enjoyed it, and he enjoyed winning. I managed a swollen, painful ironic smile at myself. He ran a casino. Maybe that should have been a clue.

I didn't manage to sleep. The naked light from the bulb, the feelings of nausea, the awkward, uncomfortable position with my arms cuffed behind the tube, and the all-pervasive pain in my body and in my head made that almost impossible, but I did manage to doze fitfully, slipping feverishly in and out of consciousness. By regulating my breathing and focusing my mind on images of ice and freezing water, I managed to put myself into a mild, hypnotic trance, slow my heart rate and cool my body. It's an optimal state for the body to repair itself, and it allowed me to get through the next few hours without suffering too much.

Eventually, I became aware of a change in the sound of the engines. The boat seemed to shudder suddenly and the pitch dropped to a deeper, grinding sound. That continued for maybe five minutes and then the engine cut out altogether. It dawned on my fogged, bruised mind that this was a bad thing. It meant more torture, and possibly death. And that meant that I had to do whatever it was I had to do to free myself from my cuffs.

I had, when Peter had handcuffed me, tensed my thumbs, but even so, the diameter of my hand was half an inch more than the diameter of the cuffs. There is a technique, which I had not mastered, by which you bring your fingers and your thumb together into a point and it narrows the circumference over which the cuff needs to slip. With enough practice, you can increase the elasticity of your hand so that it all but collapses in on itself. It does take a lot of practice, practice which I had not done.

I tried. I pushed my fingers and my thumb into a point, took hold of my left cuff in my right hand and began to maneuver it down toward the widest point of my hand, twisting it back and forth. By the time it got to the base of my thumb and my little finger, it was biting hard, and the bridge formed by my knuckles was a barrier I was just not going to get past.

I took hold of my left hand in my right and crushed the knuckles hard, pulling with my left arm at the same time. It shifted maybe a quarter of an inch, bit deep into my flesh and hurt like hell. Now it was stuck. I couldn't move it forward or back and the pain was becoming intolerable. I bit hard on my teeth to stop myself from yelling, screwed up my eyes, clambered to my feet and yanked hard, putting all my weight behind it.

The pain was excruciating. I felt the steel bite deep into my skin and the slick warmth of blood running over my hand. I squeezed harder with my right, crushing my knuckles again, leaned back and rammed my whole body forward. The cuff, made slippery by the blood, slipped over the base knuckle of my thumb.

Two sets of heavy feet tramped overhead. I slid back to a sitting position, panting from the pain in my hand. Gregor came down with his slow, deliberate steps and turned to face me, with his dull, yellow eyes peering out of his gleaming, shiny head. Behind him, Peter descended, squeezing past his boss, who did not move to make room for him, and sat on a crate to leer at me. Gregor spoke.

"You have thought?"

"However much I think, Gregor, it doesn't change anything. I can lie to you if you want, but the box will still be in New York."

I was breathing hard and my voice sounded weak. Peter grinned.

Gregor nodded his big, hairless head. "Pain sometimes make things change."

I sighed. "Sure, but pain won't change the fact that the

box is in New York with my attorneys. The only thing that will change that is my presence and my signature."

"Good. That is good. If that is true, it is good news for you and good news for me. Now I am go talk to Emily. We see what she is say. If she is confirm your story, then we are make progress and we go to New York. See? Everything moving in right way."

"And you'll kill her because you won't need her anymore."

"Maybe is possible."

"And if she doesn't confirm my story?"

He lifted his big shoulders. "We improvise. Probably bad news for you, good news for sharks. We see. One step at the time. For now, is good for me that you are in much pain. Pain make people cooperative. I tell Peter: not remove the fingers, not damage the eyes, and not kill." Something that might have been a smile touched his mouth. "This at least is comfort for you."

"Yeah, that's a big comfort. Thanks."

"Now I leave you with Peter. He will make lot of pain. I will be maybe two hours. This will seem like long, long time to you. I hope, when I am return, you are cooperative, Mr. Walker. Good bye."

He climbed up the ladder, back onto the deck. He left the hatch open and I could smell the cool, night air. I could hear the lapping of the water against the hull and the creak of the rigging. A few voices shouted. After a moment or two, there was the sound of the launch, rising, then fading into the night. Peter sat looking at me with no expression on his bearded face, taking his time over his cigarette. He was thinking that the anticipation of pain is almost worse than the pain itself. He was wrong. Nothing is worse than pain.

Finally, he dropped the butt on the floor and trod on it. I pushed myself to my feet. Peter stood, and as he stepped closer to me, I held his eye and carefully and deliberately spat in his face. The astonishment in his eyes was total and, as I watched it turn to rage, it made me smile.

"Surprised? Let me tell you something, Peter. Whatever you do to me, the fact will always remain that when I was un-cuffed, and there were two of you, I bitch-slapped your girlfriend, busted her eardrums and pistol-whipped you. The only way you have the balls to take me is if I'm cuffed. You're nothing but a chicken shit, candy-ass piece of pussy. I know that, and so do you."

Gregor might have been deep and hard to read. Peter wasn't. I saw the rage build beyond endurance in his neck and then flood his cheeks under his scraggy beard. His eyes were bright and he telegraphed every move he was going to make. Why shouldn't he? I was cuffed to that big old pipe. I was his prisoner.

He balled his fist, clenched his teeth, pulled back and hurled a punch at my head that would probably have cracked my skull. As it was, I bellowed, lunged to my right and wrenched the cuff the last couple of inches off my hand, as his fist smashed into the steel pipe.

His jaw dropped open, his eyes bulged and he made a nasty wheezing sound in his throat as he pulled his shattered hand back toward him. The pain in my own hand was intense and debilitating, but I had no time to think about it. I grabbed his ponytail in both hands and smashed his nose into the tube, just about where his fist had hit it. Then I went down on one knee, dragging him after me, so that he sprawled, lying with his head thrown back over my right thigh. I let all the pain and the rage do the rest of the work, and smashed the cuffs into his windpipe.

He rolled and dropped to the floor, trying to gasp but unable to pull in air, clawing at his throat with his fingernails, tearing the skin. He flopped onto his back, thrashing and kicking convulsively. His face turned purple, his eyes bulged out of their sockets and his tongue, like a swollen plum, protruded from his mouth.

I reached under his arm and pulled out his Glock. Then I searched him for my Fairbairn & Sykes and slid the blade deep into his carotid artery. He bled out quickly. It was more compassion than he had planned to show me.

I turned off the light, pulled myself up the ladder and peered out. Two thirds of a moon was rising over the ocean, touching the black water with silver light. The breeze was cool and soothing on my burning face. Deep, quiet voices came to me from the stern. It was hard to distinguish how many voices, but there were more than two.

The lights had been turned out in the main cabin, but there was a glow coming from the far end, and I figured he had a few guards keeping watch on the deck. Peter had said something about a dozen men. His death made that eleven. If Gregor had taken two with him, that made it nine, though I was willing to bet he had taken more than two. So I was looking at somewhere between nine and seven men. Were they all up and about, or were they taking shifts?

Shifts was more likely.

I had the moon on my left, so I slipped down to the right

side of the cabin and dragged myself slowly and silently toward the stern. About two thirds of the way along, a chair began to come into view beyond the corner of the cabin. It was one of those collapsible, steel-tubing chairs that have a seat and a back made of stretched plastic cloth. I inched a little farther and saw it was occupied by a guy in a black roll neck sweater, with a black woolen hat on his head. He was holding five cards in his hand and had a cigarette in his mouth.

I eased myself another couple of inches forward and saw that he was sitting at a table and had a glass in front of him that might have been brandy or whiskey. I looked above me and saw that I was under a window. I pressed against the wall and slid up until my head was just below the glass. Then I peered in.

It was a saloon. The lights were off, but I could make out a bar, sofas and armchairs and potted palms. I could make them out because the door was open onto the stern, and the light of a lamp was flooding in through the door and the two windows that flanked it. The lamp was an old kerosene lamp that was sitting on a table where four men were smoking, drinking and playing cards. Between them, they had an almost full bottle of Johnny Walker.

Four. Which left approximately that number again, probably sleeping, and the rest with Gregor. I peered in the direction of the shore. I could see a light twinkling, but it was impossible to tell what it was or how far away it was; a mile at most, but maybe half that distance. In any case, too far to swim, especially in the condition I was in after my beating. I needed a plan, and I needed it fast.

Suspended over the stern of the yacht, I could see a large,

rubber dinghy with an outboard motor. That was my way out. So the plan was, steal the dinghy and go ashore. The million dollar question was, how do I get to the dinghy without getting shot?

Then I had a thought.

ELEVEN

I TOOK THREE LONG, SILENT STRIDES AND CAME around the corner. Four astonished faces looked at me in the lamplight. I ignored them and, holding Peter's Glock in both hands, put a 9 mm round through the base of the kerosene lamp. Kerosene is highly flammable and the burning lead from the slug ignited it immediately as it flooded across the table. Suddenly everybody was shouting and jumping, falling backward over chairs and beating at their pants with their hands, where flaming kerosene had spilled. While they were busy doing that, I picked off two of them with clean headshots. The first keeled over backward, the second did a little dance on wobbly legs and then folded to the deck.

By that time, the other two had backed away, looking for cover. That suited me fine. I backed up too, down the side of the cabin to the nearest window and smashed it with the butt of the Glock. I knew I had only seconds before the rest of the crew arrived. I picked out the glass and pulled myself through. As I did so, I noticed on my left, at the back of the saloon, some steps going down to what I assumed were cabins below decks.

I logged them in my mind and ran four strides across to the bar. There I found a bottle of Scotch and a bottle of cognac and lobbed them both out the door at the burning table. They shattered and there was a *whoosh* as the alcohol caught and the flames started to bite into the varnish on the decking. I saw the bottle of Johnny Walker had also shattered in the heat and added to the growing conflagration. The fire was now seriously at risk of getting out of control.

A door slammed below. I crouched behind the bar and waited. There were shouts and hammering. Another door slammed and suddenly the saloon was full of the sounds of tramping feet and panicking shouts, as five guys in various stages of undress stormed up the stairs and across the room, toward the flames that had engulfed the table and were beginning to spread across the deck. Beyond them, I could see the two who'd been left outside, waving their arms and pointing.

I didn't waste the opportunity. I had five backs turned to me. They dithered maybe half a second before one of them turned to run for the fire extinguisher, but it only takes two seconds to shoot four motionless men. And that was what I did.

By the time I'd shot the fourth, the guy with the extinguisher was screaming and running at me. He swung the canister and knocked the Glock from my hands. Then he lashed out in a powerful front kick that hurled me against the wall, and I slid to the floor in severe pain. But he made the mistake of not finishing me off. Instead, he ran to the door and threw the fire extinguisher across the flames to his buddies. Then he came back to finish me off.

By then, I was on my feet again and leaning, sagging on the bar. He could see I was a mess and he sneered and came at me. He had big, powerful shoulders and fists like concrete slabs. When he was within range, he swung his right fist in a wide arc, intending to take off my head. I leaned back, and as I did so I held up the wine glass I had just shattered and rammed it into his wrist.

He screamed and backed away, gripping at the gushing wound, with a fountain of blood spraying out all over his face, the floor and the ceiling. I went after him, picked up the Glock from the floor and put two rounds through his chest. It wasn't his day.

Outside, the two guys were bringing the fire under control, one with an extinguisher, the other with somebody's jacket. That was good, I needed them to do that. I went and leaned on the doorjamb and let them slowly become aware of me. When they realized who I was, they paused, staring. I waved the gun at them and said, "Finish!"

They finished dousing and beating the last of the smoldering wood, put the extinguisher and the jacket down and raised their hands. I stepped out and pointed the gun at the nearest guy. I said, "You speak English?"

He shook his head. "*Nyet.*"

I shot him in the forehead and he keeled over backwards. The other guy gaped and his eyes bulged. I pointed the gun at him and asked, "Do you speak English?"

Obviously he had grasped the lesson, because he nodded and said, "Little."

"Good. It's your lucky day. How many guys did Gregor take with him?"

"Three man."

"Three?"

He nodded. "One drive boat," he made a gesture like driving a boat. "Two with gun." He pointed his fingers like a gun. He was good. "Three and Gregor."

"Where have they gone?"

He pointed toward the small, glimmering light. "House. Maybe two kilometer. Woman there."

"OK…" I nodded and waved him toward the door with the gun. He looked scared. I shook my head. "It's OK. Go to the bar."

He inched around the smoldering table and crossed the saloon, looking down at the scattered bodies, then up at me like I was some kind of freak. Maybe he was right and I was. He went to the bar. I said, "Irish whiskey, big."

He pointed uncertainly at the bottles. I nodded. He picked up two glasses and showed them to me. I nodded again and he splashed whiskey into both of them, then handed me one. I took a long pull and felt the warmth ease its way through the pain. He took a slug and smiled uncertainly.

I asked him, "What's your name?"

"Vlad."

"OK, Vlad, cooperate with me and you live. Be stupid and you die. We understand each other?"

He nodded. "Is OK."

"How did the woman come here?" He stared blankly and looked frightened. I pointed in the direction of the house. "The woman…"

"Emily."

"Good. How did Emily come to Mexico?"

"Plane." He held out his hands like small wings. "Boat plane. Plane go on water. Boat—plane."

"I got it. You're doing good." A trace of a smile. He took another swig. I could see his hand was shaking. He knew he was walking a tightrope. That was good. "Have another drink."

He refilled his glass and I let him give me another drop. I started talking again.

"So, Vlad, in the house..." I held up my thumb. "Emily." I put up my index. "Gregor." My other three fingers. "Three men... How many more?"

"Pilot and two man looking at, looking for..."

"Looking after."

"Yes, looking after Emily."

"Guarding her?"

"Yes, guarding."

I sighed and wanted very much in that moment to sleep for twelve hours. Instead, I said, "Vlad, do you believe in God?"

Vlad was getting rapidly drunk. The question scared him and his face went pasty white.

"Yes..." He said it softly.

"I don't. I'm an atheist. Maybe I'm a Buddhist, or a pagan. I have no idea. When I die, I want to go to Valhalla, drink ale, sing songs and have wenches sit on my knee. You have no idea what I am talking about, Vlad, do you?"

He gave his head small shakes. "No... You are going to kill me now?"

"Not today. I am going to give you a chance. An opportunity. Can you sail this yacht on your own?"

"With motor, not sail. And two girls downstair can help."

"OK, good. Now I am going to go and kill Gregor and his men. I want you to think that today, God has spared your life. God has let you live instead of me killing you. You have a chance, an opportunity, to start again. Take this yacht, go somewhere, and do something useful with your life. OK? Because next time I see you, if you are still a gangster, I will kill you."

He stared at me with round, drunken eyes. The jab caught him right on the tip of his slack jaw. His legs turned to spaghetti and he went down. I did a tour of the boat and found a dozen handguns, six assault rifles and enough ammunition to start a small war. I selected an AK-47 because they are so reliable. There was also a nice little Galil which I slung over my shoulder for backup. It's small and light, but has little recoil, so it's accurate and surprisingly punchy.

I stuck two Glock 17s in my belt and went out to lower the dinghy into the water, then drew it around to the retractable ladder and secured it there. Finally, I went back to where Vlad was lying on the floor of the bar. I stood for fifteen seconds, staring down at him. The smart thing to do would be to kill him. If I didn't, when he came around he could alert Gregor, and that could cost me and Emily our lives.

Instead I went forward, started the engine and put her on a heading northeast, toward Florida. Then I clambered down the ladder, jumped into the dinghy, and as the yacht slowly disappeared into the darkness, I fired up the engine, made a sharp turn and opened the throttle, speeding toward the small light I could still see flickering in the darkness ahead of me.

The water was flat, still and black, and I skipped over it fast, enjoying the cool wind on my bruised face. I figured I was doing about 20 MPH, which should get me where I was going in about four or five minutes at most. I had no idea what I was going to find there, or how I was going to deal with it. I was going to have to make it up as I went along. At least, for the moment, I had the element of surprise on my side.

After three minutes or so, I began to see the pale glow of the white sand in the moonlight and, anchored just off shore, near a short wooden pier, was a small de Havilland Otter. I reduced the speed of the dinghy and, when I was a couple of hundred yards from the beach, I killed the engine and started paddling. Now I could see that the glimmering light of the house was in fact two lighted windows, approximately thirty feet apart. The house looked like a modern, cubed structure on several levels, set back among palm trees and some kind of undergrowth.

I paddled to the pier and tied the dinghy on the far side, where it was out of sight. Then, hitching the two assault rifles over my shoulder, I sprinted across the sand for the cover of the trees and bushes thirty feet away. In among the ferns and the palms, I dropped to the ground and lay waiting and listening. There was nothing but the lap and sigh of the waves, the soft breeze among the leaves and a distant bird that might have been an owl. I got to my feet and peered along the long, luminous ribbon of sand. I figured the house was forty or fifty paces away. I could see the glow from the windows on the sand, but from where I was, the structure itself was not visible.

I began to walk, staying close to the fringe of undergrowth, where I could take cover if I needed to, but also where it was easier to walk. Slowly, the shape of the house began to emerge. It seemed to be three large, concrete cubes balanced one on top of another at odd angles, like a toddler's bricks, giving the impression that if you sneezed, they would all topple down.

Now that I was closer, I could see that the bottom cube, which was the size of a large bungalow, was set among rolling green lawns within a fence of evergreen hedges. The second cube gave the impression of being precariously balanced on the first, and was tall and narrow, with long windows set up one side. Closer inspection suggested it was a stairwell and elevator shaft.

Set across the top of this cube, like a 'T' section, was the third cube, balanced some thirty feet above the ground, with the sea-facing wall taken up almost entirely by plate glass windows. But these were not illuminated now. The light was coming from two windows set in the bottom cube.

I sprinted to the hedge, dropped on my belly and listened. Now I could hear the soft murmur of voices. In fact, it seemed to be just one voice, deep and slow, and two got you twenty it was Gregor.

I found the gate and went in. Now I could see on the far side of the lawn there was a grove of palm trees, and to the left of them, half-surrounded by them, was a large, irregularly shaped swimming pool. As prisons went, it wasn't bad.

One last sprint took me to the cover of the palm trees.

There I dropped to my belly and crawled to within seven feet of the pool. From there, I could see a floodlit patio at the back of the house. Gregor was there, sitting in a white, wrought iron chair beside a round table with a closed parasol stuck in the center. There was a glass beside his elbow and he was talking to somebody in a monotonous, lecturing tone. I crawled a little farther around the pool and saw who he was lecturing. Emily was sitting in another white, wrought iron chair, listening to him. She had one leg crossed over the other, and there was what looked like a gin and tonic sitting in front of her.

Some distance behind Gregor were two guys dressed in black with black woolen hats, holding assault rifles. Presumably, that left four guys inside the house: the pilot of the plane, the pilot of the dinghy, and the two men who guarded Emily. I tried to listen to what Gregor was saying, but his voice was still indistinct.

I inched closer until I was lying in the shadow of the outermost palm tree. The base was thick, a good four feet across, and provided me sufficient cover so long as nobody came to the pool. I could just see Emily's chair past the corner of the house, her profile, and her havaiana dancing nervously on her foot.

I lay very still and listened. Gregor's low rumble came to me.

"We are go in circles. Soon my patience is end. You make deal with me, Emily. You offer me this thing. I give you money. Lots of money. Now suddenly, this men is appear. Give me back money, kill my men, say no deal, we have now auction. He call the CIA... This is not acceptable way to do business. You cannot play this kind of game with me, Emily.

It is very dangerous for you. You should not listen to this men."

"I am sorry, Gregor. I am as much a victim as you are. You can't hold me responsible for what Lacklan Walker has done. The man was recommended to me, but he is out of his mind. He is out of control..."

He grunted. "Why you send him to make exchange? Why you not come?"

"Let's not be naïve, Gregor. I needed insurance. What was to stop you killing me and keeping the money and the NPP?"

He shrugged, spread his hands and made a long, 'Pffff...!' noise. "Why for? Is only few millions. I don't know, Emily. I think there is more. How you know him?"

She seemed to hesitate. Her havaiana danced furiously for a moment. "He is a friend of a friend."

"Friend of your father? He tell me that man is your father."

She looked up sharply. "No. Just a friend."

"He say..."

"I know what he said! It was a sob story. I wanted his sympathy, so I told him a story about finding my long lost father. It is none of your concern."

Gregor was silent for a moment. Then he said, "Who is your friend, father, advisor...?"

"I told you, it is none of your concern."

He seemed not to hear her. "How somebody like you comes to Freeport? Why you are there, with Jerry..."

"Can we stay on task, please? Do you want the damn NPP or not?"

He didn't answer for a long time. They just sat staring at each other. Then Gregor said, "I have kill Jerry."

Her foot froze.

"Was that necessary?"

"Yes. I torture him, to make him call you. I think he was in love with you. But after that, he is big liability to me. I have to kill. Where is it?"

She looked up at the sky and groaned. "For the thousandth time, Gregor! As long as you have me imprisoned here, you will not get the box. And every day you have me locked up here, the price goes up. I will not cooperate as your prisoner."

He sighed noisily through his nose. "I think you don't have box. I think Walker has box. I am torturing him now. He will talk."

She laughed. "He won't, because he doesn't know where it is. The thing with torture, Gregor, is that the victim will always tell you what you want to hear. But whatever he tells you, *I* know where it is, and he doesn't." She was quiet for a moment, then asked, "You have him on the yacht, here, now?"

"Mm-hm..."

"And he says he has organized an auction?"

He shrugged. "Is what he says. CIA people are there. I don't see nobody else. Not yet. I cannot let you sell to them. You must sell to me."

"Then you better start treating me with a little more respect, Gregor. I told you, as long as I am your prisoner, we cannot do business." She paused then and frowned at her foot. "Why don't you bring him ashore, we can talk to him together."

"For what?"

"So that I can prove to you that he hasn't got it. There is only one way that this thing will play out, Gregor. You take me back to Houston, you set me free, you compensate me for this abduction, and then we make the deal."

He gave a small, humorless bark and shook his head. "So that you can trade with all world and his mother? No. There is other way. I call my boys. We hold you down on table and we start to remove your fingers."

"Then you will never get it!"

"Wrong. I am tired of playing game. You have it or Walker have it. Tonight, one of you tell me where it is."

Her foot stopped dancing and she sat up straight. "Listen to me! I sent it to my attorney in Washington! If he doesn't hear from me by Friday…"

Gregor was laughing loud. "I hear same story from Walker. But he tell it better than you! Him, I almost believe. Enough of bullshit." He called in through the open French door and said something in Russian. Four guys trooped out. Emily was on her feet talking incoherently, repeating over and over, "No! Stop! Listen! *Listen to me!*" The guys had her by her arms and Gregor stood and swept the glasses off the table. They shattered on the floor and the four men lifted Emily bodily and lay her on the table. By now she was screaming. Her voice was high and shrill. Gregor said something and one of the boys went inside. I figured he was going for some pliers or a knife.

I had the Galil in my hands. It had less recoil than the AK-47 and at this distance, it would be more accurate. I needed a nice, clean shot. I unfolded the stock, wedged it against my shoulder and lined up the guy holding Emily's right arm. He had his back to me and was half leaning over her. I breathed out, held and gently squeezed the trigger. It gave a single thud and the front of his head exploded and showered all over Emily.

Everyone stood staring. Emily was hysterical, screaming. The guy sank to his knees and keeled over. I spoke loudly.

"Gregor, if you twitch, I will blow your head off. So just nobody move, everybody stay very calm and don't do anything stupid."

Emily rolled off the table and fell onto the ground. She was still screaming in a kind of spasmodic hysteria, with her face, covered in blood and gore, screwed up and her hands up by her shoulders. Everybody watched her stand, run across the lawn toward the pool and jump in. Then she bobbed up and down, giving little screams interspersed with bubbles as she pulled off her clothes and rinsed her face and hair.

I heard a muttered voice and saw one of the two guards who were carrying assault rifles swing his weapon gently around in my direction. He obviously planned to spray the area and try to take me out. The Galil thudded again and the back of his head erupted in a pink plume.

"I said, nobody do anything stupid. Now, everybody put down your weapons or I start spraying, and I swear I'll cut you in half, Gregor."

He raised his hands and said something to his four remaining men. Three of them pulled handguns from their belts and threw them on the lawn. The fourth tossed down his rifle, and then followed up with a hand gun. I stood, switched to the AK-47, and stepped out from behind the palm tree.

TWELVE

His eyes narrowed but his mouth sagged. He said: "I not understand..."

I walked toward him, keeping the AK-47 trained on his belly. "It's simple, Gregor. I killed everybody on your yacht, and I have set it on a course toward Florida. The Coast Guard should find it in the next couple of hours."

"...How...?"

"A creative mix of kerosene and whiskey. Now tell your boys to lie face down with their hands on their heads."

He frowned a moment longer, licked his lips and turned and spoke to his boys in Russian. I guess he told them to lie down with their hands on their heads, because that's what they did. Behind me, I heard the slosh of water, followed by the pad of bare, wet feet, and a moment later, Emily appeared, soaked and dripping, in her bra and panties. She stared at me for a moment with a 'what is wrong with you?' face, then went into the house, trailing water behind her.

I said to Gregor: "Sit down." He sat gingerly, like he

thought something had happened to reality and he had to be extra careful. When he was sitting, I said, "I'm thinking about having one of your boys cut your fingers off."

He looked startled. "What for?"

"I think you need a lesson in empathy."

"What is?"

One of his boys lying face down on the grass lifted his head. He had short hair, a goatee and large, round eyes. He said something that sounded like, "*Soperezhivaniye...*"

Gregor turned in his seat to look at him. "*Soperezhivaniye?*"

"*Da, Soperezhivaniye... sostradaniye...*" He pulled the corners of his mouth down and moved his head from side to side, then said more emphatically, "*Soperezhivaniye...*"

Gregor shrugged. "*Spasibo, Yuri.*" He turned back to me and shook his head. "I think is no necessary, empathy. In our work..."

I sighed and reminded myself not to try and be funny with Russians. Emily came out in a fresh pair of jeans and a sweater. I pointed to her chair. "Sit down, Emily."

She sat and said, "This is not what it looks like."

"Really?" I smiled. "How many divorces do you think have been kicked off with that phrase? Guy gets home early from work, finds his wife naked in bed with another man. 'This is not what it looks like, honey. This is Dr. Brown, he was just testing my core body temperature.'" She didn't answer, so I asked, "What do you think it looks like, Emily? Because I'm still trying to work it out. I'd like somebody to explain."

Gregor shrugged his big shoulders again. To him, everything was simple. "What to explain? One of you has box. I must have box. I don't understand why you are complicating. Give me box, I give you money. Who has box?"

I pulled a pack of Camels from my pocket, shook one free and poked it in my mouth. I lit up and inhaled deep. As I blew out the smoke, I looked at Emily. "Yeah, Emily, who has the box?"

She didn't answer. She slipped her hands between her knees and looked down at her boots. I looked back at Gregor.

"Here's the problem, Gregor. Whoever hasn't got it dies, right? That's why you had Emily shacked up in a luxury villa and me cuffed to a pipe, because you thought the odds were on Emily having it."

"Torture one, be nice to other. Sometimes it is working."

"Yeah, only this time, you got it the wrong way around. You should have been nice to me."

"Perhaps this is true."

"Now, here's what happens next. I ask both of you questions, you answer. If you lie, I'll know and I'll start removing digits."

Emily looked up in alarm. "From me too?"

I narrowed my eyes at her through the smoke from my cigarette. "So don't lie. It's not so difficult. You should try it sometimes. Eventually you might get the hang of it."

Gregor shook his head. "I no lie to you never. I am always tell you truth. People lie when scared. I never scared. So I always tell truth."

"Yeah, especially when you drugged my whiskey."

Yuri began burbling in Russian. Gregor turned to listen to him and started nodding, "*Da, da...*"

"What?"

"He say is your fault. You come to us with aggression, hitting people, insulting. You started it…"

Yuri managed to shrug with his hands still on the back of his head. "*Chto on ozhidal!*"

Gregor spread his hands. "*Amerikantsy! Tipichnyy!*"

"*Mudak!*"

There was some stifled laughter. I said, "Are we done?"

"He says you are shit head."

"That's nice. Now, tell me how you and Emily got acquainted."

I watched Emily while he spoke. She was keeping her eyes fixed on her knees, where she had her hands clasped again. Gregor seemed to be amused. "Jerry was come and make introduction to us. He say he has something valuable maybe we want to buy. I tell him I am think about, then I make Peter follow him. I see he is meet discreetly sometime with pretty girl. So I am send Peter to bring girl to me. My instinct is right. Emily is boss and Jerry is just…" He turned to Yuri, "…*lakey?*"

"*Da, 'lackey.'*"

"*Lackey? Tak zhe?*"

"L-A-C-K-E-Y."

"Hah! *Tak zhe!* Is the same, lackey. In Russian lakey. Only 'c' is different."

"What is this, Beavis and Butt-head?"

"No, his English is good. I ask him."

"So you realized Emily was in charge. What else?"

"So we make deal. She is happy. Everybody happy. Then you come…"

"*Mudak…*"

"Can it, Yuri."

"And everything go to shit."

"So are you telling me, Gregor, that Emily was never in your employ?"

"In my employ?"

"At your gym in New Jersey?"

"I have no gym in New Jersey. I have casino in Texas, why I want gym in New Jersey?"

I turned to Emily. "You want to explain to me how the girl-next-door, fleeing from white slave traders in Jersey, wound up trying to sell an NPP to the Russian Mafia in Texas?"

She wouldn't meet my eye, but said, "So you believe him, but not me..."

"You know what? I have to agree with Gregor, apart from the small matter of drugging my whiskey, he has not lied to me so far."

"Why I would?"

"Exactly, why he would? Like he said, people lie when they are scared. And until now, Gregor has had nothing to be scared of. So right now, I am thinking that Gregor is telling the truth, and I would like to know, A, how you come to be in Freeport, and B, how did you get hold of the NPP?"

She didn't answer. Instead, she chewed her lip and continued to stare at her knees. Gregor, on the other hand, sighed noisily and said something in Russian, then added, "This conversation is no interest me no more. I have just one thing which I am need to know. Who I am dealing with for NPP?"

I frowned at him for a moment. "How many men do you see here who are armed?"

"This is true, just you."

"You're dealing with the guy with the gun."

He lifted his shoulders, pulled down the corners of his mouth and danced his head slowly from one side to another. The gesture was oddly Italian, and somehow suggested maybe I was wrong. I frowned and noticed Emily was staring hard at my chest. Gregor said. "Things change now, Mr. Walker. You are not only men with gun. Look at your chest, please."

I looked down and saw the little red dot dancing slightly to the left of my sternum. Gregor said, "I prefer you are alive, but situation is intense and if I have to kill you, I do. Men is in trees. He know if you do stupid thing, he shoot you. I tell him this when you first arrive. You tell me, 'Say your boys to lie down.' I do this, and also tell Stephan, 'Wait, I want to hear what American *mudak* will say.' Is good, yah?"

"Real good."

His boys got off the grass and retrieved their weapons. I sighed and put the AK-47 and the Galil on the table. I saw Yuri move toward me and I spoke.

"This changes very little, Gregor. So you are armed now and I'm not. But you still have the same problem. I have the NPP. I am scheduled to contact my New York attorneys tomorrow afternoon. If I don't, he will post a package for me."

"Post? To where? To CIA? I don't believe this. You will not give box to CIA."

"No, you're right. I actually have no idea where he will post it."

"This make no sense."

"It makes perfect sense, Gregor. I instructed him to select an attorney at random anywhere in the world and send him, or her, the package with instructions to throw it into the nearest river, lake or ocean. He thought I was crazy. Maybe I am. But that is what I told him to do."

Emily had gone the color of old tofu. "You're not serious."

"Wrong. I am. I am the only person here who doesn't know what the NPP is. I am also extremely rich. So that makes me the only person here who has *not* got a vested interest in the NPP. What I have got is a vested interest in getting out of here alive. Are you following this, Gregor, or do you need Yuri to translate?"

"I am follow."

He put his hands on his knees and grunted. Emily was still staring at me. She shook her head once and said, "You can't, Lacklan. You have no idea…"

Gregor said again, "I am follow, I am understand…"

Emily said, "We have to stop that happening…"

"I am understand, but I am run out of patience." He stood. "Tonight you both talk, or I cut you in small pieces."

She stood and gripped my arm in hands like talons and hissed savagely, "*You have to kill him!*"

Gregor waved his hand at her. "OK, put on table. We take off thumb. Right thumb."

The two Glocks were burning a hole in my back. I was thinking I had to pull off at least four shots in about three seconds. And then there was the sniper hidden somewhere in the trees. I knew I couldn't do it. It was that simple.

Then, as the three other guys dragged Emily onto the table, Yuri pointed at me and said something to Gregor. Emily was kicking and thrashing and kept screaming. "*Lacklan! Lacklan! Do something!*"

Gregor frowned. "Yuri say you still have hand gun."

I held both hands up, speaking as I did so. "Yes, I have, but you don't need to do this. Just hold on, Gregor, we can talk..."

"I am boring with talking..."

"Yes, you are, I agree..."

As I said it, I pulled one of the Glocks from my waistband with two fingers, stepping forward and to the side, placing Yuri between me and the sniper. I handed him the Glock. Emily was on her back on the table and the three guys were holding her down, looking at Gregor, waiting for instructions. She was screaming incoherently now and writhing furiously. Yuri reached out, took the Glock, frowning at my chest, aware the red dot had gone, and I was still talking, fast.

"But you don't need to do this, Gregor. You want the NPP. I've got the NPP. I can give you the NPP. Just let Yuri help me!"

Time slowed down. Yuri and Gregor frowned, confused by what I'd said. I seized Yuri's right hand, and the Glock in it, with both of mine. I headbutted the bridge of his nose and shot the guy holding Emily's feet, using Yuri's finger on the trigger. Keeping Yuri between me and the sniper, I aimed at the guy holding her right arm. I fired, but he was already diving for cover and the plate glass, sliding door shattered behind him.

Emily jumped, clawing at the remaining guy's face, drawing red lines of blood. He let go and ran. I swung Yuri's arm around and aimed at Gregor, but he was scrambling for cover. I fired anyway, to keep them lively, and yelled at Emily, "*The beach!*"

I kneed Yuri in the balls and dragged him backward toward the table. There I head butted his nose again and grabbed for the AK-47 with my left hand. As I let him drop to the ground, I sprayed the trees with hot lead and followed Emily down the side of the house at a sprint, followed by a wild volley of bullets.

At the far corner of the house, I turned, dropped to one knee and opened up without aiming, shouting at Emily over my shoulder to make for the plane. I needn't have bothered. She had vaulted the fence without waiting to open the gate and was running through the sand toward the cover of the trees. I followed, jumped the gate and plowed through the sand toward the palms and the deep shadows. The air around my head popped, the tree trunks ahead smacked, chipped and splintered and ricochets whined into the night.

I dropped, rolled and came up on one knee again, facing back, and sprayed indiscriminately. Glass shattered and I heard somebody cry out. I gave a second burst, turned and ran. Emily was barely discernable up ahead, a bobbing shadow among the black forms of the undergrowth. Now the pier became visible in the wan moonlight, with luminous surf breaking around it and, not far off, the bulk of the seaplane, our ticket out of there.

Behind me, I heard the crackle of automatic fire and on my right, lead tore through the foliage. I shouted to Emily: *"Get down! Wait for me!"*

I heard her drop. Half a dozen strides carried me to where she was lying and I dropped beside her. I couldn't see anybody approaching, but I guessed they were among the trees. She was breathing hard. I glanced at her and her eyes were wide with fear.

I said: "Are you hurt?"

She turned her big eyes on me and shook her head. I pointed toward the sea.

"We have to get across the sand. You understand? We'll be slow-moving and we're going to stand out against the whiteness, that will make us easy targets."

She gave several quick nods. "What do we do?"

"We're going to make it in three dashes. We head for the far side of the pier. I have a boat there. We have to be quick. When I say run, you run like hell, count to four and drop." I counted out four steady seconds: "One and two and three and four—got it? Then we repeat two more times. OK?"

She nodded and swallowed. "OK."

"OK, *run!*"

I stood and opened up with the AK-47, hammering the area where I thought they must be. She ran, half crouching, and I kept pace with her, running sideways, spraying the palms and the ferns with a hail of fire. I counted four, then shouted, "*Down!*"

She dropped and I dropped beside her, facing the trees. A second passed and then they opened up. There was only one rifle, but there were handguns as well. The rounds came close and kicked up sand around us and made the air sing. It was terrifying, but I noted where the fire was coming from. I figured I had half a magazine. I opened up and shouted, "*Run!*"

We ran another four seconds, raining fire on their position, forcing them to take cover. On the count of four, I shouted, "*Drop!*"

She screamed, "*No! We're there!*"

I bellowed back, "*No!*"

I was pulling the trigger and getting dry clicks. I needed to reload. Then I saw the flames spitting from the trees. We were still twelve or fifteen feet from the pier. I turned and hurled myself at Emily, wrapped my arms around her legs and we sprawled in the mud as bullets kicked up showers of wet sand and water just inches from us.

"*You stupid bitch!*" I shouted at her. "*When I say drop, drop!*"

I scrambled around, staying flat, pulling the Galil from my shoulder. I could see three, maybe four figures running toward us, eighty or a hundred yards away. I opened the stock, nestled it and fired two short bursts. I didn't wait to see if I'd hit anyone. I screamed, "*Run!*" got to my feet and started running backward toward the pier and the dinghy, firing short bursts as I ran.

Then we were waist-deep in water, with the small swell breaking around us behind the wooden supports of the pier. The dinghy was there. I grabbed Emily by the scruff of her neck and the seat of her pants and hurled her into the boat, then slashed the rope holding it to the struts and jumped in. "*Stay down,*" I snarled, "*and do as you're told!*"

I fired her up and we sped, bouncing over the small waves, staying close to the wooden structure. I heard the crack of gunfire, but the shots went high and wide. Then we were skimming around the end of the jetty, out in open water and speeding toward the aircraft. Now I knew the risk was high. We had no cover and we were highly visible in the moonlight. I veered and danced erratically, aiming to move behind the plane. Shots peppered the water around us, sending up great plumes of foam.

I came in under the belly of the plane. A couple of shots

hit the fuselage and whined into the night. I clambered onto the float on the far side from the pier. On the shore I could just make out the guy with the rifle. He was running to get a line of fire on me. I yanked open the door and shouted at Emily, "*Get in! Fast!*" As I said it, I reached down and hauled her up. She scrambled into the cockpit and clambered over to the far side. A shot sent a shower of spray cascading over me, and a second smacked into the fuselage. Emily screamed, "*Get in! Let's go!*"

I pulled myself onboard, released the anchor and powered up the engine as a hail of bullets rattled against the side. I prayed to all the gods I didn't believe in that nothing essential was getting hit. Next thing, the props were thudding and we were accelerating away from the beach into dark ocean, smacking over the waves in showers of spray. And then we were rising, rising up high above the sea, toward the stars, and banking toward the moon.

THIRTEEN

THE ENGINE DRONED IN THE NIGHT AS WE climbed. She cried convulsively for about five minutes, maybe a little more. I didn't speak. I kept the plane on a heading slightly east of north, with the moon to my right casting a long, silver path across the blackness below.

Slowly, her sobs subsided and eventually, the only sound in the plane was the steady drone of the engine. It was an oddly peaceful sound. After a while, she looked at me and said, "Your face..."

"It's looked better."

"Why did you come...?"

"Don't flatter yourself. The smart thing would have been to take the plane and get the hell out of there. Maybe it's what I should have done. But I aim to find out what this damn business is all about."

She looked away. "I've caused you a lot of trouble."

"Yeah. You caused Jerry a bit of trouble, too. Why do I get the feeling it's something you do a lot of?"

"I'm sorry."

"Tell Jerry that. Sorry doesn't cut it, Emily. I keep warning you and you just keep lurching from one sack of horseshit to the next. Maybe you don't give a damn that people all around you keep getting killed. But sooner or later —probably sooner—that person getting killed will be you." I glanced at her and said without smiling, "Keep pushing me and I'll do it myself."

She frowned and looked genuinely shocked. "Don't say that!"

I grunted and after a moment she added, "This isn't my fault. I had no idea things would turn out this way. I'm sorry I lied to you, but I have been so scared..."

"You sold me that line already, Emily. Don't try and sell it to me again. I was there listening when you were talking to Gregor, remember?"

"You must realize that was an act!" She studied my face and her expression was incredulous. "Tell me you realized that was an act!"

"Why the hell should I, Emily? All you have done, from the moment the Colonel introduced us, is lie! I don't think you'd know how to tell the truth if you had to!"

She sighed and looked out at the moon. "I can't blame you for taking that view, I suppose. But not everything I said was a lie."

"Name one thing that wasn't."

"Harry, the Colonel, he really is my father."

"Yeah, right."

"He is, and when I said I wanted to stay the night with you, that was genuine, too."

"Don't try to play me, Emily. That is a bad plan right now."

"I wasn't trying to play you."

"That whole story about your mother dying, about working for Gregor, about the Colonel…"

"Some of it was true, Lacklan. I did live in Jersey, and my mother did die. When I looked through her things, I did find that Harry was my father…"

I was losing patience and I interrupted her. "Who was Jerry, and what was your business with him?"

She didn't answer for a moment, and the only sound was the hum of the engine as we moved slowly above the sea below. Far off to our left, small lights glimmered along the coast. I looked at her and asked savagely, "Are you working out the next story, the next collection of lies? Just tell the goddamn truth for once, will you!"

She looked at me resentfully and blinked tears from her eyes. "No, I am not. I was thinking about Jerry and how I am going to miss him. We were friends. We had been colleagues for a long time. Jerry was an IT expert."

"So now you worked in IT?"

Her voice became shrill. "What is the point of demanding that I tell you the truth if you are going to sneer at everything I say?" She was silent a moment, then turned to stare at the windshield. "I majored in Information Technology at NJIT. Jerry and I were both software developers in the field of artificial intelligence."

"So what were you doing in Freeport?"

She looked away, toward the coast. "I don't want to tell you."

"Why not?"

"We were working on a project that was highly classified. It had government backing, though it was also partly private sector investment, too. We weren't supposed to talk about it."

"So it's OK to sell it to the Russian Mafia, but it's not okay to talk about it?"

She sighed and turned hooded eyes on me. "You can be a real asshole sometimes, Lacklan. Do you know how damn self righteous you sound sometimes?"

"You going to answer the question or just insult me?"

"If you got down off your damned high horse for five minutes, maybe you'd realize that what I have been trying to do since I met you was *not sell the goddamn thing to the Russian Mafia!*"

I ran through everything that had happened since the Colonel had introduced us and realized that what she'd said was true. She waited for that to sink in and then went on.

"Yes! OK! I used you and I am sorry, but you're a soldier, Lacklan. And a special ops soldier at that! It's your job to get used, and to put your life at risk for the greater good! Sorry, but it's true."

"The greater good?"

"Jerry made a mistake. He contacted Gregor to make him an offer. It was a stupid thing to do. Then we didn't know how to get out of it. It was a mess. When Harry told me about you, and that you were on Galveston Island, I thought maybe I..."

"Maybe you could use me, manipulate me, risk my life and it would be OK because I was a soldier, I'm meant to be used and it's for the greater good anyway."

"You make it sound awful."

"No, it is awful, Emily. It stinks. Before you put a man's life at risk, you talk to him, you tell him the *truth!* And you give him the option to say no."

"I'm sorry."

"So basically you were selling a top secret device you had stolen from the U.S. government."

"No, it wasn't like that."

"What was it like?"

She buried her face in her hands and I thought she was going to start crying again. Instead she rubbed her face, ran her fingers through her hair and said, "What is the point? You won't believe me anyway."

"The point is," I snarled, "if you don't tell me, I'll open that damned door and push you out! Start talking! Were you selling a U.S. Government device to a foreign power? Yes or no?"

"No!" She looked genuinely horrified, then closed her eyes and sighed. "It wasn't *meant* to be like that, but it got out of hand."

"I'm still waiting for you to explain, Emily, and you had better not be cooking up another damned story."

"Jerry and I both worked at QPS..."

I frowned. The name meant something to me, but she went on before I could think about it.

"We were developing software for a device that can inter-face between the human brain and various different IT and robotic systems."

I nodded. "I've seen this on TV. It's used for prosthetic arms and hands."

She nodded, then shrugged. "Amongst other things. It can also be used to communicate with computers, and enable computers to talk to each other. If you can interface with a powerful computer that has the capability of communicating with other computers, you effectively turn the whole network into a cybernetic organism controlled by your brain. The potential is vast. You could take control of satellites, space shuttles, banking systems..."

"And this is what you made?"

She laughed. "No, we are some way off yet, but what's in the box is a prototype. If the Russians got hold of it and reverse engineered it..."

I scowled. "And you were planning to *auction this*? Are you out of your mind?"

"*No!* Of course we weren't, Lacklan!" She put her hands to her head. "Jerry had this insane idea. If we offered it for auction but remained anonymous, then we could sell the highest bidder a dud, bank the money in an offshore numbered account and make a fortune, without ever putting the homeland at risk. He had the whole thing worked out and tied up in bows."

"That has to be the stupidest idea I ever heard in my life."

"I agree, and you don't need to rub it in. I told him it was crazy and I told him he was going to get us both killed, but he was..." She stopped, wiped her eyes and sniffed. "He was Jerry. He thought he was immortal and indestructible. He had a huge IQ and he was sure he could outsmart everybody. It took Gregor less than a day to persuade him to go to the casino, find out who he was, and tell him that if he went to auction, he would gut him like a fish."

"So who else did Jerry contact?"

"Nobody, as far as I know."

We stared at each other for a long moment. Finally, I told her, "The CIA are in Freeport for the auction."

She sagged. "I guess Jerry must have contacted them, then. I don't know. Gregor scared the hell out of us and we panicked. We were sure that when we handed the NPP over, he would just kill us. Especially when he told us the arrangement for the handover. So when I reached out to you, I guess Jerry reached out to the CIA. He wasn't a great communicator. He just went ahead and did things, and didn't always tell me what he was doing."

I thought for a while. I'd been watching the gauges. I asked her, "Have you any idea where that house was?"

"The one we just came from?"

"Yes, the one where they were holding you."

"Yeah. It was about two hundred and fifty miles south of Freeport. We made the journey in just over an hour and forty-five minutes, cruising at a hundred and forty MPH. Why?"

I looked at her curiously. "Not a lot of people would notice a thing like that when they've just been abducted."

She shrugged. "That kind of information can save your life when you've just been abducted. Why are you asking?"

"Yeah," I said, studying her face. "And you'd know that, being a software developer." She ignored the irony. I looked back at the gauges. "I think one of the slugs might have damaged the fuel tank, we're losing fuel faster than we should be. I don't think we're going to make Freeport."

Realization of what that meant began to dawn on her. "Will we at least get out of Mexico?"

"Yeah, of course. We must have been just inside the border,

east of Matamoros. We're already over U.S. waters, but I'll have to call the coast guard, get them to come and rescue us. You can be pretty sure they'll notify Rand—that's the guy from Central Intelligence, he'll want to talk to us, to you in particular."

She nodded and was quiet for a bit. Eventually, she said, "I understand. It was never our intention to sell government secrets, Lacklan. That's why I asked you for help, and why Jerry contacted the CIA. You do understand that, don't you, Lacklan?"

I grunted. "I understand that it's the story you're telling me now, Emily. It sounds plausible and I want to believe you. But the jury is out until I get some proof that you're telling me the truth." I turned to look her in the face. She held my eye. "Lying comes just a little too easy to you. It's like your go-to response to any situation, and I am not convinced you've told me the whole story, let alone the truth. You're not just a software developer. You have skills you don't learn at software development school."

She didn't answer and we lapsed into silence. I kept my eye on the fuel gauge and after a time, I saw it slip below the half way mark. Emily was staring out the side window at the lights along the coast. Up ahead I saw a bright, luminous cluster. She pointed to it.

"That must be Corpus Christi. Can't we land there?"

I smiled. "You have a talent for suddenly disappearing. I figure you, in Corpus Christi, with me looking like this, in a plane that's registered to a Russian mobster... I can think of any number of ways you could use that set up to weave an interesting story and disappear again."

"I don't want to disappear, Lacklan. I want to get the

NPP to the authorities, clear my name and get Gregor off my back."

"Good." I managed a bruised, swollen smile. "In that case, we'll ditch in about an hour, about fifty miles outside Freeport. It could be a long night. To pass the time, you might want to think about telling me the rest of your story."

She sat and observed me for a long time while the engine droned and the ocean crept slowly beneath us. She observed me, but she didn't say anything. After a bit, she looked away, at the lights of Corpus Christi inching by. We flew on in silence. The moon, having reached its zenith, now slipped a little lower, but aside from that, and the slow procession of lights along the coast, little seemed to change outside the cabin, giving the illusion that we were motionless in space. But what did change was the full level, and as the tank approached empty, I pulled my cell from my pocket and instead of calling the Coast Guard, I called Rand.

He answered immediately.

"Lacklan, I've been wondering where you were."

"If I had a dollar for every time somebody said that to me."

"I bet. Where are you?"

"About to ditch in the Gulf. I figure we're about fifty miles southwest of Freeport, on a direct trajectory from the beach east of Matamoros. We're in a de Havilland Otter."

"How very interesting of you. When you say, 'we'...?"

"Emily is with me."

"Of course she is. And you would like me to come and get you."

"No, I'd like you to send the Coast Guard to get us. Let's

not complicate things, Rand. I called you as a gesture of good will. Play nice."

"Feel like telling me what you were doing at Matamoros?"

"You mean apart from wiping out fourteen of Gregor Ustinov's men?"

"You made your point, Lacklan. You're a badass. I'm terrified of you and I will play nice. What were you doing down there?"

"Just send me the Coast Guard and we'll talk when we get back. I'm sending you my location."

I hung up and shortly after that, the engine began to stutter and we began the gradual descent into blackness. As we came lower, the stuttering stopped and the engine died, though the sensation of speed increased. It was impossible to see what we were speeding toward, because below us, there was nothing but darkness. All I could do was watch the altimeter. When it told me we were a few hundred feet off the surface, by the limpid light of the moon, I began to detect small white crests and turquoise troughs in the inky ocean. And then, quite suddenly, we were racing over the waves, there was a thud and great plumes of spray exploded all around us. We slowed gradually and finally came to a halt.

Then there was silence.

After a few minutes, Emily asked me, "Will I go to prison?"

I moved around in my seat so my back was against the door and I could look at her. She was exquisite. Not beautiful in the way a supermodel is, but delightful to look at. I tried to imagine her after fifteen years in prison. It wasn't nice.

"That's the least of your worries, frankly, Emily. The way things stand right now, you'll be lucky to make it to a trial."

"What do you mean?"

"You just heard me warn a senior government agent to back off. Right now, you have the Russian GRU, the Russian Mafia, the CIA and God knows what other government agencies all really pissed at you. And I would say that the two things they all have in common are that they want the NPP, and they'd be very happy to send you on a six foot holiday to get it. As things stand, fifteen to life is the best outcome you can hope for."

She gazed out of the windshield at the golden path the moon was laying across the sea toward us. It looked beautiful, but I knew well that moonlit paths always lead you astray. They always lead to darkness.

FOURTEEN

She looked weary. She rubbed her face with her hands and ran her fingers through her hair. Outside, I could hear the wet lap of the waves against the floats. She said:

"I don't know what you want from me, Lacklan. I've come clean, I've told you the truth. What else can I do? What's the point in threatening me with death and prison?"

I nodded. "I used to have an aunt, my mother's sister. My mother is English and her sister lived in a small village near Oxford, in a pretty cottage with a rose garden out front and a big lawn out back, with a pond and a weeping willow. She was a sweet, kind woman and whenever people were in trouble, they would always go to her for help and advice. She was that kind of woman, you know? She was always smiling and had big, rosy cheeks, and she would always tell people the same thing: trust the Universe—Universe with a capital 'U'—trust the Universe and everything will work out.

"When I was twelve, and I was beginning to have problems with my father, we had a chat and she told me the same thing: trust the Universe. So I asked her, 'Is this the same universe where power is gained through violence and eighty percent of murders are committed by people who love each other? The same one that created ebola, leprosy and tapeworms? Is this the same universe where life is designed so that living creatures have to eat each other in order to survive? The same universe where, as often as not, the animal that gets eaten is still alive?'"

She stared at me like I had just farted loudly in the presence of the First Lady. "What a horrible thing to do. Why did you do that? What did she say? I hope she slapped you 'round the back of the head!"

"I agree. I had no right to destroy her faith, however absurd it was, especially as I had nothing to replace it with. She was very upset. She stopped giving people that piece of advice, and about a year later, she got cancer of the liver and died. I always felt bad about that."

"Why are you telling me this horrible story?"

"Because sometimes, the only way to get out of a really ugly situation is to recognize just how fucking ugly it really is. If we have hospitals and welfare systems today, it's not because people prayed for them or trusted the 'Universe', it's because three hundred and fifty years ago, a bunch of guys in England came up with a thing called empiricism and said, 'Hey, it's not God, it's gravity.'"

"Are we done with the lecture?"

"Maybe. You tell me. We have a little more than half an hour. Are you going to start getting real or are you going to keep telling me to trust the Universe?"

"Jesus! You are one persistent pain in the ass!"

"You're not the first person in the world to tell me that, though often 'persistent' is replaced by something shorter, with fewer syllables. My aunt, after she had turned to gin and marijuana to dull her existential angst, used to call me..."

"I get it!

"...a loathsome pain in the ass."

"I get it."

"Who do you work for?"

"Nobody. Me."

"That's a lie."

"It's true."

"The Company won't ask nicely. If you want my protection, you have to come clean. Who do you work for?"

"Nobody—anymore..."

"Stop playing games, Emily. We are running out of time. Who did you work for?"

"QPS."

"Who, or what, is QPS?"

"Was. QPS was a high security facility. Ostensibly, it was a software research and development company, contracted to the government. In reality, it was part of the military industrial complex, answering directly to the Pentagon."

"What was your role there?"

"I was senior management, and I was directly in charge of developing the NPP."

This finally had a definite ring of truth about it. "What happened?"

She gave her head several little shakes, then shrugged. "That's the thing. I don't know. Neither Jerry nor I had any idea. In fact, nobody seemed to have any idea. No explanation was given and when we asked, we were blanked." She raised her hands and dropped them in her lap in a gesture of helplessness. "One day, we turned up for work and there was an unscheduled meeting of all the senior management. We were informed that the company was closing. No reason was given. Nothing. We were just told to pack up and leave within two days. Our contracts were terminated summarily and we were given a substantial redundancy package, but in exchange, we had to sign an undertaking not to seek legal redress. That was it. End of story."

"So you and Jerry decided to take the NPP with you."

She took a deep breath, held it and frowned out the windshield. The horizon was turning grainy. "It was kind of weird..."

"What was?"

She bit her lip and shifted her eyes to study my face, like she was wondering whether to tell me. "There was a lot of confusion. It was like, one day we were this slick, well organized corporation and the next day, we were a shambles. And, get this, they had invested millions, *millions* into our project, but nobody asked us for it. We were instructed, the whole company was instructed, not just us, to hand over all research and research materials to our senior supervisors." She gave a small laugh. "But I *was* the senior supervisor, and all our research was digitalized. There was practically nothing on paper. So there was practically nothing to hand over.

"Me and Jerry discussed it on the second night. I was cagey but he was gung-ho, typical Jerry. He just put the damned thing in his pocket and walked out with it. Nobody said a damned thing to him. We were stunned. It was like they didn't know what research was going on there, or what they even had. We were kind of reeling. Holy shit! You know? We just walked out of a government facility with a *multi-million* dollar project in our pocket, and nobody said a damned thing to us! More than that, Lacklan, nobody even seemed aware that the project existed."

"Until later."

She nodded. "Until later, after Jerry had offered it to Gregor."

"So you *were* planning to auction it."

"Look, Lacklan, sincerely, we didn't know what the hell to do with it. The government didn't seem to know they even had the damn project. I told Jerry we should wait till the dust had settled and then contact the Department of Defense anonymously. But I already told you, he was rash and reckless and he was in a hurry. He thought the quickest way of getting the government to notice us was to offer it to the Russians."

"He may have had a point."

A sudden sadness clouded her eyes. "Yeah, but that point cost him his life. Worse."

"So what about all the research that went into the project?"

"I told you, it was all digital, practically nothing on paper. It's all on the computers at QPS."

"So the value of the NPP is that it can be reverse engineered?"

"Yeah. And it is the only physical prototype that was made."

I smiled, then gave a small laugh.

She said, "I'm telling you the truth, Lacklan."

"I think you probably are, or some near version of it. So if all this is true, how does it tie in with New Jersey, your mother, the Colonel..."

She puffed out her cheeks, then nodded. "It's basically true, Lacklan. I may have elaborated here and there, but the story is basically true."

I shook my head. "No."

"What do you mean, 'no'?"

"It is too much of a coincidence, Emily. The one company in the U.S.A. conducting that kind of research and development is located just where your long-lost dad happens to be living? Come on!"

"It's not a coincidence, Lacklan. It was deliberate. I was working for QPS in Jersey. They have a small research facility there. I am damn good at what I do. When I found out about my father, I asked for a transfer. The plant here wasn't *that* close, anyway. It's at least halfway to Houston, probably a bit more. I had a few interviews and they thought I'd be a good fit, so they agreed to the transfer. That was a couple of years ago, and I was promoted twice during that time. Like I said, I am good."

It made sense. I wasn't taking what she said on faith, but it actually made more sense than she realized. I still had my doubts about the details, but I figured the substance was about right. I already knew the answer to the question I asked next, but I was curious to see what she would say.

"Why didn't you print the research and smuggle that out, too?"

She laughed. "Apart from the fact that it would have taken a couple of small trucks to move it all, even if we'd tried to print only the most essential findings, we couldn't have. They had shut down the whole system. The computers were all dead."

"You got anything on your own computer, or Jerry's?"

"No, that was strictly forbidden. Why are you so interested in the research? All the essential stuff can be gleaned from reverse engineering."

I nodded. "Yeah, I guess it can. Pandora's box is open. Everything inside it has been unleashed. Now all we have to do is study it and replicate it."

"I don't know what you mean."

"Never mind. Tell me something, without the help of reverse engineering, could you recreate the NPP?"

She raised her eyebrows, and blew gently between her lips. "Yeah, probably, but it could take years. Don't forget, this was just a prototype, and it was the culmination of several years' work that had been carried out before I joined the team. Also, there were lots of specialists, each working on their own, discrete part of the project, often with no idea of what everybody else was doing. If I could assemble most of the original team, with the right facilities and budget... yeah, probably." She puckered her brow, trying to work out what I was getting at. "But the research exists. They have it on their system. Like I keep telling you, the value of the NPP is in the possibility of reverse engineering it."

"Yeah, I understand that."

She stared at me for a while as the eastern horizon turned from dark, grainy gray to a paler blue-gray, while in the west it was still dark night and the moon was still luminous in the sky. Finally, she asked me, "So what are you going to do?"

I held her eye. "Do you trust me?"

She didn't hesitate. "Yes."

"I'll talk to Rand, argue your case and advise him that you are more use to the government outside than inside."

"Thank you, but..." I waited, knowing what she was going to say. She said it, "What about Gregor?"

"What about him?"

"He will never stop coming after me, especially after tonight."

"I don't know what you think I can do about that."

She hesitated. "I don't know. Tonight..."

I waited, wondering if she would come out and say it.

"You were so... You were incredible."

"I don't know what you're trying to say, Emily. Be clear."

She averted her eyes, looked down at her knees, shoved her hands between them. "Can't you... Couldn't you just..."

"Are you asking me to assassinate him?" She raised her eyes to meet mine and chewed her lip, but she didn't answer. I said, "I have assassinated people professionally. They were enemies of the U.K. or the U.S.A., terrorists or heads of cartels. But that doesn't make me a hit man. I won't kill somebody just because they are an inconvenience to somebody else. Killing somebody, or having them killed, is not some magical way to dodge your responsibilities. You created this mess by being stupid. Now you have to clean it up by being smart."

Her cheeks colored and there was bright anger in her eyes. She couldn't hold back the acid in her voice. "Yes, Daddy!"

I nodded. "We still don't know the real Emily yet, do we?"

"Oh, stop it, Lacklan! For God's sake, stop pontificating!"

"I won't kill Gregor for you."

"Thanks."

On the northwestern horizon, a bright light appeared suddenly. I said, "The Coast Guard are here. I'm going to tell you one last thing, and you would be smart to listen to me."

She still looked resentful. "What?"

"You have created this mess by being stupid, and you keep repeating that same stupidity and digging yourself deeper into the mess. Stop. Be smart. Do something different."

There was still a glimmer of sarcasm in her eyes. "What is that, something you learned from your sensei? Is that like Zen wisdom? Only kill when the government tells you to?"

I shook my head. "No, Emily, it's common sense. Just stop being stupid."

We sat in silence after that as the light approached steadily through the predawn, growing brighter until after about fifteen minutes, we could eventually see it was two banks of spotlights mounted on two boats. One was a forty-seven foot Coast Guard MLB, the other was a tug which I figured would take the plane back to port.

We were helped aboard the Coast Guard launch, taken below deck and given hot coffee and donuts. The small complement of crew looked at us curiously, tended to the cuts and bruises on my face, but made a point of making no observations and asking us no questions. I figured they'd been briefed to mind their own business by Rand.

Shortly after we'd started our return journey, the skipper

came down from the bridge to see how we were. He was a man in his mid forties, with gray hair and intelligent blue eyes. He studied us both a moment, taking in my injuries, and said, "You were lucky we have good weather at the moment. If we'd had a storm, you would have been in trouble." He paused, then added, "It might have made more sense to land in Corpus Christi."

I held his eye. "That wasn't an option. I'm guessing Rand Peabody has spoken to you already."

He nodded. "Yup. So has the sheriff. They both want to see you when we get in—both of you. But I haven't been instructed to arrest you."

I raised an eyebrow at him. "Is there any reason why you would have been?"

He gave me a smile that said he knew my type and if it were up to him, he'd have us all arrested. "Not that I'm aware of."

"Thanks for the heads up."

"Sure."

He turned and made his way back to the bridge, and after that Emily and I were left alone. We were at a table, sitting on a bench. She was sitting next to me. She dunked the last bit of a donut in her coffee and then stuffed it in her mouth and chewed slowly. She looked exhausted. Before she'd finished chewing, she drained her coffee, swallowed, leaned over and rested her head on my shoulder. Within a few seconds, she was asleep.

I closed my eyes too, but I couldn't sleep. I kept running over in my mind everything that had happened, and everything that she had told me. It wasn't just credible, it was all too credible. The problem was, if it was true, the implications were far reaching. I thought of my father, all those years ago, bringing us here for our holidays. It was about that time that things started to go bad between him and my mother. I turned and looked at Emily, her tired head resting on my bruised shoulder, and wondered how much she knew, and how much she was simply a victim of circumstance.

FIFTEEN

AT NINE O'CLOCK THAT MORNING, WE WERE sitting in an office at Freeport City Hall. Two large windows overlooked a patch of wasteland and the Freeport Marina. In front of those windows, there was a functional, melamine desk, and behind the desk sat the Sheriff of Brazoria County. He didn't look happy. He had a paper cup of coffee in front of him and he was looking at the contents like they had let him down badly. When he spoke, he seemed to speak to the coffee.

"I kind of had a feeling we'd run into each other again, Mr. Walker." he said. "You seem to turn up at the damnedest times."

I didn't know how to answer that, so I said nothing and tried to look innocent. I was sitting across the desk from him in an uncomfortable, low-backed chair made from steel tubing and blue synthetic wool. Emily was beside me and Rand was sitting on a brown vinyl sofa at the far end of the room.

The sheriff tore his attention away from his paper cup and spoke again. "You want to tell me what you was doing down in Mexico, Mr. Walker?"

"I was abducted and taken there."

He flopped back in his chair and sighed. "You was abducted. Who abducted you, and while you're telling me, maybe you could explain why. Why," he said again, before I could answer, "would anybody want to abduct you?"

I chose to answer his second question and said, ambiguously, "I don't know."

"You don't know who abducted you?"

"Yes, I was abducted by Gregor Ustinov, the man who runs the Caribbean Island Casino."

Rand said, "The man has known ties to the *Shulaya* clan of the Russian Mafia, Sheriff. We have suspected for some time that the casino is being used to launder money, and possibly to move drugs, guns and prostitutes, too."

"That so? And what would make the Russian Mafia abduct you, Mr. Walker? What would you have that he wants?"

It was a remarkably incisive question which I had no intention of answering. So I ignored it.

"I had appealed to him on behalf of Miss Burgess for him to leave her alone. He had apparently been attempting to force his attentions on her. She had told him she was not interested, as you can imagine. But he became insistent and even threatening."

The sheriff frowned at Emily. "That so, Miss Burgess?"

She nodded. "Yes."

"Why didn't y'all come to us, or the police department?"

"I'm afraid that's my fault, Sheriff. I advised her not to. I happen to know that there's not a lot the police can do, aside from talk to them. After all, it is not against the law to court a woman. On the other hand, I happen to have some experience with the Russian Mafia, and I know they are contemptuous of the police, they do not take 'no' for an answer, and they can be very dangerous if crossed. I advised Miss Burgess, whose father is an old friend of my family, to let me deal with it."

He leaned on the desk with his elbows and frowned at me.

"Is that a fact? You have some experience with the Russian Mafia, do you? We might come back to that, but first of all, how about you tell me just exactly how you planned on dealing with it, Mr. Walker?"

"Sure. I went and had a conversation with him, in which I advised him to leave Miss Burgess alone. I have to admit that the outcome was not what I had expected."

Rand spoke again. "On the face of it, Sheriff, it would seem that Gregor Ustinov was so enraged by Captain Walker's courageous intervention that he killed her friend, Jerry, perhaps mistaking him for her lover, abducted her and took her to Mexico. He then abducted Mr. Walker, for the purpose of brutalizing him and torturing him, as we can plainly see from his face and hands."

I nodded. "I was drugged, Sheriff, taken on board his yacht, handcuffed to a steel pipe and beaten. During the ordeal, he told me that it was indeed him and his men who tortured and killed Jerry, for the purpose of luring Miss Burgess into a trap."

The sheriff sat quietly for a while and then shook his head.

"Nope," he said. "There's something missing here. "If you'll forgive the expression, ma'am, nobody sets up a whole rodeo just to ride one cow. You might be awful pretty, Miss Burgess, but he don't need to kidnap y'all and take you down to Mexico to seduce you, and to beat seven bells out of... *Captain* Walker." He turned to Rand. "And if what you're telling me is right, Mr. Peabody, and he's using the casino to run drugs, guns and women, then that just confirms what I am saying. He don't need to go to Mexico to do what he's doing. So, why the sailing trip?"

I smiled at him. "That's a very good question, but I am afraid you'll have to ask Mr. Ustinov, because I don't know the answer."

He raised an eyebrow over an ice-cold eye and then shifted it to Emily. "How about you, Miss Burgess? Why'd he take you all the way to Mexico?"

"I have no idea, Sheriff. You will have to ask him."

Before he could answer I said, "We are very tired, Sheriff. We will be happy to make full and detailed statements, but if you want to interrogate us, that will have to wait until we have rested. We have been through quite an ordeal."

He sighed. Rand said, "In any case, I think you'll find that Central Intelligence will be very keen to supply you with all the evidence you need to bring in the Bureau, arrest Ustinov and close the casino. It will be quite a feather in your cap, Sheriff."

He gave Rand the same look he'd given his coffee a little earlier and took our statements without any further questions. We signed the statements and Rand accompanied us downstairs, through the lobby and into the parking lot, where his red Jaguar was gleaming in the morning sun.

We climbed into the car in silence and slammed the doors. He pulled out of the lot and we headed across the bridge toward Baldwin Road. He didn't say anything until we'd turned onto the 332 and were headed for the coast road. Then he said, "We're going to have to talk."

I said, "I agree, but not now, Rand."

"I'm not talking to you, Lacklan…"

I turned to face him as we approached the Bluewater Highway. "But I am talking to you, Rand. You want to talk to Emily, you talk to me."

He raised an eyebrow and echoed the sheriff. "Is that so?"

He turned left onto the highway and the big Jaguar engine growled as we accelerated toward my house. After a moment, he glanced at me. "What's going on? You still the auctioneer?"

"What's going on is that I have been beaten to a pulp, I have killed fourteen men, escaped from a yacht, been chased across a Mexican beach and then escaped again in a seaplane. I need drink and food and sleep."

"You're a real James Bond. My heart bleeds for you. But you know that's not what I'm asking."

"I have the NPP, Rand. You want it, you talk to me, not Emily. And before you ask, no, she has no idea where it is."

"So you're the man to talk to."

"Not for the next six hours, no. I'll tell you what you can do in the meantime, though. Put eyes and ears on the casino. Gregor was stranded at Matamoros with no plane and no boat. He'll have to come back somehow, and I need to know when he does."

"What happened to his boat?"

"Long story, I sent it off toward Florida."

He laughed. "You're such a son of a bitch."

He slowed as we approached my beach house. I went on, "Put a BOLO out to watch for his return. Don't let them take him. I want this son of a bitch, Rand. I want him and I want his operation. And something else, put somebody on my house for the next six hours so I can sleep. Somebody good."

"You're giving a lot of orders there, boss."

"Yeah. I have the NPP. That makes me the man."

He nodded slowly. "You the man."

He pulled off the road and I saw the Zombie parked under the house among the stilts. Rand said, "I had it towed back for you. Don't worry, I didn't take anything. You still have your full arsenal in the trunk. So are we doing a deal or what?"

I scratched my head. "Not for another six hours, Rand. Then, probably. Thanks for bringing my car back."

I climbed out and Emily got out with me. Rand turned the car around and leaned out of the window. "I'll be in touch, in six hours. Four thirty P.M."

I gave him a thumbs up and we moved toward the front of the house. We dragged ourselves up the wooden steps and I pushed open the sliding doors. The place was pristine. All the furniture was brand new. I led her through the living room to the bedrooms at the back and opened the door to the guest room. She stood in front of me with sagging shoulders and stared at my sternum. Then she put her arms around me and rested her head on my chest. After a moment, I realized she was crying quietly.

I took her shoulders in my hands and gently pushed her

back so I could look into her face. "Get some rest, things will look better after you've slept a few hours."

"It's not that."

I sighed. I desperately needed sleep. I didn't need an existential conversation.

"What is it?"

"You act like such a badass, ruthless killing machine, but underneath you're a good person. You're dead on your feet and you're still looking out for me, despite everything I've done."

"What can I tell you? It must be your big, blue eyes."

She smiled. "They're brown."

"See? I really am a son of a bitch."

"Lacklan, I am not coming on to you."

I laughed. "In this state?"

"I'm serious. Please, let me sleep with you. And I do mean sleep. I am scared. Just to feel that you're there... I don't want to be alone. Please..."

I snorted. "It's usually me making that speech. I must be getting old. Come on. And you'd better not snore or I'll strangle you in your sleep."

I followed her into the bedroom, we pulled off our boots and fell back on the bed. She put her head on my shoulder and I was too tired to care. I closed my eyes and within a few seconds, I was deeply asleep.

SIXTEEN

I OPENED MY EYES AT TWO P.M. AND COULD NOT GO back to sleep. Emily had rolled over and had her back to me. She was snoring softly. I got up and made my way to the bathroom, stripping off as I went.

I stood under the shower for ten minutes, turning it from hot to cold and back again, shocking my body into full wakefulness. Then, I spent another ten minutes soaping and shampooing myself, trying to wash away all the pain and the blood. Finally, I toweled myself dry and went back to the bedroom. Emily was still asleep. I dressed, threw my old clothes in the dirty linen basket and went down to my car. I checked the trunk. Everything was there. I put my spare Sig in my waistband and then checked under the chassis and the hood to see if there was a bomb. There wasn't. I figured in any case that right then, most people wanted me alive for a change, but it pays to be careful.

I climbed behind the wheel and drove back to Lake Jackson. Lake Jackson is in the shape of a big letter 'C'. Emily's house was pretty much at the top of that 'C', the Colonel's was right down on the bottom tip, on Lake Road. It was a sprawling mansion set among broad, well tended lawns dotted with palm trees and silver birches. The driveway was long and paved, and opened around a fountain in front of a flight of four broad steps up to an arched, oak door.

I rang the bell and glanced at my watch. It was three P.M. I remembered Rand saying he would return at four. I knew he would, and felt vaguely uneasy about him being alone with Emily.

The door was opened by a young, Mexican girl in a blue uniform with a white apron. She smiled a nice smile, though her eyes said she wasn't crazy about my bruised, swollen face.

"I'm here to see the Colonel. Tell him it's Lacklan Walker."

Her eyes widened. "Oh, he is waiting for you to call..."

But as she said it, a door opened across the spacious hall and Harry stepped out. "Lacklan! Is that you?"

He hurried across the terracotta floor with his arms held out. "My God, man! What happened to you? Is Emily with you? Is she all right? Come on in..." He held my shoulders and gazed at my face. "My God..." he said again. "Who did this?"

I smiled. "You should see the other guys. Colonel, I need to talk to you. Can we go somewhere...?"

"In my office. Maria." He turned to the girl. "Bring some coffee to my office, will you?"

He led me back to the door he'd just come out of. His study was more like a comfortable living room than an office. It was agreeably shabby. There was a big, old, oak desk, beside an open fireplace, which was littered with papers and books. The air was rich with the aromatic smell of pipe tobacco, and there was a cold pipe in an old brass ashtray half buried under the papers. Against one wall there was a big sofa, and a couple of mismatched, overstuffed arm chairs were placed around the room. Two walls were taken up by a couple of thousand books stacked on oak bookcases, floor to ceiling, and sunlight streamed in through French doors that opened out onto a gleaming swimming pool.

On the sofa, the *Houston Chronicle* and the *New York Times* lay partly dismembered. I made some room and sat in the corner, half turned so that I could face him. He stood at his desk and started to pack his pipe. He spoke without looking at me.

"Is Emily OK, Lacklan?"

I nodded. "She's sleeping right now, at my place, and she has a couple of CIA agents watching over her."

He struck a match and held it to the bowl, puffing, sending thick billows of sweet-smelling smoke into the room, watching me all the while. When the pipe was alight, he came and sat.

"The CIA?" He shook his head. "Why are the CIA watching Emily?"

"That's what I am trying to find out, Colonel. She and Jerry were involved in something pretty deep. That much she has admitted to me. It's possible she was drawn in unwittingly, not really knowing what she was getting herself into. I don't know, but make no mistake, she has got herself into an unholy mess."

"What kind of mess? The CIA? That's counter espionage. They operate abroad..."

"They operate wherever they need to operate and they

do whatever they need to do. They are not people you want to be playing games with. Harry, I need to ask you a few awkward questions, and I need you to tell me the truth. No BS."

For a moment, he looked offended, then sighed and bit hard on the stem of his pipe. "Of course," he said.

"Have you had a paternity test done for Emily?"

He nodded several times. "Of course. I wasn't going to simply accept her word for it. I have also seen the letter her mother wrote me, but never sent. I am her father."

"Can I see the results of the test?"

He expostulated. "It was two years ago, Lacklan! I'd have to search for the letter..."

"OK, don't worry. Who had it done, you or her?"

"Well, um, I don't know, we sort of did it together."

"Sure." I smiled. "That makes sense. What can you tell me about her work, Colonel?"

He laughed. "Not a lot! I'm a fifties child. I still think in terms of levers and pulleys! I know she used to develop software for QPS. Oddly enough, they were the company that leased my land, out past Chenango. How about that for divine intervention? So after she had made contact with me, she had herself transferred there."

"And you provided her with the house on the lake?"

"Of course. It was the least I could do. I only wish Ruby —that was her mother—I only wish she had contacted me when she knew she was pregnant. I would have gladly taken care of them."

"Why didn't she? Did Emily ever explain that?"

He shrugged and shook his head. "Pride? Who can understand women, Lacklan? I know I can't."

I grunted. "Tell me about it."

"Their emotions fluctuate constantly and they have no real understanding of loyalty, except where their children are concerned."

"Did she ever discuss her work with you?"

"No!" He laughed again. "Even if she had, I would not have understood. I mean, it's essentially applied quantum physics, isn't it? Not even *they* really understand how it works. They just know that it does."

"Sure, but I mean more things like, relationships at work, people she dealt with... Did she ever come in complaining that so-and-so was a pain in the ass, this guy was really cute, that guy asked her out, Mary-Jane is a bitch...? You know the kind of thing."

His face was completely blank. "Now that you mention it, no, she never did. She really never talked about work."

"And you told me she never mentioned Jerry to you, either."

"No, never..."

There was a tap at the door and Maria came in with a tray of coffee. The Colonel stood and smiled at her. "Just leave it on the desk, I'll serve."

He moved some papers, she set down the tray and left. As he poured, he said, "Lacklan, these questions you're asking..." He set down the pot and looked at me. "Forgive me for saying so, but they are a bit odd, to say the least. Don't you think it's time you shared your thoughts with me?"

He brought over the cup and handed it to me. Then he returned to pour his own.

"Did she often work late?"

"Occasionally."

"And she has no boyfriend?"

He smiled as he sat. "I was rather hoping you might solve that problem. Are you going to answer me or just keep asking odd questions?"

I was quiet for a while, staring down at the black brew in my cup. "I keep trying to fit all the pieces together so that they make sense, and they keep not making sense. Emily had a friend at QPS. He seems to have been a close friend, more like a close ally. When QPS closed, she and he decided to steal a piece of hardware, a prototype, that could be worth a large fortune to any number of foreign powers."

He was staring at me like I had started speaking ancient Sumerian at him. *"Emily stole from the company?"*

I nodded. "The way she tells it, it was Jerry's idea and she got carried along. Their plan was to sell it back to the government. Instead, Jerry got either impatient or greedy, and tried to set up an auction. The Russian Mafia, in the form of Gregor Ustinov, the owner of the casino up at Caribbean Island, decided they wanted this device, and that's when things started to get badly out of hand."

He put down his cup and rubbed his eyes. "This is a lot to take in. I can't believe Emily would be involved in something like that. Surely there must be some kind of mistake."

"No mistake, Colonel. But it's not the only thing about this whole affair that is hard to believe."

He stared at me for a long moment, like he hadn't really heard what I'd said, then shook his head. "So what happened to her? And to you." He gestured at my face. "These bruises..."

"Her friend Jerry was abducted and tortured by Ustinov's men, forced to call her and arrange a meeting at her house. That was the call you thought you heard. When she returned to her house, they killed Jerry and abducted her. They took her down the coast, across the Mexican border, to a house they have there. It's pretty remote. After that, they abducted me and took me there, too. You see, I had told Ustinov that I had this device. My aim was to take the heat off Emily. It didn't work too well. Ustinov's plan was to play us off against each other in some way, torture one and offer the other incentives, something like that."

He frowned, shaking his head, "Incentives for what?"

"To give him the device."

He kept frowning. "Am I to understand that you, and not she, have the device?"

"I have the device. But neither Ustinov nor the CIA are one hundred percent sure that's true. They think maybe Emily still has it."

"But she hasn't?"

"No, only I know where it is."

"So that means Emily is safe, right? They won't hurt her if she hasn't got it..."

"I wouldn't be too sure. She has become a pretty dangerous witness."

He sighed and seemed to sag. "This is very worrying news, Lacklan. What do you propose?"

"If she is smart, she will put herself in the hands of the federal government. It is the FBI who should be investigating this and not the CIA. She needs to give evidence against Ustinov, hand over the stolen device and try to get protection and immunity. If she does that, I think she stands a pretty good chance."

"Immunity from prosecution and protection against the Russians."

I nodded.

His eyes shifted from my face and he gazed out the French windows at the pool and the lawn. The afternoon sun reflecting off the turquoise water made odd, wavering patterns on his face. His brow suddenly contracted. "How much is this damned thing worth?"

"It's impossible to say, Colonel. I am not even sure what it is. But it's worth millions, at least."

"What is it?" He asked it almost savagely, glaring at me suddenly. "What is this damned thing? You must have some idea!"

"From what she says, it's a prototype of some kind of neural transmitter that allows the human brain to interface with computers."

He looked disgusted. "It's science fiction!"

I gave a short, dry laugh. "We left science fiction behind a long time ago, Colonel. That's one of the things that worries me. Listen, I am going to arrange a meeting where I want to resolve this whole affair for once and for all. I'd like you to be there with Emily. I think she needs a lot of emotional support at the moment. She's pretty shaken up, as you can imagine."

"Of course, just tell me where and when."

"I'm not exactly sure yet, but I'll contact you and let you know."

"She's at your place now?"

"Yeah, and I need to get back to her."

I stood and the Colonel stood with me. "Lacklan, may God forgive me for what I am about to say. The FBI, the

CIA, military intelligence, they cross the line sometimes. I know they do—we did. Sometimes you have to in order to preserve national security. It's the way the game is played. But the bottom line is, I trust the American government to do the right thing." He stopped dead, staring at me, appealing to me with wide, frightened eyes. "But the Russians, Lacklan... I *know* what those people are capable of. I *know* what they would do to Emily if they got hold of her. The only thing that has stopped them so far, if what you tell me is true, is fear of losing this... *device!*"

"What are you saying, Colonel?"

"We have to do something..."

"We?"

"Help me, Lacklan! May God forgive me, but help me to eliminate Gregor Ustinov! I can't bear to think of my little girl in that *animal's* hands!"

I sighed. "One thing we do not need right now, Colonel, is somebody else going off the deep end. Let's just keep cool and do this by the numbers. The sheriff is already interested in Emily. You kill Gregor and you and Emily could both go down for twenty to life. That's not a good play."

"Would you do it? You're a professional. I'd pay you handsomely."

"Stop it, Harry. I'm not a paid assassin. We do this my way and everybody wins. If you and Emily start going off half cock, we wind up with a tragedy on our hands. Just cool down and wait for my instructions. Understood?"

He closed his eyes. "Just, please, promise me you'll keep her safe."

"Count on it."

I left him looking disturbed and unhappy at his front

door and drove down Lake Road toward the coast. As I drove, I called Rand.

"Where are you? My boys told me you left."

"On my way home. Any news of Gregor?"

"Yeah. He's back at the casino. He flew in to Scholes this morning in a private charter jet. From what we can gather, he's out for your blood."

I was quiet long enough for him to ask if I was still there. I said, "Yeah, I'm here. Listen, Rand, do you know what this NPP is?"

He didn't answer straight away. When he did, he said, "Do you?"

I allowed a smile to inflect my voice. "That's what I thought."

"Lacklan, we need to cut the crap. If you have this thing, you need to hand it over."

"I agree. But who am I handing it over to, Rand? You have no jurisdiction in this country. Why are you not accompanied by a Federal Special Agent? Why are the Feds not here?"

"This is too sensitive for the Feds."

"Bullshit. When a man like you uses the word 'sensitive' it means it's something you have a vested interest in keeping under wraps. I'll bet the federal government doesn't even know this damned thing exists, does it?"

"You're playing with fire, Lacklan."

"You know what happened last time I played with fire, Rand?" He didn't answer, but I told him anyway. "Everybody got burned, especially Jean-Claude Timmerman,[1] but

---

1. See *Kill Two*

a lot of computers got fried, too. My advice, Rand, is to humor me and trust that I will do the right thing."

"Don't threaten me, Lacklan. The right thing for whom?"

"I'll be in touch. We'll have a meeting. It's time I handed this thing over to the relevant authorities. You'd better be representing those relevant authorities, Rand, or things could get ugly. I'll arrange a meeting and let you know. In the meantime, call your boys off. I don't need them anymore."

"A meeting when?"

"Tonight."

I hung up and turned left on the Bluewater Highway. I didn't stop at my place. I kept going, toward Jamaica Beach and the turn off for the bridge to Caribbean Island.

SEVENTEEN

I GOT THERE AT FIFTEEN MINUTES AFTER FOUR. THE evening rush hadn't started yet and the parking lot was almost empty. I parked the Zombie beside the grotesque fountain again, opened the trunk and pulled out the Smith & Wesson 500. This revolver weighs about four and a half pounds, has an eight inch barrel, takes 50 cal ammunition and can shatter a concrete block with a single bullet. I loaded it with 700 grain flat nose rounds and sprinted up the steps.

A clone of the pretty girl I'd seen last time I was there was standing behind the reception desk. She looked unhappy about the state of my face. I leered at her, showed her the Smith & Wesson and said, "What's your name?"

She swallowed hard and said, "Cindy."

"Cindy, there is something really important that you need to do across the other side of the parking lot."

Her eyes were wide. "What...?"

"I don't know, but I have a very strong gut feeling that it

would be a really good idea for you to go and do it, and not come back until you see me leave. OK?"

She nodded and I nodded with her. She slipped around the desk and hurried into the parking lot. I sprinted up the stairs and blew the door half off its hinges without pausing in my stride. I stepped into the office and saw Gregor sitting behind his desk with his mouth open. One of his goons was sitting on the sofa and the other had been pouring a dark drink from a decanter into a balloon glass. They were all staring at me wide-eyed.

The next few seconds seemed to go into slow motion. That often happens at times of extreme violence. The guy on the sofa was only about ten feet away. It was an easy shot and his whole head exploded like a watermelon. The recoil on the 500 with a 700 grain round is huge and the revolver jumped. It took a whole second to settle again, but when it did, I had the guy with the decanter lined up. I blew the top of his head off too, and tore a hole the size of a grapefruit through the oak cabinet behind him.

As his body sank headless to the floor, I strode across the room toward Gregor. I have often seen terror in a man's face, but I never saw it so eloquently expressed as I did in that moment. He looked like a terrified goldfish, with his mouth forming a perfect 'O' opening and closing on silent words. He got to his feet as I arrived at the desk. I dropped the revolver on the surface and took hold of his head in both my hands, then slammed it face-first onto his blotter. I lifted him up, saw that his nose was busted and bleeding and slammed him down again, twice. After that, I shoved him back in his chair. His face was smeared with blood and he kept saying, "Oh... Oh..." as he put his hands to his nose and his mouth.

I picked up the revolver and put it to his head. "Two people offered to pay me to kill you today, Gregor."

He made an incoherent noise which might have been, "Please... stop..."

"You know what? While your man Peter was beating me on the boat, I never once asked him to stop. You think if I'd asked him, he would have stopped, Gregor?"

He made a wise choice and changed the subject. "What are you going to do?"

"I'm going to ask you a couple of questions, then I am going to make you an offer."

"What questions? What offer?"

He had pulled a white handkerchief from his pocket and was mopping the blood from his nose and lips.

"Who first approached you about the NPP, Emily or Jerry?"

He gave a small laugh. "Trouble in paradise. It is Jerry who makes first approach. But he was crazy, so I insist I want deal with Emily. What else?"

"What did they tell you the NPP was?"

Now he looked surprised and frowned at me. His eyes narrowed and acquired a look of cunning. "You don't know what is..."

I nodded a few times. "I know what is, Gregor. I just wonder if you do."

"What you are talking about?"

"What am I talking about?" I dropped into the chair opposite him. "It's a good question, Gregor. And I'll confess I am not one hundred percent sure yet. But I think somebody has been playing us all like fools, and you were the biggest fool of them all, because a key part of the game was that you get killed. The one person you should have trusted and worked with, Gregor, was me, because I was the one who was supposed to kill you."

He eyed his bloody handkerchief and muttered, "Are you sure, Mr. Walker?"

"And instead you tried to kill me."

He raised an eyebrow. "Kill you? Who would want kill somebody like you?"

"You still want the NPP?"

"Yes, of course I want."

"What's it worth to you?"

"Original price. Five million. You cause me so much damage, I must mitigate."

"The CIA are offering me a damn sight more than that. I had a meeting with their representative today. You have to do a lot better than five million and excuses."

"Ten..."

I laughed and went to stand.

"Fifteen!"

"You're getting closer."

"Twenty is maximum I can offer."

"Try twenty-five and a ten percent stake in the casino."

"Five percent."

"Fifteen!"

"OK! OK! Ten percent."

I sat smiling at him wondering how far I could push him. "We meet this evening. I'll let you know where. You come alone. I'll kill any man who shows up with you, and then I'll kill you." I gave a small laugh. "Though I don't think you have many men left, have you, Gregor? You bring the contract and a laptop. You make the transfer, where I can see you do it, into my Belize account." He nodded unhappily and I stood. "I'll be in touch this afternoon. Be ready."

I left his office and trotted down the broad staircase, feeling better than I had that morning. In the parking lot I saw the pretty, cloned receptionist sitting on the fountain, smoking a cigarette. I said, "Did you do what you had to do?"

She said, "Is this place going to shut down, mister?"

"Probably, it's running out of staff."

She sighed, dropped the cigarette and trod on it. I climbed behind the wheel and headed for home.

I drove slowly, smelling the sea air and letting the breeze soothe my mind. Fifteen minutes later, as I parked the Zombie among the stilts beneath the house, I realized I hadn't eaten since I'd had the donuts that morning. I climbed the steps, thinking about a good steak and a cold beer.

I wasn't surprised when I got to the terrace to find the door open and Emily gone. I knew Gregor didn't have her. We were well past that, and I knew Rand didn't have her either. He was too smart for that. So that left only one possibility.

I smiled to myself and pulled a large, fat sirloin from the fridge and an ice cold beer. I figured I'd earned them.

After lunch, I drove to Sweeny, a small, leafy town about twenty miles northwest of Freeport as the crow flies, but considerably farther by road. On the way, I made a detour past an arts and crafts shop in Freeport and bought some black lacquer. Once in Sweeny, I made my way to the post office on East 2nd Street, left my car in the parking lot and went inside to collect the mail I knew I had waiting for me in my PO box. It was a parcel, about two feet long.

I took it outside and threw it in the trunk. I put the Eagles on the sound system and headed north out of town, with the band telling me I couldn't hide those lying eyes. At State Highway 35 I turned west, through West Columbia and East Columbia and came finally to Angleton, where, with the sun turning coppery and the shadows growing long, I joined the 288 north to Chenango.

A mile past Chenango, I turned onto a side road, followed it through broad, flat fields for half a mile and then plunged into dense, dark woodland for another mile. When I came out the other side, I was at a crossroads. The only signpost was a red one that said, 'stop'. A cloud, the first I had seen in a few weeks, moved across the low sun. The fields ahead and to my right were empty, as was the road. A red barn two hundred yards away looked back at me with black, empty doors half closed. Everywhere, there was absolute stillness and silence.

I looked to my left. The road went west, straight, as far as the eye could see. Another flat field spread out to the right of the road, dotted with copses of oaks and poplars. About half a mile away, dead center of the field, I could make out a low, modern, red brick building, maybe two stories high. I turned left and cruised slowly, looking for a gate that would give me access to the grounds. I found it half a mile up the road, with a small sign beside it that said 'QPS.' It was a tall, white, metal gate. I climbed out and went to inspect it. It was locked, and also secured with a chain and a large padlock.

I went to the trunk, pulled the Maxim 9 from my kit bag

and returned to the gate. I stood back, blew out the lock and then blew the padlock off the chain. The Maxim has a built in suppressor and barely made any noise. I put the weapon back in the trunk, pushed the gate open, drove through and closed it again behind me, looping the chain through the bars to look like it was locked on the inside. Then I drove toward the building.

It was at the end of an asphalt drive, about a quarter of a mile from the gate. The building was unremarkable: a red brick, two story, oblong office block surrounded by lawns on three sides, with a large parking lot at the rear. The windows were all dark and the only access was through double plate glass doors that opened onto the parking lot.

I left the car by the door, climbed out and sat on the hood, looking at the building and wondering if it had an active alarm system. If it had, it clearly wasn't connected to the gate. I went and peered through the nearest windows. It was gloomy inside. I saw a large, open-plan room with maybe thirty partitioned cubicles, not a lot more. I went to the door and peered in through the glass. I saw a large reception area. There was a desk on the left, a flight of stairs and a couple of elevators straight ahead.

I stepped back and a steel staple in the ground in front of the door caught my eye, and I looked up above my head. There, I saw a steel roller blind sitting in its casement. I wondered why it hadn't been pulled down and secured. Something told me it had been, and then it had been rolled up again. I turned and looked behind me, across the parking lot. There were lawns, and then what looked like dense woodland. There was nobody for at least a mile in any direction.

I made up my mind, collected the Smith & Wesson 500 from the trunk and blew out the lock from the door. The 500 is a hand-held cannon and made a hell of a noise. I put it back in the trunk and sat for a while on the hood, listening. There was no alarm in the building, and there was no wailing of sirens approaching from Angleton. There was just the quiet and the stillness of late afternoon. I thought that was really interesting. So I went and pushed inside.

It was about as unimaginative on the inside as it was on the outside. The ground floor was taken up with the reception, two very large, open plan areas which were connected by plate glass doors, and along the inside wall, four rooms with large tables, which were presumably intended for meetings and conferences. Both of the large, open-plan areas contained approximately thirty cubicles, each with a computer terminal. I tried switching a couple of the units on, but they were dead. Windows all along the far wall looked over empty grounds flanked in the distance by tall, dark poplars. The feeling of isolation was total.

I went to examine the conference rooms. Each was identically nondescript. I flipped one of the switches inside the door and, as I had expected, the lights came on. I smiled. The roller blind was up, the alarms were off, the power was on, but the computers were down.

I made my way back to reception and climbed the stairs to the upper floor. It was much like the ground floor, except that there were no conference rooms. As downstairs, there were two big, open-plan areas with cubicles, connected via plate glass doors, but at the back of the second room, there was a collection of offices, eight of them, all told. I inspected each one in turn until I found what I was looking for. They were all abandoned, empty, devoid of everything except the desk, the chair and the dead computer, but the fourth one I went into was different.

There was a mattress on the floor, with bedding and, on the desk, as well as the computer terminal, there was a laptop attached to a black box by a short cable. Against the wall, there was a small fridge. When I opened it, I found beer and pizzas, and coke. There was also a microwave oven and a sports bag full of clothes.

This, then, was where Jerry had lived and worked. This was the place from which he had contacted Gregor, and later the CIA. This was the place from which he planned to organize and conduct his auction. There could be little doubt he had both the skill and the equipment to avoid having his IP address discovered. And the last place on Earth they would ever think of searching for him was right in the building where the NPP had been made.

Here, at last, was concrete evidence of something.

I went to the elevators, called one and when the doors hissed open, I examined the buttons. There was the ground floor and the second floor, where I was, and then there were two basements, and each basement button required a key. I had seen no stairs leading down, and there was no underground parking, so the only access was via these elevators. Two got you twenty that those basements were the labs where Jerry and Emily had developed and tested their device.

I returned to the office, sat in Jerry's chair and went methodically through the drawers until I found what I was looking for: two small keys that would fit the buttons in the elevators. Then I sat for a while with my ass on the desk, smoking and thinking. Finally I picked up the phone and called Rand.

"What?"

"Do you know where I am?"

"What do you think? I spend my time tracking you on GPS?"

"I know you wish you could. I'm at the QPS factory."

"Oh..."

"You want to hear an interesting story?"

"Always. It's what I live for."

"Then you do exactly as I say. Deviate one jot and you wind up with nothing but egg all over the Company's face. Deal?"

"What can I say? Deal."

We talked for another five minutes, then I called Emily. It rang twice and she answered on the third ring. She didn't say anything for a moment. I waited and finally, she said, "Lacklan, I'm sorry. Are you mad at me?"

"No. Listen, there's something I need you to see."

"What? Where? I woke up and you were gone."

"That's not important now. I need you to come to the QPS building."

"... You mean out by Chenango?"

"Yes, Emily, where you used to work."

"But it's all closed up now, and vacated."

"I'm aware of that. I need you to come out here. How long will it take you?"

"I don't know, twenty minutes?"

"Where are you?"

She was quiet for a bit, then said, "I'm at home. The

carpet is still stained…” She began to cry. “Lacklan, I can’t take much more of this…”

“Call your father. Tell him to pick you up. I want you both to come here together.”

“Why, Lacklan? What’s going on?”

“I’ll expect you in at six. That gives you plenty of time. You’ll find the door open. Go upstairs to the offices. I’ll be there waiting.”

I hung up and immediately called the Colonel. He answered on the first ring, like he’d been waiting by the phone.

“Lacklan!”

“Emily is going to call you in a moment, Colonel. I want you to pick her up from wherever she is and bring her to the QPS site.”

“The QPS… why? That place is closed down.”

“I know. There is something here I need you to see. You and Emily both.”

“Very well. Is everything OK?”

“Sure. I’ll expect you in at six. Not before, and don’t be late.”

I hung up, spent a moment running through things in my head and called Gregor. When he answered, he was lisping.

“You break my nothe, and two teeth I have lotht.”

“Count yourself lucky you can still talk to complain. You know where the QPS building is?”

“Yeth, I can find.”

“Be here in…” I looked at my watch. “Be here at six fifteen. Bring your laptop and be ready to make the transfer.

If you follow my instructions to the letter, you leave here with the box. Do you understand what that means?"

"Yeth. I make tranthfer to your account in Belize. Twenty-five million, and contract, ten perthent of profit from cathino."

"And, Gregor, you come alone. You bring your boys or try any smart moves, things get very ugly. You better be very clear about that."

"I clear."

"Half an hour."

I had about an hour to prepare. I went downstairs, climbed in the car and drove to the gates. I removed the chain and pulled them back enough to admit a vehicle. Then I drove back to the building and parked outside the door. I opened the trunk and took out the parcel and a couple of other things I thought I might need, including the 500. I carried everything up to the office and spent a quarter of an hour preparing the room, after which I opened the parcel, checked the contents and put it into the desk drawer.

Then I checked my watch. I had half an hour before Emily and the Colonel were due to arrive. I used it to go to the elevators and try the keys. They worked and carried me down to the basements.

As I had thought, they were two labs. I didn't have long to inspect them in any detail. But in any case, the equipment in them, which all looked like cutting edge, high-tech electronics, was such that even a detailed inspection would have told me very little. I spent about ten minutes in each, did what I needed to do, and then rode the elevators back to the top floor. There, I flipped on the lights in the areas with all the cubicles and settled to wait. From where I was sitting behind the desk, I had a clear view right across to the elevators and the stairs, and the windows at the far end of the building, fifty or sixty yards away.

At a couple of minutes past six, as the last of the light was fading from the sky outside, I saw Emily and the Colonel appear, hesitant and unsure, at the top of the stairs. They looked oddly small and vulnerable in that large, bright space. They looked around for a moment, hesitated some more, and then moved across the big room, Emily slightly ahead of the Colonel. They vanished from sight for a moment and then appeared again, large in the doorway. They both stood, looking around the office as I watched them from behind the desk. Emily asked:

"What is this…?"

I held her eye a moment and said, "Come in and sit down."

They were still hesitant, but after a second, she came in and he followed. They sat, staring at the mattress, and the microwave and the fridge, though Emily's eyes kept returning to the laptop on the desk.

The Colonel said, "What is this about, Lacklan? What's going on?"

"I was hoping Emily would be able to explain that, Colonel."

"What?" He frowned and stared at her.

Her face was rigid. She was staring at me fixedly. "What are you doing, Lacklan?"

"What is this room, Emily?"

"I trusted you."

I laughed. "That's funny, because I never trusted you. That might be because every time you open your mouth, it's to tell another lie. Answer the question. What is this room?"

"I have no idea."

"You're lying."

The Colonel blustered for a moment. "Now hold up there, Lacklan!"

I sighed and reached down. I pulled open the drawer, took out the black, featureless box and placed it in front of me on the desk.

"Pandora's box. What do we do with it? Do we open it? Do we leave it closed? Do we hand it to the federal government? Do we hand it to the CIA, the Russians, do we auction it and live happily ever after on the proceeds? What should we do with Pandora's box, Emily? Shall we unleash what is inside it?"

She had gone very pale. There were beads of sweat on her brow and she kept swallowing. Her eyes were riveted to the box. I glanced at the Colonel.

He was frowning hard. "What is that?"

I shrugged. "Right now, it's a box. Maybe Schrödinger's cat is inside it. Maybe the cat is dead. Maybe it's alive. Everything is possibility until we open it. Isn't that right, Emily?"

She still didn't answer. The Colonel turned to her and said, "Emily? What is all this about?"

I nodded. "Yes, Emily, what is this all about?" I placed my hand on the lid. "This is mine right now. What I do with it depends to a large extent on you. I am not going to charge you millions of dollars for it. Right now, all I want is information. Tell me what I need to know, and you can have the box, to do with as you please."

She was trying to read my eyes, trying to see if I was lying or telling the truth. The Colonel's face was starting to flush red. "I think you need to start explaining yourself, Emily."

I said, "This room. It's where Jerry was working from, wasn't it?"

Her voice was barely a whisper. "Yes..."

"What was he doing here?"

"If I tell you, will you give me the box?"

"If you tell me the truth—and I will know if you're lying—if you tell me the truth, you can have the box."

She nodded. "Jerry was using this place to organize the auction of the NPP."

EIGHTEEN

THE ROOM WAS SILENT FOR A LONG MOMENT. Then, she pointed at the laptop.

"That's his computer. He had developed a device that rerouted him all over the planet once every fifteen seconds. So it was impossible to trace where he was. He was quite brilliant at IT. But he was a fool when it came to dealing with people. Gregor wasn't, and he managed to manipulate him into a face to face meeting. I told you that already. Jerry was as arrogant as he was brilliant and he was convinced he could pull off an act where he pretended to be from California. Obviously Gregor had him followed, and before long, they had established he was from Freeport, and that he knew me. It didn't take them long to find out that we had both worked at QPS..."

She left the words hanging. I nodded a while. "So before you could proceed to the auction..." I waited and she filled in the gap.

"Yes, before we could proceed to the auction, we needed to find a way of getting free from Gregor."

"Before we get into that, just tell me a little about the basements."

"What about the basements?"

"They are labs, right?"

"Have you been down there?"

"Would I get a different answer if I hadn't?"

"Of course not."

"Of course not. So what's the answer? Are they labs or not?"

She closed her eyes and hesitated. "Yes, you know full well that they are."

"Are they still functional?"

She stared at me for a full fifteen seconds.

Finally, I said, "I am going to take that as a yes, but I have noted that you were unwilling to be honest about it." I laid my hand on the box. "And that might have repercussions when the time comes to decide who gets the box."

Her face flushed with anger. She took a deep, unsteady breath and said, "The labs are still operational. We haven't used them since the place closed down, but theoretically, we could continue the research into the NPP if we had the right funding."

I smiled and nodded. "That was what I was wondering about. This isn't just about getting a big pay off, is it? It's about getting a contract to continue that research."

She thrust her hands between her knees in that characteristic gesture of hers, looked down and said, "Is that so surprising?"

"Not at all." I shook my head. "You turn up for work

one day and you find that overnight, the plug has been pulled on the research you've been doing; research that could change the world, transform the way people live." She glanced at me under her eyebrows. I ignored her and went on. "No explanation is given, no warning, no reasons, nothing. And, to make matters worse, all the computers you've been using to store your data have been shut down. Your world-changing project is dead in the water. But what you want, more than anything in the world, is to continue that vital work, which will not only change the world, but will also put you at the forefront of your field. What to do?"

I paused and waved a finger at her. "You'd heard that the Russian Mafia had ties to Putin. Maybe you even knew that the *Shulaya* clan had ties to the Russian government. You hoped that if you played your cards right, you might get access to the Kremlin through Gregor. But that wasn't just naïve, it was plain stupid. I'm guessing the first thing he asked you was what the NPP was, and you spun him some bullshit story like the one you spun me. Gregor might be all kinds of things, but he is not stupid, and he realized that what you had was a hundred times more valuable than you were making it out to be. He understood right away that you were using him to get to the Kremlin. You'd tell *them* what you had, but not him. Once you made your connection at the Kremlin, he'd be out in the cold. If you were saying it was a way of interfacing with computers, which is cutting edge modern technology, then it had to be something even more radical than that."

Her brows twitched into a frown. "I already told you, that's what it is."

"And I already told you, that's bullshit." I gave a small

laugh and shook my head. "The technology you described, Emily, I happen to know that that kind of technology is not radical anymore. There has been research going on into that kind of interface for a long time. I have been personally responsible for destroying a lot of it. No, what you described just wasn't radical enough to be stirring up the kind of interest you were getting from Gregor and the Company."

Her next question surprised me. "Who *are* you...?"

I smiled. "The last person on the planet you should have asked for help. What happened? Did you end up telling Gregor what the NPP really was?"

"Jerry did. He said it was the only way. Another one of his brilliant ideas."

"And Gregor told you the way it was going to be. He would pay you enough so that you would be able to retire in style, and he would then take the NPP and sell it to the Kremlin."

She nodded.

"So you decided you had to kill him, or, more accurately, have him killed."

"Yes."

"And that's where I came in."

"Yes."

"Your plan from the very start was that I would make the drop, Jerry would spark a firefight and I would kill Gregor. Then, either I would be killed in the exchange—that would be the best option—or I could be bought off afterwards, perhaps with a little seduction from you." She drew breath to say something, but I plowed on. "What really blows my mind is that you actually thought Gregor would be present at the exchange."

"That was the deal. I would be there in person if he was."

"And your first reaction was to get somebody else to go in your place. It didn't occur to your criminal mastermind that he might do the same."

"Jerry was convinced he would go..."

"Jerry is dead."

"You don't need to remind me of that."

"Apparently, I do. This has been a catalogue of stupid decisions and stupid actions that hasn't ended in total catastrophe because one of those stupid decisions actually played out in your favor, if you only had sufficient intelligence to recognize it."

"You've made your point, Lacklan. I am stupid. You can stop insulting me now."

I glanced at the Colonel. He hadn't said anything for a while and now he was staring at the floor like he was trying to burn a hole in it.

I pulled my Camels from my pocket and took my time lighting one with my old Zippo. I inhaled deep and blew out the smoke through my nose. Between their heads, I could see the row of black windows at the front of the hall. I was watching a bright light approach and slow as it reached the gate. After a moment, it turned in and moved slowly toward the building. I shifted my eyes to Emily.

"So what is it, Emily? What is the NPP?"

"It's a prototype. I told you."

"You told me it was a device for interfacing your brain with computer software. But we both know that kind of technology already exists."

"What there is is mainly theoretical or very basic."

"A prototype is little more than that. Stop bullshitting me. To command the kind of prices this thing is commanding, and the kind of interest it's getting, it has to be a lot more than that." I shook my head. "Every time you bullshit me, this box slips further away from you. This is the end of the line, Emily. You tell me, or you lose the box."

The Colonel turned to look at her and said, "Tell him, Emily."

She closed her eyes and sighed. "If I tell you, will you end this nonsense and let me take the box. It is *my* device. I created it, for God's sake!"

"What is it?"

She opened her eyes and raised an eyebrow at me. Her tone was a little patronizing. "It's an NPP. You know everything else, I'm surprised you don't know what that is."

I spread my hands. "You going to tell me?"

"It's a nano-particle processor."

"And what is that?"

She gave a small laugh. "The holy grail, the philosopher's stone, the key to creation..."

"Cut it out, Emily..."

As I said it, I saw Gregor's huge form appear at the top of the stairs, holding a briefcase. He saw us and moved on massive legs across the room, vanished from view as Emily and the Colonel had, and then reappeared vast in the doorway. The Colonel turned and saw him, then jumped to his feet, knocking over his chair. Emily gave a little scream and turned to stare at me.

"Lacklan! What is this?"

"Come in, Gregor. Grab a chair and join us."

He pointed at the box on the desk. When he spoke, I

noticed he'd had provisional false front teeth installed. "This is it?"

"Yes." I raised the Smith & Wesson and showed it to him. "And at the moment, possession is nine tenths of the law. Bessie here is the other tenth. Are we clear? Sit down."

Gregor grunted and moved across the office to sit in a chair that looked far too small for him. The Colonel picked up his chair and sat down, too.

"What do you think you're playing at, Lacklan?"

I raised an eyebrow at him. "Russian roulette?" I turned to Gregor. "Emily was just explaining to me what an NPP is. We had got to the philosopher's stone and the key to the universe. I was starting to fall asleep at that point. You want to start again, Emily, without the manure?"

Gregor said, "Is not manure."

"A nano-particle processor was, until recently, little more than a theoretical proposition, almost a thought experiment. What would happen if… Some people had looked into it on a theoretical level and had been manipulating and tuning nano-particles using optical field interactions for some time, mainly for use in electronics and photonics. They had achieved scalable, direct, and optically modulated nano-particle patterns of comparatively high precision using pulsed nanosecond lasers. But we are talking about structures so small you need a microscope to see them."

I shook my head. "I have no idea what you're saying."

"I'm saying that around the world, labs had made instruments that could program electrons and other particles to align themselves in certain shapes. That was awesome! It was incredible, because it meant we were learning how to shape the building blocks of reality. But we were doing it on such a small scale, it makes practically no difference. The applications were very few and very small."

She reached out her hand and pointed at the box, and I saw her hand was trembling.

"What I have created there is a tool that, given a little more research and development, can build a wall, can make bricks, can turn lead into gold, because it can change the structure of atoms and molecules. It is the prototype of an actual, real nano-particle programmer. It programs electrons, protons, atoms and it brings them together to *create matter!* Have you any *conception* of what that means?"

I sank back in the chair and went cold from the top of my head to the soles of my feet. Gregor spoke suddenly.

"This is like Industrial Revolution times one billion. It revolutionize the world. No poverty. Nobody ever have to work. Unlimited energy, food, water. Fix ozone, fix global warming. Is potential unlimited." He stared at me a moment and then added, "But is necessary Communist government. You have competition with this thing and it comes the end of the world. Only one government can have this thing."

There was a ghastly, twisted truth to what he was saying. I looked back at Emily. "How true is this?"

She shrugged. "It's a little sensational, but that is the basic theory. It has never been tested on anything bigger than a grain of sand. But the theory is that it brings together particles and programs them into atoms. It's a very simple theory."

"And that little tablet does all of that?"

"Not exactly. That's like the CPU. It needs a bigger computer to work through. We were at the testing stage.

That's what the labs are for downstairs. But then they shut us down."

"How close were you to the nightmare Gregor described?"

"I don't know, years. A few years. We were about to start making complex inanimate objects—almost like using a 3D printer, only it's more like a hologram. You program the holographic image and then the hologram takes on a solid form. It's hard to describe. I guess in three to five years we could start giving it practical applications, given the right funding and the right political support."

Gregor made noises in Russian that could only have been obscenities. "If this thing is in hands of United States, you know what will happen. Military application, licensing to mega-corporations, military industrial complex, Pentagon, exploitation, it will be disaster. People like Bush, Clinton, Trump using to control the world. You cannot allow!"

I burst out laughing. "This from the head of the *Shulaya* clan, who had me chained to a steel pipe while his thugs beat me senseless. I like your style, Gregor."

"Come! Enough bullshit. I have the transfer ready, and the contract. We make exchange now."

Emily was on her feet, and the Colonel beside her.

"Lacklan, you can't! You said I could take it if I leveled with you and told you the truth!"

And the Colonel was shouting, too: "*You can't be serious! You can't sell a thing like this to a foreign government! Have you any idea what that would mean!*"

I said, quietly, "Sit down, both of you."

They both sat. I looked at Emily. "You're right, I said

that. And straight away, you started lying and trying to hide the truth from me." I turned to Gregor. "And as for you, the price we agreed was based on something very different." I gave a small, un-amused laugh. "You're asking me to sell you the next Industrial Revolution for a string of beads. That ain't going to happen." I pointed at the box on the desk. "What you guys are talking about is worth not millions, not even hundreds of millions. It's worth billions—more than that. This thing will change the world. It will change the way we manufacture, the way we live. It will change everything, and whoever controls it will be master of the world."

I looked at each of them in turn. I could see Emily's chest rising and falling. Her eyes were bright. I wondered what she was going to do. The Colonel also was tense, watching me like a cat watching a mouse with an AK-47.

Gregor said, "What do you want? Anything you want, I can arrange. I can make you a prince. We had agreement. You must honor that agreement."

I studied him a moment. "How much are you authorized to transfer right now?"

"Twenty-five million dollars."

"Make it thirty."

"You give me the box."

"The box stays where it is until you make the transfer."

"I don't trust you. You all making tricks together."

"Tell me something, Gregor. If I change my mind, and hand the box over to Emily, what happens next? How many men have you got surrounding the building?"

"Seven."

I nodded. It had been predictable. I slid the box along the desk. "Make the transfer, Gregor."

He opened his attaché case and started typing. Emily was shaking her head. "You can't do this, Lacklan! This is my life's work! I'd have got the Nobel Prize. You can't let this *animal* take it!"

He stood and put the laptop in front of me. He tapped the enter key and I watched twenty-five million dollars transfer into my account in Belize.

I pointed at the box. "There it is. Pandora's box. If I were you, I wouldn't touch it with a barge pole. Don't say I didn't warn you."

He pulled a Desert Eagle from under his arm and pointed it at me, then at Emily and the Colonel. "No more tricks. I have bought. Is mine. You leave me alone. I leave you alone. You have your money. Now this is mine."

I laughed out loud. "Aren't you even going to check it's in there? Don't you even want to see what it is you just bought?"

A spasm of alarm constricted his face. He fumbled and dropped the case, then opened the box. Emily stood. I said, "Is that it, Emily?"

She peered in and Gregor immediately backed away. She turned and scowled at me with an expression of utter loathing. Gregor snapped the box closed, grabbed his case and ran on big, lumbering legs. I watched him reach the elevators and then turn and rush down the stairs.

I stood and opened the window. A chill breeze crept in. Emily began to speak. I raised my finger to my lips. After a moment, I heard shouted voices, then a volley of car doors slamming and the hum of an engine as Gregor and what was left of his Russian army receded toward the gate.

NINETEEN

EMILY WAS ON HER FEET, SCREAMING AT ME. THE Colonel had also stood up. He looked pale and was shaking his head, muttering support for what Emily was saying. While all this was going on, I pulled out my phone, ignoring them both, and dialed a number on my speed dial. A second later, there was a massive detonation that rattled the glass in the windows and reverberated through the floors and the walls.

Then there was total silence, but through the windows at the front of the building, I could now see the wavering, orange light of flames from a large fire. Emily and Harry both turned and stared. Then the Colonel slowly sank into his chair. Emily looked back at me, struggling to understand what had just happened, blinking furiously. Her mouth was working but nothing was coming out of it. I put my phone on the desk. Her blinking slowed and she drew a breath.

"What did you do?"

"I put a pound and a half of C4 into the box, painted

with black lacquer. It looked pretty much like the NPP. I warned him not to take it. I also warned him to come alone. If I hadn't given him the box, he and his men would have tried to kill us."

Suddenly her eyes were wide, her mouth smiling. She rushed forward. "Then, the programmer is still all right? You haven't destroyed it?"

"It's safe."

"But Gregor is dead?"

"It seems likely, doesn't it?"

She turned to the Colonel, grabbed his hands and dropped on her knees. "Then we're OK, Daddy! It's what we wanted all along..."

Her voice trailed off and the Colonel shifted his eyes to look at me. I raised an eyebrow. "It's OK, Colonel. I'd figured it out already. Just tell me something. Were you a member, or just a friend?"

Emily whispered an apology and leaned forward with her head on his lap. He stroked her hair for a bit. "It's OK, baby." To me, he said, "I was never rich enough or, I guess, smart enough to be a member. Your dad was a good friend to me. He sponsored me, put in a good word, but I never made it past 'Friend'. I didn't resent it. I was never in their league, and they did help. I made a lot of money with their help." He smiled. "Hell! This research center, they could have put it almost anywhere, but they put it here, on my land, and I can tell you that that deal was worth a pretty packet. Your dad always looked after me. He was a good man. I know you had your problems, but he was a good man, Lacklan. Loyal."

"Was this your idea?"

He shrugged. "When Emily and Jerry came to me and told me what'd happened... Well, your dad was gone, and Ben had disappeared, there was nobody left to go to for advice. And the management of QPS had all changed. They were all French and German now. I didn't know any of them as friends. Not like your dad. So I didn't know what to do. And while I was still thinking about it, the management just all upped and vanished. Not a word, not a trace."

He looked at me for a long while, as though challenging me to say that what he had done was wrong. "How can that happen?" he said.

"Omega is finished, Colonel. It has been all but destroyed. You know my father is dead, but you probably don't know that Ben is also, and all his colleagues." Emily raised her head and stared at me. I went on. "The reason all your computers died was not that they had been switched off or disconnected by Omega. It was because the central Omega computer was infected with a virus known as a neutron bomb, that spread to all the computers that were connected with it. The whole Omega system was wiped out in a matter of a few days. That's what triggered the European stock exchange crash, and brought down your network. This was an Omega research facility."

It was as though she hadn't heard a word I'd said. She asked, "You know about Omega?"

The Colonel said, "His father was a big shot in Omega, honey."

"Omega owned this plant. They were funding my research."

I said, "I know. You're their kind of scientist, Emily. But they're gone now. It's over. It's finished."

She smiled. "No." She shook her head. "Gregor is dead. The NPP is safe. We can start again. You can help us."

"No, Emily. I can't."

Across the long room with all the cubicles, a figure emerged from the stairwell, followed by a man in a suit. They saw us and began to walk toward us. They disappeared from view and then Rand and a tall, well-dressed man I had never met before, appeared in the doorway. There was reproach and pleading in the Colonel's face as he watched me watch them. Emily was looking up at them too, uncomprehending.

Rand spoke: "Good evening, people. This is Special Agent Jeremy Foster, of the FBI. I think it's time we all had a talk, don't you?"

I gestured to the empty chairs and they came in and sat down. Foster crossed one long leg over another and said, "That was quite a stunt, Mr. Walker. Was it necessary?"

"Yes. There was no way I was going to give him the NPP, and if I didn't give it to him, my life, and these people's, weren't worth a damn. I have already been Ustinov's guest once, I have no intention of going there again. I told him to come alone and I warned him not to take the box. He made his choices. You want to prosecute me, go ahead, but I wouldn't advise it."

"Take it easy, Walker. I have no intention of prosecuting you, but Gregor would have been a useful prisoner."

I shrugged. "I gave Rand the heads up, I'm assuming you recorded everything that went down."

"We did." He turned and regarded the Colonel and Emily for a moment. "I am still trying to work out, Colonel, whether you and your daughter are actually guilty of a crime. Since the company you stole the NPP from was not a legitimate legal person according to the law, and was probably an enemy of the state, it's possible it didn't constitute theft at all. Trying to auction it to a foreign power..." He shrugged. "It's a gray area, as is the ownership of the NPP. Where is it, by the way?"

I showed him a face that was mildly surprised. Rand was watching me like a hawk. I pointed across the long room where the black windows still showed wavering orange fire-light. "In pieces, in Gregor's van."

Emily frowned at me. Rand scowled. Foster almost smiled, as did the Colonel.

I shrugged at Rand. "He paid me twenty-five million bucks for it, Rand. It would have been immoral not to give it to him. You wouldn't want me to do anything immoral, would you?"

He closed his eyes and shook his head. "You son of a bitch, Walker. Have you any idea how much that research was worth? Do you know what it could have done for this country's position in the world?"

I observed him a moment without expression. "What do you think, Rand? Do you think I had any idea about that? But, you know what? If it's all the same to you, for now, I'd like to keep the lid on Pandora's box, get my meat from the field and my vegetables from the ground. You can have your dystopian nightmare when I'm dead and buried."

He narrowed his eyes. "Let's hope that's many years hence, Lacklan."

I took a long second to gaze at the Smith & Wesson cannon sitting on the desk. Then I shifted my eyes to look into Rand's. "Are you threatening me, Rand? Do we have a problem?"

His face went pale, but I knew he wasn't going to back down. "You can shoot me dead, Lacklan, but you can't destroy the whole of the CIA. There are powerful interests involved here. Don't cross the Company, Walker, or we will come after you and we will eliminate you."

I smiled. I made the smile as patronizing as I could manage. "You want to tell me about those interests, Rand?" He opened his mouth to answer, but I didn't let him. I kept talking. "I have a few powerful interests of my own. Senator McFarlane is one that has the president's ear. There are others. You going to go after them, too?"

"You think we can't? You think it's never been done?"

I laughed. "I think you're full of shit, Rand. I think you're a superannuated has been who fondly remembers the days of the Bay of Pigs and the Cold War, when the CIA was a law onto itself. Times have changed, Rand. Next time you threaten me, I'll have your job."

He sat forward, a nasty curl on his lip. "You think times have changed, Lacklan? You're living in a dream. I can have you, McFarlane *and* the damned President any day I want. Don't fucking cross me!"

I shifted my smile to the man from the Bureau. "Special Agent Jeremy Foster, you were present during Rand Peabody's statement just then."

"I was, but I am inclined to think it was just bluster."

"Your opinion of his motives is not relevant, Agent Foster, your recollection of his words is."

Rand snarled, "What the hell is this?"

I picked up my phone, scrolled through to the appropriate app and pressed the stop button on the screen. I smiled at Rand.

"I just turned off the bugs, Rand. The ones I put under the chairs to record everything that went down this evening. I'm sure the president will be very interested to hear the recordings, I know Cyndi will—that's Senator McFarlane to you. The bugs, I am sure you're familiar with them, they use cell phone technology. The recording was made on my laptop, about a thousand miles away from here."

He had gone very pale.

"Anything happens to me, to Emily, to the Colonel, to Cyndi or the president for that matter, you and your interests will be about as dangerous as Gregor is right now."

"You can't do this."

"I can and I did. Get out, Rand."

He stood, stared at me for a long moment, and then walked out. I didn't watch him leave, I kept my eyes on Foster. "Have we got a problem, Special Agent?"

"I hope not. My instructions from the Bureau were to do whatever I could to avoid Miss Burgess being employed by Central Intelligence. I am authorized to offer her a job with the Bureau."

I looked at her. She had her head in her father's lap again. "I wish you luck with that." To the Colonel, I said, "She's going to need care and looking after. If anybody comes after her, the Company, Military Intelligence, you call me. Don't let this happen again."

He shook his head, then turned to Foster. "Give me your card. We'll be in touch, but I don't think she'll be going to work for anybody for a long time. She's not well."

He nodded and stood, handed me one of his cards and

held out his hand, too. I stood and shook it. "You ever need a witness, you know where to find me."

He left and I sat on the edge of the desk, looking down at Emily and her father. He spoke while stroking her hair. "She told me once her mother had been forced into prostitution. She told me all sorts of stories. I was never sure what to believe, how much was fantasy, how much was lies to get me to do something... All I knew was that I loved her. She was my little girl and she'd come home to me, and I had to protect her as best I could." He looked up. "But I also knew she was damaged. So something in those stories was true, wasn't it? You don't get like this without something bad happening to you, do you?"

I shook my head. "I guess not, Colonel."

She looked up at his face. "I don't feel well, Daddy, can we go home now?"

I gathered up my stuff, switched out the light and we made our way across the long room to the stairs and the elevators. Emily paused a moment to look at the elevator doors. She smiled. "The labs are still intact. We could start there, start to piece it all together again. I can remember some of it." We began to move down the stairs. "It's a shame Jerry isn't here. Between us, I'm pretty sure..."

Down in reception, I switched off the lights and we stepped into the parking lot. The Colonel and Emily climbed into their car. I watched the headlamps come on and after a moment reverse and turn, and then they were just a fading glow in front of two red lights that vanished around the side of the building.

I got into the Zombie, slammed the door and took a moment to light up a Camel. I took a deep drag, opened the windows and reversed out of the parking lot. As I came around the side of the building I saw the smoldering wreck of Gregor's SUV. I pulled up beside it, climbed out and peered in. It was hard to identify the bodies. One and a half pounds of C4 in a small, confined space does a lot of damage, but I was pretty sure that the big, bald mess in the back seat was him.

I went and sat against the trunk of the Zombie and pulled my cell from my pocket. I went to speed dial and pressed number two. There were two muffled reports and some of the windows on the ground floor of the building shattered. Emily, if she ever recovered, would not be using the labs at QPS.

I stood smoking a while, then dropped the butt on the road, crushed it and climbed back in the car. I didn't go home. I drove to Pier 32, found a spot in the parking lot and pushed through the door. It was full and noisy, with voices and laughter raised above the country music. I found a space at the bar and got a beer from JD.

"And send me a burger out to the terrace, will you?"

He nodded. "How's things?"

"Good." I nodded back. "I'm taking a boat out tomorrow to do a bit of fishing. You want to come along?"

He smiled at the glass he was filling with beer from the pump. "You mean you want to use my boat."

"Well, as you're offering. Ten A.M.?"

"You supply the beer and the sandwiches."

"You got yourself a deal."

I carried my beer out to the terrace, found a table and sat, looking up at half of the moon hanging like a broken Christmas bauble over a flat, silver ocean. It was done.

Gregor was finished, Emily and the Colonel were safe—which was frankly more than they deserved—and the world had at least another ten years to breathe before some other lunatic scientist decided to invent hell.

I took a long pull on my beer and wondered why I still felt unsatisfied, why the business still felt unresolved. Why?

TWENTY

IT WAS TWO IN THE MORNING BY THE TIME I GOT home. I left the car among the stilts and climbed the wooden steps, feeling the cool sea breeze on my skin and listening to the gentle sigh and crash of the surf. As I climbed, I wondered to myself if it wasn't time for me to think about going home. My period of rest and recuperation had not gone exactly to plan. Perhaps what I needed after all was to be at home, with Rosalia and Kenny, and learn to find peace there.

I reached the deck, unlocked and opened the door, and thought about having a nightcap on the terrace. I would sleep late in the morning and then phone Kenny to tell him I was coming home. He and Rosalia would be pleased. She would bake a steak and kidney pie, and a plum pie for after. I smiled.

I flipped the light switch and my four lamps came on. By their amber glow, I could see that my bedroom door was open. I knew I had left it closed. I pulled my Sig from my waistband, cleared my throat and stepped over to the drinks tray, where I noisily poured myself a whiskey. I then took two long, silent steps toward the bedroom.

In the dim light, through the half-open door, I saw movement on my bed. Then, very slowly, I saw Emily sit up. She remained motionless, looking at the floor. I moved closer and gently opened the door a little further. She looked up at me.

"Emily, what are you doing here? You should be at home, with your father."

"You took a long time to come home. I had to lie down. Everything is a bit of a mess."

"You can't be here, Emily. You have to go home."

She smiled, then gave a small laugh. "You think I've gone crazy. I haven't. I'm just tired, sleepy, and maybe a little drunk. Can we just hang out for a bit and talk, and you help me understand what the *hell* just happened to my life?"

I sighed. "OK. And then you go home."

"Boring." She held out her hand. "Put your gun away Mr. SAS, and help me to my feet, will ya?"

I helped her up and she walked unsteadily into the living room. I pulled open the drawer in my bedside table and dropped in my weapon. Then I closed the door and followed her to the living room. She stood a moment, then dropped onto the sofa.

"Offer me a drink, Mr. Tough Guy."

"Don't you think you've had enough?"

She mimicked me, making me sound like an old man. "Don't you think you've had enough, young lady?"

I sighed and rubbed my face. I was suddenly very tired and longing to be in my bed. Alone.

She said, "No. I don't. Offer me a drink and I'll leave you in peace and go home, Mr. Mean Man."

"What would you like to drink, Emily?"

"Gin and tonic. You have one, too, and sit here beside me and talk to me."

I made her a weak gin and tonic and poured myself a tonic. I handed her her drink and sat at the other end of the sofa.

She pouted. "You're not being very nice to me."

"You'll thank me later."

"I suppose, Mr. Sensible."

"Does your father know you're here?"

"Yup. He tried to stop me, but I said I needed to talk to you." She smiled at me. "Only known you a few days but we've been through a lot together, huh? Kidnap, gunfights, escaping from Mexico in a seaplane..." The smile faded. "My life's dream, my life's work, up in smoke. You're kind of like a tornado, aren't you?"

"I just do what needs to be done. I am not a good person to get involved with."

"Don't you ever get lonely?"

I shrugged.

She went on, "Tell me the truth. Did you really destroy it? Was it really in the box, with the C4?" She shook her head, then wagged a finger. "I don't think it would have fit. What did you really do with it?"

"I destroyed it. That's all you need to know."

She put her drink beside the sofa on the floor and slid up to me. She took the scruff of my neck in her fist, in mock threat, and leaned really close, so her lips were an inch from mine.

"Don't patronize me, mister. I am not crazy and I am not a helpless female. I am probably the smartest woman you've ever met, and I have a right to know what happened to my life's work."

I was bruised, inside and out, I was tired and lonely, and suddenly the thought of sharing my bed with Emily that night didn't seem like such a crazy idea. She rested her forehead against mine and ran her hand over my chest. There were tears in her eyes as she spoke.

"Come on, Lacklan, my life just got handed to me in a fucking urn. Give me some latitude."

She straddled my legs and sat on my lap. My body wanted her badly and she was left in no doubt about that. She smiled and leaned close to me, stroking my face with her fingers. "Do you know what I did? Have you any idea what I achieved? I made the key that opened the door to Olympus. Little old me. Little Emily. I made it possible for humans to become gods. And today, all of that, all that work, everything..." Her smile faded again and the tears ran freely down her cheeks. "It was all destroyed, with no hope of ever getting it back. All I'm asking, all I want to know is, where is she buried? What have you done with her?"

I shook my head. "Emily, you have to stop. We can't do this. You can't play me and I am not going to exploit your vulnerability. It's not going to happen."

She closed her eyes, groaned and rolled away from me to sprawl on her back on the sofa. She lay motionless a moment with her hands over her eyes and then shouted, "*God!*"

I stood. "Come on, you're going home."

She removed her hands and glared at me. "Why are you so... *stupid!*"

"Get up."

"A man like you, with your skills, your strength, your intelligence—*Jesus!* You could do whatever you like with me, and in the morning go on to become, not a millionaire, but a *billionaire!* And what do you do?" She mocked me again. "I will not exploit your vulnerability...!" She spread her arms and her legs wide. "*Exploit it, you asshole! Take me! And in the morning, let's sell the damned NPP and be rich!*"

"Get up."

She sat up. Her face was expressionless, but her eyes were rich with contempt. Her voice was loud and flat.

"He'll never tell me. It's useless."

I frowned at her. Behind me, the door to the guest room opened and Rand and the Colonel came out. They were both holding guns. Rand grinned.

"Not the first mistake you made tonight, old buddy. You could'a got laid and become a very rich man. Instead, you're gonna get tortured and you'll be lucky to come out of this one alive."

I frowned at the Colonel. "Harry?"

He scowled. "Don't look at me, you dumb schmuck! You could'a had everything. But you're just like your father said, a self-righteous asshole. Now we have to do this the hard way."

I stared at Rand. "You're all in this together?"

"Last minute allies. It could have been you. But you blew it."

Emily stood and came close to me. "How can a man like you be so *naïve?*"

The Colonel shook his head. "You got rid of Gregor for us, *in the end*, and I really thought for a moment there tonight, you might just give us the NPP. But no, you're flawed, Lacklan. Your father always said so. You're a flawed man. At heart, you're weak."

Emily grabbed me and pushed me onto the sofa, then stood over me with narrowed eyes. "Before we get started, just explain something to me, will you? Why did you go through the whole moral high ground charade of saying you wouldn't kill Gregor, and then you went and blew the son of a bitch to pieces? I don't get it!"

I sat a moment, cursing myself for my own stupidity. Then I shook my head and told myself there would be time for that later.

"I said I would not kill him *for you*. I am not a hit man. I don't kill people for money. I killed Gregor because it became clear he would not desist. He was a clear and present threat."

Rand stood opposite me with his ass on the dresser.

"I'm going to blow your kneecap off, and then I am going to cut through every joint in your body with a blunt knife. You know, I know, we all know, that you will tell me where the NPP is, and where the goddamn computer is with the recordings from tonight's Lacklan Walker Show. Save yourself the pain. Tell me now and then take us to the recording."

I knew that if I said no, if I gave him a wiseass answer or hesitated too long, he would blow my kneecap off and from there on, it would all be downhill. So I nodded and said, "OK, you win. Don't blow my kneecaps off. Let's do this." I glanced at Emily. "Is it too late to have sex and become an equal partner?"

She winked. "That ship sailed, honey. You blew it."

Rand wasn't smiling. Neither was the Colonel. He said, "Quit stalling. Where is it?" He cocked his revolver. "I'm counting to five."

"It's in the trunk of my car."

Rand snarled. "You're lying. I checked it while you were in Mexico, remember?"

I shook my head. "Uh-uh. I kept it in my jacket until Emily had Jerry turn my place over. After that, I kept it in my bedside cabinet, and after you checked my car, I put it in the trunk. It's common sense, Rand. Always keep it in the place that has just been searched."

They looked uncertain.

I shrugged. "It's simple. Let's go look."

Rand laughed an ugly, sardonic laugh. "Sure. You have a whole goddamn arsenal in there. I've seen it."

I made a 'give me patience' face and said, "Yeah, genius, that's why I put it there, for just such a situation as this."

They exchanged glances. The Colonel said, "OK, give me the key. I'll go get it."

I smiled, reached in my pocket, pulled out the keys and tossed them to him. "It's booby trapped." There was no way they could know, or find out, if I was lying. I watched them exchange more glances with each other and said, "When the guys made it for me, I had them fit traps in the trunk. There's a button you have to press. If it's not my thumb, bad things happen." I shrugged. "If you don't believe me, go ahead. But just remember what happened to Gregor. I warned him and he wouldn't listen either."

The Colonel handed me back the keys. "On your feet. We all go." I stood. He said, "Put your hands up."

I raised my hands and we walked in an absurd procession into the darkness on the terrace. I was in front, the Colonel and Rand were right behind me and Emily was behind them. As we started down the steps, Rand's voice sounded above and behind me, in odd contrast to the gentle sound of the surf.

"I don't need to remind you, Lacklan, that I am a superb shot. You try and run, I'll take both your legs."

"I won't run, Rand. You can be sure of that."

We came to the bottom of the steps and I led them through the dense shadows under the house to where the Zombie was parked. My hands were still up. I shook the right one with the keys in it and looked at them in turn.

"I'm going to open the trunk. Don't shoot me, OK?"

I leaned forward and smiled as they all crowded in. I inserted the key, turned, withdrew the key and very elaborately placed my thumb on the release button. I pressed and there was a clunk. I said:

"OK, now I am going to open the trunk and step back. The NPP is in the kit bag."

I did exactly as I said. I opened the trunk and stood back. They did exactly what I expected them to do. They all crowded forward and peered in. I had Emily on the far right, Rand in the middle and the Colonel on my far left.

I didn't waste time. I lunged forward on a wide stance and smashed my knuckles into Rand's kidneys, putting every ounce of my two hundred and twenty pounds into the punch. A punch to the kidneys is one of the most painful blows a person can receive. He gasped and his knees buckled, but by then, I had jumped up, grabbed the top of the trunk and smashed it down on the Colonel's head. He staggered back a couple of steps, holding his head in his hands, still clasping his revolver.

I seized his wrist in my left hand and the barrel of the weapon in my right, and levered back savagely. I heard his finger snap and he screamed. I wrenched the gun away and in the same movement drove my right foot into his crotch. He went down on the sand in the fetal position. I didn't waste any more time on him but turned on Rand. I was acutely aware that he was slumped half inside a trunk full of weapons. He turned his head toward me. His eyes were red with rage. He moved his right hand and I saw he was clutching the Smith & Wesson 500.

In that instant, Emily screamed. It was a high-pitched, hysterical shriek and she threw herself at me with teeth bared and her fingers hooked like talons. She clawed at my face, reaching for my eyes. I staggered back in the sand, stumbled over the Colonel's prone form and fell on my back with Emily still clawing at my face, and her body weighing heavy on my right arm, pinning down the revolver I'd taken from Harry. I fought to drag her off me, but her hysterical thrashing made her impossible to control. I grabbed her hair with my left hand and dragged her back, yanking my right arm from under her at the same time.

As I did that I saw Rand getting to his feet, leveling the huge cannon of the 500 at me. My first shot went through his wrist. He fired, but the shot went wide into the night. My second shot went through his eye. He swayed and fell back with a dull thud into the sand.

It was only then that I became aware that Emily was sinking her teeth into my wrist. The pain was excruciating and I raised the revolver to club the back of her head. It dawned on me half a second too late that she had pulled my fighting knife from my boot, and now, as she clenched her teeth, biting deep into the bone and searching for my artery, she rammed the knife home into my thigh. I screamed.

She climbed off me, squatting in the sand, keeping hold of the Fairbairn & Sykes with both hands. My body was going into spasm with the pain. I stared at her. She had blood smeared over her mouth and chin. Her eyes were bright and manic. She snarled, "I am going to twist!"

All I could say was, "No, no, *no...!*"

"*I am going to fucking twist!*"

"Emily, no! If you twist, I'll bleed out, you'll never find it!"

She was still screaming. "*I'll never find it anyway! Will I? You won't tell me! You won't fucking tell me!*"

"All right! I'll tell you! Just don't twist! For God's sake, Emily!"

"Where is it?"

I looked at the knife. She was still holding the handle with both hands. It was about three inches in, buried in the muscles at the back of the thigh. She had missed the artery by about an inch. I held her eye a moment and said, "Here." I raised the revolver and put a round right between her eyes. The back of her head erupted and she gently keeled over on her side.

I pulled off my belt, slipped it around my thigh and pulled it tight till it hurt. Then I yanked out the knife and for a moment thought I might pass out. I dragged myself to the trunk of the Zombie and hauled myself onto my right foot, then rested against the open trunk.

Panting and dizzy with pain, I watched the Colonel uncurl himself from the fetal position and slowly get to his hands and knees. He was staring at his revolver, which I had dropped on the sand while applying the tourniquet to my thigh.

"Don't do it, Colonel. There's been enough killing. Let it go."

"Fuck you. What have I got to live for? You've taken everything from me."

He staggered forward a step. His broken right hand was just an inch from the butt.

"I don't want to kill you, Colonel."

"Fuck you and what you want. You're just like your father said: a wimp, a pussy, a girl in boy's clothing. A shame and a disappointment to everybody." He was kneeling, holding the gun in both hands now, shaking, trying to take aim. "No damn good. That's what he always said about you. No damn good."

He struggled to his feet. He was leering now. "You and Robert were both shit, from that English whore of a wife he had. The one he loved, the one he doted on, the one he was proud of, was Ben. Ben was to be his heir." He laughed suddenly. "And you think a piece of shit like you could kill Ben? You really think you could bring down Ben, your father's son and heir?"

I nodded. "Yeah."

I pulled the Maxim 9 from the trunk and shot him the way I had shot his daughter, through the middle of the forehead. Then, as his body sank to the sand, I pulled my cell from my pocket and called Special Agent Jeremy Foster. I told him I needed him, a couple of meat wagons and an ambulance, sooner rather than later.

Then I slid down into the sand and passed out among the dead.

EPILOGUE

THE SUN FLASHED AND SPARKLED ON THE turquoise water. Small waves slapped softly at the wooden hull of JD's old fishing boat and, while a cool breeze soothed my still tender, swollen face, seagulls wheeled overhead, laughing raucously at some private, evil joke.

He swung his rod, the reel whirred and after a couple of seconds there was a soft 'plop!'

The 'plop!' was followed by a soft hiss as I cracked an ice cold bottle of beer. I wasn't fishing, I was propped up against my jacket in the back of the boat, trying to ignore the ache in my left leg. JD's question had been a simple one, but answering it was not so simple.

I thought about it for a while and eventually said: "My father was not a good man. He was a very complicated man. He was a law onto himself."

JD smiled and stroked his beard. "Hmmm... reminds of somebody, damned if I can think who, though."

"His marriage with my mother broke down pretty early

on and I think he decided he didn't like her or the kids he'd had with her."

"I remember your brother Robert. I don't think anybody liked him very much. What happened to him?"

I almost told him, but shrugged instead and said, "He died 'round about the same time my father did. Thing is, my dad got involved with an organization who were basically a gang of thugs with big IQs and a lot of money. The Colonel wanted to join the gang, and my dad, whatever else was wrong with him, was a loyal friend, and tried to get him in. But neither the Colonel's IQ nor his bank balance were up to the mark, so he became what they called a 'friend' of the gang, and my dad used to give him a helping hand. After my dad died, the gang looked after him."

"Kind of like the Masons."

"Except instead of charity, they murder people."

"OK, like the Illuminati."

"A bit like that."

"So, I am guessing at this next bit, but it seems to make sense. When the Colonel discovered he had a daughter, he pulled strings with the gang and got her a job with QPS, because QPS belonged to the gang and was doing research for the gang. She was smart enough for the job—in fact, she was a genuine genius—and her department's research came up with a device that, if it had been fully developed, had the potential to give whoever owned it absolute temporal power. Kind of like the ring in the Lord of the Rings."

"Kind of like that." I took a swig and set about peeling a packet of Camel. I offered him one and he shook his head, fingering his long, straggly hair from his face. I lit up and inhaled deeply, enjoying the gentle sun and the peace. I went on, "I have no idea if it would actually have worked or if it was just one of her crazy fantasies. I don't know how much testing they had done or how far along they were. I don't know, but she and Jerry were convinced it would work, and they convinced the Colonel."

"So what went wrong? How come QPS shut down?"

I laughed. Then I laughed a bit more. "That was my fault. I put a virus into the gang's central computer network. I had no idea how far it would spread. But the QPS computer network was hooked up to the gang's, the virus got in and wiped the whole network clean. Everything, their accounts, their passwords, their research—you name it, everything. The whole damn thing went down. So they had to close the research facility."

"So Emily and the Colonel..."

"And Jerry, they come up with a plan. They were going to try to contact my father's old friends and get some funding for Emily and Jerry to continue their research. But what they didn't know, what they couldn't possibly have known, was that all my dad's friends were gone..."

"How come? What happened to the gang?"

"Best you don't know."

He shook his head. "You are some kind of a son of a bitch."

"I guess. Anyway, so Jerry, in frustration, contacts Gregor, and while he's at it, he contacts the CIA as well. The kid is out of his mind. He has no conception of how dangerous these people are. Pretty soon, Gregor has taken over, and he is about to take possession of the device. He's told his pals back in the Kremlin what Emily has got, and they are as excited as hell about it."

JD snorted. "Meantime, you roll back into town, and the Colonel hears from me that you're here and he figures you can help him and Emily out."

"By getting rid of Gregor, that's right. Gregor had arranged the drop, and I think Emily was right. He probably intended to eliminate her and hand the device over to their own people to develop. The rest is history."

We were quiet for a bit. Then JD asked, "So what are you going to do with the twenty-five million?"

"I thought I'd set up a fund to help vets, their widows and orphans."

He nodded. "Makes sense." He was quiet again for a bit, then gave a small laugh. "Must have been a shock, though, when the old man turned up with that creep from the CIA."

"Yeah, I should have seen that coming. She was a damn good actress. I wonder if even she knew who the real Emily was."

He shrugged and shook his head. "Don't ask me about women, Lacklan. You think you know one, and five seconds later, she's a different person."

I nodded. "I'd known Rand for a few years. We'd crossed paths a few times. I knew he was a dangerous son of a bitch. The Colonel surprised me, though. He knew a lot more about my father than I had expected. Seems they'd been pretty close, and I never knew."

"He knew about your other brother, Ben."

I nodded. "Said he didn't believe he was dead."

"What do you think?"

I was quiet for a long while. I didn't know what I thought. "I'm beginning to realize, JD, that everything I thought had started when my father died, when he sent Ben to get me from Wyoming[1], was actually just ending. The whole thing started many, many years ago, when I was a kid." I stared out at the distant, hazy blue horizon. "When Marni was a kid, and Ben was a kid, too. And my parents were not much older than I am now. That's when it all started."

JD snorted. "Dude, stories never start and they never end, they just keep rollin' along." Suddenly, he reached down between his knees and felt around in his canvas shoulder bag. After a moment, he pulled out a shiny, featureless black cuboid, about twelve inches long, three inches deep and six inches across. The sun gleamed off the high-polished surface. We both stared at it. I smiled.

He said: "So you had me put this in my fridge, and you posted the case to yourself at a PO box you had your butler open in Sweeny."

"What magicians call misdirection. You sure you don't want to try and sell it to the government? According to Emily and the Colonel, it's worth billions."

He gave his slow, rasping laugh. "You know what I'd do if I were the richest man in the world?"

I jerked my chin in a 'what?' gesture and swigged my beer.

He gazed out at the vast, blue sea. "I'd open a bar, on the Gulf of Mexico coast, I'd play country music and serve cold beer and whiskey, and on my days off, I'd take a boat out on the water and do some fishing."

I smiled and grunted. "He is a lucky man indeed who has what he wants, and an even luckier one who knows he

---

1. See *Dawn of the Hunter*

wants it." I held out my hand. "You think we're far enough out?"

We both looked back at Freeport, small and slightly misty in the distance.

"I reckon."

He tossed it to me and I stood with care, trying to ignore the pain in my left leg. The weight was good. I drew back my arm and hurled the NPP in a high arc, out into the ocean. It plopped into the sea and sank quickly below the waves.

I sat carefully down again and leaned back against my jacket. JD cracked another bottle of beer, swigged and sighed. "So you're telling me that thing could just kind of produce anything?"

"That's what they claimed."

"Can you imagine," he said, "If a shark ate that thing, and suddenly started farting tractors, and cars..."

I burst out laughing.

He started to laugh too, wiping the corner of his eye, and went on, "...and like, long strings of yellow rubber ducks..."

"And inflatable sex dolls..."

"This fuckin' shark, sailing through the ocean...!"

"And all these things every time it farts...!"

And we sat and laughed, and drank beer, and wiped the tears of mirth from our eyes.

Don't miss THE OMICRON KILL The riveting sequel in the Omega Thriller series.

Scan the QR code below to purchase THE OMICRON KILL.

Or go to: righthouse.com/the-omicron-kill

NOTE: flip to the very end to read an exclusive sneak peek...

DON'T MISS ANYTHING!

If you want to stay up to date on all new releases in this series, with this author, or with any of our new deals, you can do so by joining our newsletters below.

In addition, you will immediately gain access to our entire *Right House VIP Library,* which includes many riveting Mystery and Thriller novels for your enjoyment!

righthouse.com/email

(Easy to unsubscribe. No spam. Ever.)

ALSO BY BLAKE BANNER

Up to date books can be found at:
www.righthouse.com/blake-banner

ROGUE THRILLERS
Gates of Hell (Book 1)
Hell's Fury (Book 2)
Ice Burn (Book 3)
Judgement by Fire (Book 4)

ALEX MASON THRILLERS
Odin (Book 1)
Ice Cold Spy (Book 2)
Mason's Law (Book 3)
Assets and Liabilities (Book 4)
Russian Roulette (Book 5)
Executive Order (Book 6)
Dead Man Talking (Book 7)
All The King's Men (Book 8)
Flashpoint (Book 9)
Brotherhood of the Goat (Book 10)
Dead Hot (Book 11)
Blood on Megiddo (Book 12)
Son of Hell (Book 13)
Merchant of Death (Book 14)
Extinction C-14 (Book 15)

HARRY BAUER THRILLER SERIES

Dead of Night (Book 1)
Dying Breath (Book 2)
The Einstaat Brief (Book 3)
Quantum Kill (Book 4)
Immortal Hate (Book 5)
The Silent Blade (Book 6)
LA: Wild Justice (Book 7)
Breath of Hell (Book 8)
Invisible Evil (Book 9)
The Shadow of Ukupacha (Book 10)
Sweet Razor Cut (Book 11)
Blood of the Innocent (Book 12)
Blood on Balthazar (Book 13)
Simple Kill (Book 14)
Riding The Devil (Book 15)
The Unavenged (Book 16)
The Devil's Vengeance (Book 17)
Bloody Retribution (Book 18)
Rogue Kill (Book 19)
Blood for Blood (Book 20)
The Cell (Book 21)
Time to Die (Book 22)
The Reaper of Zion (Book 23)

DEAD COLD MYSTERY SERIES
An Ace and a Pair (Book 1)
Two Bare Arms (Book 2)
Garden of the Damned (Book 3)
Let Us Prey (Book 4)
The Sins of the Father (Book 5)
Strange and Sinister Path (Book 6)

The Heart to Kill (Book 7)
Unnatural Murder (Book 8)
Fire from Heaven (Book 9)
To Kill Upon A Kiss (Book 10)
Murder Most Scottish (Book 11)
The Butcher of Whitechapel (Book 12)
Little Dead Riding Hood (Book 13)
Trick or Treat (Book 14)
Blood Into Wine (Book 15)
Jack In The Box (Book 16)
The Fall Moon (Book 17)
Blood In Babylon (Book 18)
Death In Dexter (Book 19)
Mustang Sally (Book 20)
A Christmas Killing (Book 21)
Mommy's Little Killer (Book 22)
Bleed Out (Book 23)
Dead and Buried (Book 24)
In Hot Blood (Book 25)
Fallen Angels (Book 26)
Knife Edge (Book 27)
Along Came A Spider (Book 28)
Cold Blood (Book 29)
Curtain Call (Book 30)

THE OMEGA SERIES
Dawn of the Hunter (Book 1)
Double Edged Blade (Book 2)
The Storm (Book 3)
The Hand of War (Book 4)
A Harvest of Blood (Book 5)

ABOUT US

Right House is an independent publisher created by authors for readers. We specialize in Action, Thriller, Mystery, and Crime novels.

If you enjoyed this novel, then there is a good chance you will like what else we have to offer! Please stay up to date by using any of the links below.

Join our mailing lists to stay up to date -->
righthouse.com/email
Visit our website --> righthouse.com
Contact us --> contact@righthouse.com

 facebook.com/righthousebooks
 x.com/righthousebooks
 instagram.com/righthousebooks

EXCLUSIVE SNEAK PEEK OF...

THE OMICRON KILL

CHAPTER 1

Lambda, Mu, Nu, Xi...Omicron.

I wrote the names down on a paper napkin, and then the symbols: λ, Ϻ, N, Ξ...O. O-mega and O-micron. Big O and small o. Did it mean anything?

Outside, the desert was an endless, shapeless glare of heat, sand and scorching sun. Inside, the bar was still, cool, dark and quiet. My beer glass, standing on the dark, high-polished wood, was empty, the inside stained with dry froth. Further down the bar, the bartender was leaning by the pumps, staring at his phone, occasionally poking the screen.

"Get me another beer, will you?"

He lifted one elbow, sniggered at his cell, read a little more, then sighed. He set down his phone and shuffled over to the pumps. As he set down the beer beside me, he glanced at the napkin. "What's that y'writin' there? Remind me of the symbols..." He paused, waiting for his brain to catch up with his mouth. "What was that place? ...Roswell, just a little ways from here, where they found the UFO. I juss read a book 'bout it. Had symbols juss like that."

I studied him a moment. His beard reached his paunch in the two prongs of a long fork. He was bald on top but had a long, scraggly ponytail down his back. I shook my head. "Letters from the Greek alphabet. Lambda, Mu, Nu, Xi and Omicron," I said.

"Huh... This book..." He leaned his elbows on the bar and stared across the empty saloon at the desert outside. "Says all the most powerful politicians and royal families and all that shit, they's all smart dinosaurs that learned to shape shift and look like humans. And that's who rules this world. That's why they's so cruel. Reptiles is all cold-blooded."

I gave a small laugh. "It's a nice theory, but in my experience the most depraved, predatory, cruel and cold-blooded species on this planet is us. Look around you. You're not seeing lizards living in their millions in the cities, it's all humans."

He gave me a curious look and nodded. The door opened onto the blistering afternoon and four men walked in making noises about beer and heat. They were big, hard guys, used to working cattle in an unforgiving desert for a living, who rode longhorns and broncos for sport. They were men I had a basic respect for, but not a lot in common with. I didn't pay much attention to them. Three went over to a booth and the fourth slapped his hand on the bar and said, "Gimme four of your coldest beers there, Gastank!"

As he moved away, I said, "And give me a whiskey chaser when you get a chance, will you?" and turned my attention back to the paper napkin.

I could feel the newcomer staring at me. I ignored him,

but after a moment he spoke. "You mind waitin' till he's finished serving me before you give him your order, pal?"

I turned to look at him a little more closely. I figured six one in his boots. His T-shirt revealed a strong torso and powerful arms. His neck was thick and his freckled face had two pale blue eyes, though there didn't seem to be an awful lot going on behind them. I guessed he just wanted to be respected. I nodded. "Sure."

I turned back to my Greek letters, in particular Omega and Omicron, but his voice broke in on my thoughts.

"See, I think it's disrespectful."

I turned to look at him again.

"If I'm talkin' to Gastank here, makin' my order, and you butt in makin' an order of your own. See? That is a lack of respect toward me."

Gastank sighed. "Let it go, Jesse. Man didn't mean nothin' by it. We was just talkin', he didn't butt in."

"You should shut your mouth there, Gastank. Man can talk for hisself. You can talk for yourself, can't you, mister?"

I calibrated him a little more carefully. He'd be slow and telegraphic. He'd waste a lot of energy. I was pretty sure he'd charge like a bull and go for a take down. There was a warmth in my belly I recognized as adrenaline, and I was surprised to realize I was hoping he'd attack me.

I gave my head a small, sideways twitch and spoke quietly. "This isn't a problem for me either way. I meant no disrespect by ordering a whiskey chaser. But if you want to take it that way, that's your problem, not mine."

He looked over his shoulder at his buddies, who were watching him and looking bored. "Does that sound respectful to you? That don't sound like a sincere apology to me."

I sighed and turned back to my napkin.

His petulant voice broke in again. "Don't you look away from me when I'm talking to you, you goddamn pussy."

I knew then there was no way out. I was going to have to neutralize him. I felt a stab of excitement in my gut that I didn't like, but accepted anyway. I climbed off the stool and turned to face him. "Why don't you put your estrogen back in your ovaries, Jesse, pick up your beer and go and sit quietly with your pals."

He obviously knew what estrogen and ovaries were, and wasn't down with gender fluidity, because his freckled cheeks flushed and he reached for the scruff of my neck with his left hand, while he drew his right back for a massive cross. If it had connected, it would have taken my head off. But for that I'd have had to wait around while he put the punch together and delivered it.

Instead, I snatched hold of the baby finger of his left hand and bent it back against the joint. He could feel it was about to snap and went up on his toes. His eyes and mouth opened wide and he went, "Ah... ah... ah..." a lot.

I took hold of his wrist in my left and bent the finger harder, pressing gently down. He started to bend at the knees. I looked over at the booth, where his pals were standing up. I shook my head and they paused. Jesse was kneeling now, staring at his finger, still saying, "Ah... ah..."

I said, "Right now, from here, there are eight simple ways I could kill you with a single move. There are three simple ways I could dislocate your arm and too many ways to break it for me to go through them all. The number of ways I could put you in hospital with broken bones and fractures runs into hundreds. And you know what's worrying me, Jesse? I actually want to do it. Now, you came looking for trouble with me, and you found it, and it was more trouble than you reckoned on. There is no shame in that. So, why don't you go on over to your friends and drink your beer, and leave me in peace to enjoy mine? You've had your warning, Jesse. Next time I'll break your shoulder."

I let him go and he staggered to his feet. His face was flushed red and for a moment I thought he was going to come at me, but his friends surrounded him and led him back to the booth, taking their beers with them. I returned to my stool, looked at Gastank and said, "How about that whiskey chaser, Gastank?"

As he poured it, he was watching me from under his eyebrows. "That was a pretty neat move. What was that? Kung Fu or somethin'?"

I shook my head, still trying to focus on the napkin. "Path of least resistance."

He nodded and corked the bottle, with his mouth slightly open. "Like Zen..."

I smiled. "Something like that, yeah."

He nodded a lot, like he understood, said, "Neat," and walked back to his cell phone. But what he'd said had started me thinking.

Zen: jhana in the original Pali language. It was a state. It was a state which you achieved through meditation, in which you experienced a kind of timeless, shapeless sense of simply being; being now. And this state was expressed in ancient Greece with the sound 'Ou', meaning entity, being, existence. O-micron, meant small being, contraction, or small existence. Whereas O-mega, meant big being, expansion, or major existence.

I sipped my whiskey, felt it burn and realized I hadn't eaten since five that morning. I made a mental note to eat something, and wondered why it mattered that Omega and Omicron were like opposites of each other. Either way, Omega, the organization, was broken, crippled, all but finished.[1]

All but.

I had spent the last six months drifting across the southern States, with no fixed purpose, not ready to go back to Weston, not ready to go home, and somehow not ready to accept that Omega was finished. Though for over six months they had give no signs of life.

Omicron. They had contracted in on themselves.

If Omega was big and expansive like the sun, then what was Omicron? A seed? More to the point, I told myself, who? Who was Omicron? In the Omega cabal of men and women with too much money and too much power, who liked to form secret societies, manipulate world power, and give themselves quasi-mystical names drawn from the ancient Greek alphabet, who was Omicron?

Whoever he or she was, they were based in South America. Assuming, I told myself, as I sipped my whiskey again, and this time enjoyed the burn, assuming that Omega III, which controlled Latin America, had not collapsed along with Omegas I and II.

I knew I had his name somewhere. I had a full list of the names of the members of Omega. I had one copy at my

---

1. See *Kill: One* and *Kill: Two*

house in Weston, and I had given another copy to Jim Redbeard in Los Angeles, less than six hundred miles to the west. I drained my glass of whiskey and waved it at Gastank to refill it.

Jim Redbeard, the philosopher-cum-Viking master of chaos who had helped me bring down Omega II in Europe. He would know whether Omicron was significant. He would probably also advise me to let it go, go home and take up fishing.

Gastank shuffled up and refilled my glass. I said, "You can leave the bottle."

He hesitated a moment. "I don't want no trouble in my bar, mister."

I eyed him a moment, feeling unreasonably irritable. "You won't get any, if you leave the bottle. You got any food here?"

"In about an hour," he said with a twist of resentment in his voice. "Carmen comes in 'round six. She'll cook you whatever you want."

"I'll have a beef burger and fries when she gets in."

He went away and I sat staring at the glare outside the window. I had the idea of cycles nagging at my mind, cycles of time. But I couldn't pin down why. I had picked up somewhere that 'O' or zero somehow symbolized eternity, infinity or great cycles of time. But I had never had time for philosophy, much less mystical BS. I could just about stomach the Zen I had learned while studying martial arts, and that was mainly because they advised you, "Don't think, do." That was my kind of philosophy.

But you need to know your enemy and understand how he thinks, and there was no doubt in my mind that Omega, whatever was left of it, was founded on mystical principles; mystical principles that were rooted in ancient Greek philosophy. Somebody, somebody connected with Omega, had spouted something at me about cycles of time being associated with the letters of the Greek alphabet. Was it Ben? Ben had had a taste for that kind of thing—they all had—but it had not been him. It had been after I'd killed Ben[2]. So it must have been Timmerman.

Then it came to me. We'd been on the train, traveling from Paris to Madrid, and he had told us, me and Njal, that Omega was not an organization. He'd said it was a protocol. Each protocol, he'd said, covered a period of social and technological development, and we were at the end of protocol twenty-three, Psi.

I pulled a pack of Camels from my pocket, shook one free and poked it in my mouth. Gastank looked at me and shook his head. "Hey, man, I can't let you do that..."

I gave him the dead eye. He sighed and walked away. I didn't light up.

Njal had asked him what protocol Psi was. What had he answered? I turned my ancient, battered brass Zippo around in my fingers, reaching back with my mind. He'd said it was the time when the technology for mass production and mass distribution expand and stabilized free markets. I had no damn idea what the hell that meant. I poured myself another shot and sipped it, allowing my mind to go back to the train again. Njal had asked him what came after Psi. Timmerman had told him that after Psi came Omega. Omega was the end. When technology surpassed human understanding.

---

2. See *Kill: One*

The end. So if Omega was the end, what the hell was Omicron?

Jim Redbeard would know. If he didn't know, he could work it out.

It was nearly six, the light was fading outside the window and I was surprised to see the level of whiskey in the bottle had dropped. I could hear noises coming from the kitchen and realized I felt sick with hunger, I had drunk too much and my head was not clear. Worse than that, I had a pellet of hot anger building in my belly, and I didn't know why.

A loud hiss from the kitchen, followed by the smell of singed meat and onions, told me Carmen was cooking my burger. Gastank was further down the bar serving drinks. The place was filling up. Jesse and his pals were still in the booth.

I said: "Hey, Gastank, get me another beer, will you?"

He pulled it and put it in front of me. "This one's on the house. Now, don't you think you've had enough? How 'bout you eat your burger, drink your beer and go home to sleep it off for a bit? I'll look after your whiskey for you."

I frowned at him. "What's your problem? I'm not disturbing anyone, I'm not causing a ruckus, I'm just sitting here having a drink."

He sighed. "You ain't causin' a problem, but Jesse's pals are comin' in soon, and you really riled Jesse, the way you humiliated him in front of his friends. You'd be smart to leave sooner than later."

"I'll have my burger, and my beer, in peace. Then I'll pay you what I owe you and go on my way."

He sighed again, a little more deeply.

I smiled a smile that couldn't have been nice to look at. "Don't worry, I'll pay for any damage, too."

He went away. The door opened behind me and people came in. Gastank came back after a while with my burger. He gave me a pleading look which I ignored and he left. The first bite of the burger made me feel better. But as I took a pull of the cold beer and a second bite, I was suddenly aware, through some sixth sense, of Jesse getting to his feet and crossing the room toward me. A couple of seconds passed and the room started to go quiet. I glanced at Gastank and smiled at the expression on his face. I stuffed the last piece of burger in my mouth, took my time chewing it and then drained my beer.

After that, I turned on my stool to see Jesse standing, staring at me.

"You and me got unsettled business," he said. "We gonna settle it right now."

All my training and all my instincts told me to walk away, but right then that pellet of anger and frustration in my gut was stronger than my instinct and my training; and it told me that people like Jesse get away with being assholes too often.

I shook my head. "I have no business with you, Jesse. If I bruised your..." I smiled and labored the words, "...little finger, like I told you before, that is your problem, not mine."

His cheeks colored. "You better get off that stool, mister, an' face me like a man, or I'm gonna haul your ass off it and bullwhip you till you weep like a girl."

"You and your friends?"

"I figure I got this."

I looked over and saw that his pals had all stood up. There were six of them and they were all grinning. I nodded. "OK," I said. "Come and haul my ass off my stool and bull-whip me. I think your friends would be amused by that."

His frown said he didn't understand what was happening, but he was going to pile right in and whoop my ass anyway. He came at me as I knew he would, with both hands reaching for my collar. I let him do that and when he had a firm grip, I slammed my left forearm down hard on his elbows, forcing him forward, and smashed the heel of my open hand into his jaw. He let go of my collar and staggered back a couple of steps. He was strong and he could take it. That was fine by me. I was in no hurry. I had some anger and frustration to work off. I climbed off the stool and walked to the center of the floor. Somebody locked the door. Everybody else gathered around. It didn't feel like a lynch mob. It felt like sport.

Jesse shook his head to clear it, then snarled. He rushed at me, swinging his right fist in a big arc. I could have written *War and Peace* in the time it took to reach where my head should have been. I weaved back and let it pass, then laughed.

"Man, you are not telegraphing, you are sending me a letter. C'mon! You can do better than that."

He charged again.

It takes a fist the same time to travel a full yard, as it does for your core and your shoulder to travel an inch. I planted my feet, flicked my hips and my shoulder and smashed my fist into his nose with the combined force of my two hundred and twenty pounds and his mammoth charge.

He went up on his toes and his knees did a little in and

out dance as he staggered back with blood streaming down over his mouth. I could see his pupils were dilated and he had a dull, stupid look on his face. I didn't waste time. I took two steps toward him and drove my fist straight into his solar plexus. He went down vomiting.

I looked at his six friends. They weren't sure what to do. The three who'd come in with him looked like they just wanted to get back to drinking beer. But there was one guy, bigger than the rest, whose face said he had a mean disposition and he'd decided he didn't like me. Jesse was getting to his feet, holding his belly, and he didn't look to me like he was out either. I guess men in New Mexico are made of hard stuff. I pointed at the big guy. I was grinning.

"What's your name, son?"

He didn't like me calling him son. He said, "My name's Billy, and I'm gonna whip your ass till you bleed."

I shook my finger in the negative. "I'll tell you what we're going to do. I'll take you both, and a third if anybody wants to join the party. And whoever goes down buys a round of drinks for the bar. You too chicken for that, Billy?"

There was a cheer. One of Billy's friends, a Mexican in a blue shirt and a cowboy hat, decided he felt like buying a round that night. He pulled off his hat and rolled up his sleeves. I was wondering what the hell I was doing, but I told myself this was living Zen. Don't think. Just do.

Jesse looked very pale, but he wiped his mouth on his sleeve and moved toward me. Billy and the Mexican started to circle, Billy on my left and the Mexican on my right. They were going to grab me and let Jesse have his revenge. That was their plan.

I laughed again and said to Jesse, "Third time lucky, huh,

Jesse?" It wasn't subtle. An experienced fighter would have seen it coming. But these guys were used to wrestling bulls, not professional killers. I'd spoken to Jesse, so their attention was on him. They didn't expect the charging side kick at the Mexican. It caught him in the floating ribs, lifted him off his feet and sent him crashing through the ring of watchers and into a table, sending the four chairs flying. He didn't get up.

But by the time he'd hit the floor, I was already closing on Billy. I knew Jesse was basically the walking dead, and the crowd was looking forward to their beers. The only man I had to worry about now was Billy.

I figured a bit of boxing would be fun. I run at least five miles every morning at about five AM and I have near zero body fat. I've also learned to develop a kind of trance-state, where I can just keep going for hours without getting tired.

Billy must have weighed in at two hundred and seventy pounds. He was muscle strong and I was pretty sure if he landed a punch it would be lights out for anyone. But I didn't think he had staying power, and every punch he threw was using up precious energy. I leered at him and got in close.

"C'mon, Billy. What's troubling you? You afraid of spoiling your looks for your boyfriend?"

That did it. He powered in, swinging right and left with massive crosses and hooks. I ducked and weaved and stayed a few inches out of range while Jesse followed along, trying to get his wind back. Billy's breathing was getting heavy and his face was flushed. He threw another right hook and as it went past, I leaned forward and flicked a nasty left jab at his right eye. He backed up a step and winked a few times. I stepped forward and as he threw his right again, I crouched and drove both fists into his floating ribs, one after another. He doubled up.

As I came upright, Jesse was charging me. I snatched Billy's right wrist, pulled and twisted savagely and palmed his elbow, so he stumbled and collided with Jesse. Jesse staggered back. Billy was still doubled over and I had a firm grip on his wrist. It was time to buy a round. I drove my right boot into his belly and he went down.

Jesse was gaping at me. I stepped forward and jabbed the tip of his chin. He went straight over backward.

I was surrounded by a ring of very silent men. I knew some of them were thinking about it. I gave them a couple of seconds. Nobody moved. I said, "Looks like these boys owe you gentlemen a drink."

There was a moment's silence. Then somebody laughed. Then they were all laughing and Gastank was pulling beers and looking relieved. Several guys went to drag the fallen to their feet. Gastank called over to me, "What about Billy and Jesse, and Nestor?"

"They look to me like they could use a drink. Give me one too, will you?"

And that was when the door opened and the sheriff walked in.

"What the hell is goin' on in here?" He looked around, saw me and said, "Oh, I might have guessed. You again!"

CHAPTER 2

"What is wrong with you, Walker?"

The sheriff was sitting on the edge of his desk beside his hat, looking down at me where I was sitting in a bentwood chair. He was big, his eyes were narrowed and his arms were crossed. He looked more like an angry barn than a man. He was wearing a gray uniform shirt with a star, but he had on blue jeans and boots. He was everything you wanted your sheriff to be. I decided I liked him.

"I'm not sure what you mean, Sheriff."

"You've been in my county for almost a month. I don't know what the hell you think you're doing here, but you've busted up three bars in as many weeks."

"I didn't start any of those fights, Sheriff. And I paid for all the damage that was caused, even though I didn't start the trouble."

"Which is the only reason you're still in my county. You say you don't start these things, but look how you always find your way to the roughest joint in whatever town you're in! Can't you spend your leisure time at Ma Bennett's coffee shop, or the Blueberry Family Restaurant, instead of Gastank's Hog Bar?"

"Mrs. Bennett makes damn fine pie, Sheriff, and the steak at the Blueberry is second to none I've ever eaten, but they don't sell whiskey, and they don't sell beer. So if a man wants to sit and have a quiet drink in your county, there are not many places he can choose from."

He sighed. "Well, no offense, Mr. Walker—and I do take your point—but perhaps you'd be more comfortable in another county where the local population take a more relaxed view of alcohol." He stood, walked around behind his desk and dropped into his chair. "What *are* you doin' here, anyhow? I know you ain't short of money, and I know for a fact you ain't lookin' for work!"

"I don't know, Sheriff. Maybe I'm looking for the answer to that very question."

He stared at me for a moment like he didn't know whether to backhand me or buy me a drink.

"I don't know what personal baggage you're carrying, Walker. I do know that it's my responsibility to keep the peace in my county. Twice I've cautioned you because it genuinely did seem you hadn't started things, and you made handsome reparation without being asked. But this is the third time you've managed to find yourself in a fight. You may not look for trouble, Walker, but you sure as hell find it."

I nodded. "I can't deny that, Sheriff."

He frowned. "You got a home somewhere?"

"Yeah, yes I have."

"Go there. Sort out whatever it is that's causing all..." He gestured at me. "*This!*" Then for good measure he wagged a finger in my direction. "If a man goes through life getting into fights that he ain't lookin' for, that means he's sendin' out some kind of bad message. You go home, Walker, and sort yourself out. I don't want to see you in my county tomorrow. You understand me?"

"I understand you, Sheriff. Is there a fine I need to pay...?"

"You just pay Gastank for the damage to his bar. Then get out of Cottontown."

I stepped out into the cold night and the door banged closed behind me. The sheriff's office was on the edge of town, set in a large lot that had been fenced off but not asphalted, so you had the feeling you were out in the desert. Up above, there was an astonishing number of stars, the moon was rising fat and orange in the east, and you could hear the coyotes howling at it, away in the distance.

I stopped outside the perimeter fence, by the municipal museum building, and paused to pull a Camel from my pack and light up. The sheriff had advised me to go home and sort out my problems. He had probably assumed my problems were wife-related. But all my wife-related problems had solved themselves, when my wife and my potential wife had walked away. My problem was a deeper one than that. My problem was that Omega lived on, either out there in the world, or inside me, in my mind, and I had to find the way to kill it, for once and for all.

I started walking the mile or so to the Hampton Motel, where I had a room and where I had left my car. As I walked, I called Jim. He sounded pleased to hear from me.

"Lacklan. I am just enjoying a glass of Bushmills on the

terrace. I was wondering how long it would be before you called. Where are you?"

"Cottontown, New Mexico. I just got thrown out of the only bar in town, and the sheriff told me he wanted me out of his county by sunrise."

I heard the weathered rasp he used for a laugh. "Nice to know there are still places like that left. What's on your mind?"

"Omicron."

He grunted. "General Francisco Ochoa, supreme commander of the *Brigada de Operaciones Especiales*, second only to the *Secretario de Defensa Nacional*. Or at least, that's what the Secretary of National Defense thinks."

I turned into 2nd Street and started walking south. The road was long and straight, and there was no lighting except from the stars, the moon that was creeping over the horizon, and what little light filtered out through the closed drapes of the sparse, one story houses that flanked the road. The silence was heavy, like a palpable thing that made the echo of my footsteps loud, almost startling in the stillness.

"You been doing your homework?" I asked.

"I had a feeling you'd be calling soon to discuss the Greek alphabet."

"You going to tell me what the Sheriff of Hidalgo County told me, to go home and sort out my problems?"

"That's good advice."

"Yeah, only my problems aren't at home."

"How far are you? Six, seven hundred miles?"

"About that."

"In that electric monster of yours, you could be here in five or six hours. Spend a few days here, swim in the ocean, enjoy some time with Mioko. We'll eat and drink and talk about Omicron."

On an impulse, I turned and looked behind me. There was nobody there, just the long, lonely road I had already walked, and beyond it the desert. Ahead of me the same long, dark road with no end in sight, flanked by the silent, dark houses.

"Sounds like a plan, Jim. Will Njal be there?"

"He's away on business at the moment. But we can call him back if we decide it's necessary."

"Yeah, good."

"I'll expect you for an early breakfast then."

"See you, Jim."

I arrived at the motel parking lot shortly before ten. The monster Jim had referred to was a matte black 1968 Mustang Fastback. Only, under the hood it had something different. This was a modified Zombie 222, from Bloodshed Motors in Texas. There was no roar when you fired her up, no thunder, no sound at all. But its twin engines delivered eight hundred bhp and one thousand eight-hundred foot-pounds of torque, instantly, directly to the back wheels. The acceleration was insane: from 0-60 in one and a half seconds, with a top speed of 200 MPH. And she was totally silent.

I opened the trunk and checked my kit bag. I hadn't replenished it since the affair in Freeport. I had my two Sig Sauer p226s, the Smith & Wesson 500, my Fairbairn & Sykes fighting knife, the suppressed Maxim 9 and my take down bow, but there was little else. If I decided to go after Omicron I'd need to replenish my arsenal.

I closed the trunk and went to pack my bag and check

out. For the first time in six months, I felt suddenly cheerful again.

———

I took the I-10 via Tucson and Phoenix and drove through the night. It was just over six hundred miles and though there were places where I had to go slow, from Phoenix to Riverside, the road was straight and mostly desert, and I was able to hit speeds of 120 MPH, and peaked outside Blythe at 150. I guess it averaged out at around a hundred and ten, because I left the motel at midnight and pulled up outside Jim Redbeard's house on Paseo de la Playa, in Malaga Cove, at fifteen minutes before six. The sun was rising over the San Gabriel mountains in the east, turning the pale blue sky slightly pink and washing the ochre walls of his house with bronze light. I grabbed my bag from the trunk and made my way to the door. It was already open and he was waiting for me on the step.

He embraced me, took my bag and asked, "How long can you stay?"

The smell of coffee and freshly baked bread was strong on the air. Through the large, open space that was his living room, I could see the glass doors open onto his terrace. Before I could answer, he leaned into the kitchen, gave some instructions and led me out to the terrace with his hand on my shoulder. Out there, he had a huge, old wooden table set in the shade of some palms above a garden that sloped down, threaded by a winding path, toward the edge of the cliff overlooking the cove. The ocean was vast and dark, reflecting the early sun in a winking sheen of broken light. He sat at the head of the table and I sat facing the ocean.

"I don't know," I said in answer to his earlier question. "That's kind of why I am here."

"You are feeling lost. You brought down Omega, and now you don't know what to do with yourself. All you know is warfare, and fighting."

Two young girls who might have been Filipino came out with two pots of coffee and several baskets of hot bread and croissants, creamery butter and cold pressed honey. They deposited them on the table and left. I helped myself to a hot roll and broke it open while he poured the strong, pungent black brew.

"That's just it, Jim. I am not sure that I have brought down Omega."

He grunted. I spread butter on the roll and watched it melt, spooned on thick, waxy, aromatic honey and bit into it. While I chewed, he gazed out at the ocean.

"Do you know," he asked without looking at me, "how William the Conqueror defeated the Saxons at the battle of Hastings?"

I wiped my mouth and sipped coffee. "The legend is that a Norman archer shot King Harold in the eye with an arrow."

He shrugged and turned his attention to a hot roll. "That may or may not have happened. Harold had formed an impenetrable wall of shields and spears, a common tactic of the time. The Normans, who were, as I am sure you know, Danes and Norwegians, not Frenchmen, charged again and again, with infantry and cavalry, but they were unable to break the Saxons' wall."

He bit into the soft, crusty bread and chewed thoughtfully for a while. Eventually he drained his cup and refilled it, and I began to wonder if he was going to finish his story. But he started speaking again.

"Harold's men were exhausted. They had just, only recently, defeated Harald Hardrada at the battle of Stamford Bridge, less than three weeks earlier, and had had to march almost three hundred miles to confront William's forces, where they had formed a beachhead at Hastings, on the south coast of England. Harold had about seven thousand men, many of whom he had recruited during the march. They were practically all infantry, with very few archers.

"William, a true Danish tactician, like his great grandfather, Ganger Rolf, had a well balanced army. He had about ten thousand men, barely half were infantry, and the rest were divided between cavalry and archers.

"Battle was joined on October 14th, some miles from Hastings, near the village of Battle. It lasted all day, from nine in the morning until dusk with, as I say, wave after wave of Norman attacks being repulsed by this impenetrable wall of exhausted, but determined Saxons.

"Finally, after what seemed to be one final, desperate attack, as dusk was falling, the Normans turned in disarray, and fled. Fresh from defeating Hardrada, exhausted from the march and the day-long battle, the Saxons were exultant, and they made a mistake which was to shape the history of the entire planet for the next thousand years."

Now he turned to look at me and said: "They broke ranks and they charged, pursuing their enemy. But it had been a ruse. The fleeing cavalry promptly turned and charged. The impenetrable wall had been broken, not by

Norman attack, but by the Saxon decision to pursue their enemy. The Saxons were decimated, Harold was killed, William marched on London and, despite pockets of resistance, he soon subjected the country and sowed the first seeds for what would become the British Empire."

I sat in silence, staring at the gleaming ocean, chewing hot bread and sipping strong black coffee. Eventually, I said, "I am not sure what you're trying to tell me, Jim."

"It would be presumptuous of me to tell you anything, Lacklan. You have proved yourself to be a supremely capable warrior. What I am doing is illustrating a fact which you already know: that sometimes it is advantageous for your enemy to think you are stronger than you are, sometimes it is an advantage for your enemy to think you are weaker than you are. What you never want is for your enemy to know your actual strength.

"Harold lost the battle of Hastings because he went after William, having underestimated his strength. Are you sure you are not at risk of making that same mistake?"

I shook my head. "No, I am not sure." I thought a moment longer and added, "I'm not sure of anything, Jim. I left the SAS because I was tired of killing, and all I've done since I set up in my house and my workshop in Wyoming is get rich and kill people. Is this all I am capable of? Do I feel lost because there is nobody left for me to kill?"

He leaned back in his big, wooden armchair and regarded me from under hooded eyes.

"In the first place, that is not all you have done. You inherited your money, legitimately, from your father, and you have used your energy and your resources to help bring down one of the most dangerous political organizations since the Third Reich. But..." He stroked his long beard. "It is interesting that in your eyes, that is all you've done."

"What's that supposed to mean?"

He shrugged. "Was bringing down Omega just incidental? Was the real thing for you the fight? Perhaps it didn't really matter to you, deep inside, who you were fighting, just as long as you were fighting. It can become like that for some men."

I peeled a pack of Camels and extracted a cigarette. I offered him one and he shook his head, waiting for me to answer. I flipped my Zippo and leaned into the flame. Then as I let out the smoke, I said, "I've been thrown out of almost a dozen bars in the last six months. I've been arrested six times and thrown out of three counties. All for brawling. I should have gone home to Kenny and Rosalia at Christmas, instead I've been drifting across the southern states, drinking and getting into fights. I'm worried, Jim. How long will it be before I kill an innocent man? Why can't I accept that the job is done, and it's time to enjoy the peace?"

He was laughing, but it wasn't a happy laugh. "That's a lot of different questions, Lacklan. For a start, there is no such thing as an innocent man. How long before you kill a man you did not intend to kill? That has been a question hanging over you since you were eighteen. You are just more aware of it now, because you have no defined enemy. You are a gun looking for a target, and that makes you dangerous."

He looked up at the sky, as though he were seeking guidance from the gods. "Why can't you accept that the job is done? I have no doubt, Lacklan, that if you asked a psychoanalyst that same question, he would point to your unresolved Oedipal complex and your need to kill your father and possess your mother. And no doubt there would be some truth in that. But for me, the explanation is simpler."

"I'm not crazy about the psychoanalytical explanation."

"Few people are. Personally I think Freud had it about right. But my own view, Freud aside, is that you are a warrior. Warriors are a thing the modern world has little use for. That is true of men in general, in fact. This is now a woman's world, where the great virtues are empathy, compassion, dialogue.." He made a vague gesture with his hand. "Good men are men who are caring and sensitive, who know how to listen, who emulate women. Men like you and me are largely obsolete, we are anachronisms, viewed with disfavor. The world has little use for us, and let's face it, we have little use for the world." He sighed. "As long as you were fighting Omega, you could ignore this fact. But with no enemy to fight, you look around you and wonder where the hell you are supposed to fit in. Especially..." He paused, nodding slowly at the table. "Especially since you lost your wife and Marni." He turned his eyes on me. "They, either one of them, might have given you a sense of purpose. Serving women is about the only purpose men seem to have left these days. We are born, we go to university, we get a job. Somewhere along the line we find a woman to adore and serve, and she and her children become the focal point of our lives. The highest a man can aspire to in modern society is being a good husband. That is the modern way."

I burst out laughing. "That's a pretty unorthodox view, Jim."

"That's the word, unorthodox. Does it help at all?"

I took a drag on my cigarette and thought about it. "You're right, I do feel that I have no place and no purpose.

With Omega gone, Marni and Abi, I feel like I don't know what my purpose is. Yeah, that's all true." I smiled and shook my head. "But I'm not so sure the solution for me is finding a woman and devoting my life to her."

"I wasn't proposing that, Lacklan. Omega are hurt, but they are not finished. There is a chance they are pulling a 'Battle of Hastings' ruse. I just want you to be sure, if you decide to go after them, that you know why you are doing it. If Harold's men had known why they were chasing the Normans, they might have timed it better and won the day. Don't go after Omicron because your head is full of murderous passion, go after him because you have decided to destroy him. Be systematic."

I eyed him a moment. "They are not finished?"

"You know they're not. They still have their Asian branch, their African branch and, above all, their South American branch. They may be down, I have no doubt you damaged them badly when you took out the computer system in Brussels[1], but they are far from out. In fact, I would say that right now they are possibly at their most dangerous."

My coffee had gone cold, but I drained my cup anyway. I studied the black dregs a moment, frowning, and finally said, "So you think I ought to go after them, and finish them?"

"Oh yes," he said. "I think you should study your attack carefully, then you should go in and kill Omicron, and all the rest of them; but especially Omicron."

---

1. See *Kill: Two*

CHAPTER 3

WE STEPPED OUT AFTER BREAKFAST, CROSSED THE
parking lot at the end of the road and found a trail leading
down the cliff to the beach below. It wound, with no real
sense of purpose, through a scrubland of small bushes that
looked like thyme, rosemary and lavender, rocks and small
boulders. And, further down the cliff, closer to the sand and
the sea, it wound among bigger bushes and small trees that I
could not identify. Above, seagulls wheeled and cried out to
the wind. Below, large breakers were rolling in off the Pacific
and, though they were a good hundred and fifty or two
hundred yards away, the roar and the spray were carried on
the brisk morning breeze, and both reached us.

Halfway down, Jim stopped to sit on the steps that had
been hewn out of the living rock and gazed out at the
immensity of the ocean beneath us. I sat on a boulder nearby
and listened for a while to the huge, heavy sigh of the waves
thundering onto the shore, and then retracting back into the
deep.

"If I understand the way they think," Jim said suddenly, "Omega is not the organization. Omega is the state the organization is in at the present time." He raised a hand. "Was in, until you came along."

"Timmerman said words to that effect," I said. "Each letter of the Greek alphabet represented a period of development in human society. Omega was the last stage, the stage we were at."

He nodded. "Right, so Omega, or, in English, Mega O, the big O, is the end. It's the final stage of expansion or dilation before everything collapses in on itself."

"That sounds about right. That's what they were about, wasn't it? Preparing for the big collapse."

"Yup..." He squinted at the horizon, like he was having some internal dialogue. The wind whipped his hair across his face and his beard crawled over his shoulder. "Then, you showed up..." He turned to look at me. "You didn't actually show up, did you?"

"No, my father sent Ben to get me."

"But we now know that your father was Gamma in the organization, and Ben was Alpha. And even though Ben was acting as your father's secretary, that was just a front. Ben was in fact your father's superior."

I frowned. "I guess he was."

"So it doesn't make much sense that your father would send Ben to get you..."

I stared at him. A sudden gust battered my face, carrying with it the smell of the sea. My mind reached and strained, but couldn't grasp it.

"My father..." I said, and faltered. "Marni had disappeared. She'd taken her father's research into..."

"Into what?"

"Into climate change, into the activities of Omega... Nobody is really sure."

"Except Marni."

"Yes..."

"And she had gone missing."

"She'd disappeared, left me a coded message that she was in Colorado..."

"And your father told you that he had sent Ben to get you, to go and look for her.[1]"

"Yes, but obviously, if Ben was Alpha, it must have been his decision, not my father's..." I frowned at him where he sat, turned slightly back toward me, with his hair and his beard flapping erratically across his face in the wind. "Why? Why would he do that?"

He grunted and stood. "If you'll forgive me saying so, that's a question you should have asked yourself when you first realized he was Alpha. It's an important question."

I watched him descend the steps for a while, toward the beach two hundred feet below, then I rose and followed him.

I caught up with him when we had reached the bottom of the long flight of steps, and he was standing on the sweep of white sand with his arms crossed, looking out at the towering waves, rolling, foaming and crashing in onto the shore. He glanced at me as I drew level and we started to walk, pushing through the sand. He said:

"So Omega is the end of a process, the final dilation, expansion, exhaustion of a process. Omicron—micro O, is

---

1. See *Dawn of the Hunter*

exactly the opposite. It is the contracted, initial stage of a process."

"Like a seed."

"Exactly like a seed. A seed is an omicron."

"So the implication is obvious. The new process—the new Omega, for want of a better name—will be born from Omicron."

"That's what I think."

"But why not Alpha? Omicron is the fifteenth letter of the alphabet. It is well over halfway through. Why is that the beginning?"

He smiled at me and placed a huge hand on my shoulder. "Will you, do you think, when you are finally too old to go around beating people up, will you become a philosopher?"

I shook my head. "I have no time for navel-gazing, Jim. No offense intended, but to be eternally asking questions you know you can never answer..." I shook my head again.

He rumbled a laugh. "That is mainly the European rationalists," he said. "The English empiricists were a whole different kettle of fish. And Newton was an alchemist, you know? But to answer your question, does a child begin in his mother's womb? Does it begin in the egg? Both of those are omicron. But the child, the process of the child, begins before that. It begins with alpha, the blade, penetration, insemination. But in reality, Lacklan, there is no beginning and no end. The whole thing is a cycle, and it perpetuates itself to infinity, like Jörmungandr, the Midgard Serpent, that eats its own tail."

I raised a hand. "OK, let me get my feet back on the ground. What we are saying is that, according to the doctrine of Omega, their South American arm, and in particular Omicron, is charged with putting them back on the map if somebody like me comes along, takes out the leaders and destroys their computer network."

"Yes, you could put it like that."

"Then I have to agree with you. It is essential that we take out Omicron."

"Mh-hm." He nodded a few times, watching his feet as he walked. "But it is not enough to take out Omicron. You have to take them all down, Lambda, Mu, Nu, Xi *and* Omicron. The whole South American operation will have to come down. Then, *then*, we can say that Omega is finished. It won't be easy. You'll need Njal."

We had come to a large, yellow canoe that was lying on the sand. Here Jim stopped, turned and walked a few paces toward the sea, and there sat on the sand. I sat beside him. He picked up a strand of seaweed and started turning it around in his fingers, frowning slightly.

"General Francisco Ochoa, supreme commander of all Mexican special forces. You may sneer, but they train with the Seals. They are combat hardened and very tough. He has them all at his command. And as of right now, he is the supreme commander of Omega, as well." He wagged the piece of seaweed a few times. "And you should also bear in mind that South America is not Europe or the United States. Different rules apply, and far fewer of them. It is a very thin veneer of civilization overlaid on absolute anarchy."

"I have worked there."

"Of course you have."

"Do you know who the others are?"

"Raul Rocha, Minister for Mines and Energy in Brazil." He smiled at me with hooded eyes. "They have one of those over there, a minister for mines and energy. That's Lambda, obviously he works and lives in Brasilia. Mu, Narciso Terry, Minister for Scientific Development in Argentina, based obviously in Buenos Aires. The other three are in Mexico. Nu is Felipe Gonzalez, the governor of the free and sovereign state of Sinaloa, Xi is Samuel Zapata, nicknamed '*El Vampiro*' because he is said to drink human blood. He is the current head of the Sinaloa cartel."

We were silent for a while, listening to the waves crash and thud, and feeling the spray on the wind. After a bit, I said, "It's a major operation. It will take a lot of planning, and support."

"Yes, and we have to be very careful that word does not reach them. This plan has to be hermetic. As far as the world is concerned, you are satisfied that Omega is finished, and now you're letting your hair down, having some fun, learning to be a playboy. The plan has to be developed in absolute secrecy."

"What about Njal?"

He thought for a while and answered obliquely. "Take a few days to familiarize yourself with their bios, their photographs..." He glanced at me. "I have them back at the house. You know the routine: get to know them, who they are, who their families are, what they do each day, how they spend their weekends..." He twisted up the piece of seaweed in his hands, tied it into a knot and dropped it in the sand. "Meantime, be seen around town, take some girls to dinner, go dancing, try to get noticed by the society pages. You're a rich playboy, behave like one. While you're doing that, I'll contact Njal. I'll arrange a get together somewhere discreet in a few days' time, and we'll discuss the plan." He paused, then added heavily, "Put some flesh on the bones."

————

BEING a playboy isn't something that comes naturally to me. Instead, I developed a routine of rising at five AM, running down the steps to the beach, training for an hour in the surf and then running back up the steps for breakfast at seven. After breakfast, I would take the photographs and bios of one of the heads of Omega III and digest them. I also tried to familiarize myself as much as I could with their homes, towns and workplaces via Google Earth and Google Maps. It wasn't much but it was something.

On the morning of the third day, Jim joined me for breakfast on the terrace. He asked me how I was getting on. I told him I had a pretty good basic knowledge of Raul Rocha and Narciso Terry and was working on the others. He squinted out at the sea for a while and then grinned.

"If I were Omicron—General Ochoa—I would have men watching you. I don't know if he has. I haven't seen anyone. Maybe he doesn't know where you are. But considering the damage you have caused so far, I would definitely have somebody looking for you, and ideally watching you." He turned his long, pale, blue eyes from the sea to look at me. "If he has, what is he going to see? He's going to see Bruce Lee. Up at five to run up and down cliffs and fight with the Pacific surf, then locked in Professor Redbeard's house all day. And who is this Professor Redbeard we have never heard of till now? Perhaps we should look into him..."

I sighed. "Playboy... How do you do that? It's not something that comes easily to me."

"Even if I had a damn, Lacklan, I wouldn't give one. Take Mioko out tonight. I'm pulling strings and booking you a table for two at Mélisse, in Santa Monica. It's one of the most expensive restaurants in town. After that, go to a club. Dance. And tomorrow I want you going to a show or a play or a concert. I don't give an amoeba's fart where you go, but you better be seen in town or I'm pulling the plug." He pointed at me. "Omega is dead and you are celebrating. Get over it."

He stood, slapped me on the shoulder and returned to his study.

So for the next three nights, I went out on the town with Mioko. She didn't talk a lot, but agreed with everything I said and did. At first I found that annoying and even tried to get her to complain about how Jim treated her and used her and the other girls, but she seemed to find that amusing and in the end I gave up and started to relax. We had fun, and every night, when we went home, she would come to my bed with me. She seemed to take it for granted.

On the morning of the fourth day, when I got back from training on the beach, Jim joined me for breakfast again on the terrace. We were served bacon, fried bananas and pancakes with cold pressed honey by the two Filipino girls. Jim poured himself coffee, drank and asked:

"How are you coping with the stress of having fun?"

"I'm coping. Mioko is a nice girl."

He chuckled and his long eyes swiveled to look at me as he cut into his bacon. There was something that bordered on leering malevolence in them. "I wouldn't advise you to fall in love with her."

"I don't plan to."

"You think they are my slaves?"

I shrugged. "It's none of my business. They seem to be happy."

"Mioko tells me you tried to incite her to rebel against me."

"Maybe I did. She seemed to find the idea as amusing as you do."

He chuckled again as he finished his bacon, then leaned back in his chair holding his coffee cup. "We'll go this afternoon and meet with Njal. He has a house in Arizona which we bought recently. It is secluded and off the grid, so we'll have privacy there. I've booked you on a private jet to D.C. for the sake of appearances. Somebody who looks like you will take your place, and Mioko will accompany him."

"Does this somebody know why..."

"They don't even know they are setting a false scent. They think they are going to D.C. for a perfectly legitimate purpose, to handle some business for me."

I nodded. "You're subtle, Jim. I only hope you're on the side of the angels."

He shook his head. "I'm not. I'm on the side of the valkyries." He laughed, like he'd told a joke, but his long, pale eyes were watching me. He stood and patted my shoulder. "Pack a bag and make whatever preparations you need to make. We'll leave as soon as you're ready."

An hour later, he rolled out a gray Wrangler Moab and we put the Zombie away in his garage. I threw my bag in the back, climbed in and slammed the door, and we set off through town. He didn't talk much until we'd joined the I-15 at Etiwanda and we were headed north out of town toward Victorville. Then he said, "Are we being followed?"

"No."

"Njal is at a place called Cadiz. It's about ninety miles east of Barstow, in the Mojave desert. We should be OK there. The few people he comes across, he tells them his name is Pierre and he's from Paris, the French one. That explains his accent."

"He has a Norwegian accent."

"You think they can tell in Cadiz?" He grinned at me.

"I guess maybe not."

"I want to put some flesh on the bones of our plan there. I think we might need to strike sooner rather than later."

"Why?"

"Why do I think that, or why do we need to strike?"

"Both."

"Njal has some intelligence that suggest Omicron may be active. And if he is, we may have a problem."

"Active how?"

"I'll let Njal explain that."

Scan the QR code below to purchase THE OMICRON KILL.
Or go to: righthouse.com/the-omicron-kill

Made in United States
Orlando, FL
02 January 2026

76166294R00164